Praise for Edgar Award-winner
**WILLIAM HEFFERNAN**
and
**UNHOLY ORDER**

"Heffernan can write a mean page and create a
living character in a few words."
Stuart M. Kaminsky

"[A] great tale . . . The plot . . . is wonderful."
*Providence Journal-Bulletin*

"Creepy . . . Heffernan does a good job of showing that
fanaticism in any guise can be a destructive, evil force."
*Orlando Sentinel*

"The plot twists tighter and tighter."
*Salt Lake City Deseret News*

"Heffernan knows how to create characters through
sharp and distinctive dialogue; his pacing is fast
and fluid, and his plotting is superb."
Nelson DeMille

"Fascinating . . . There's plenty for thriller
fans to enjoy."
*Library Journal*

## ALSO BY WILLIAM HEFFERNAN

**ATTENTION: ORGANIZATIONS AND CORPORATIONS**
Most Avon Books paperbacks are available at special quantity discounts for bulk purchases for sales promotions, premiums, or fund-raising. For information, please call or write:

**Special Markets Department, HarperCollins Publishers, Inc.,**
**10 East 53rd Street, New York, N.Y. 10022-5299.**
**Telephone: (212) 207-7528. Fax: (212) 207-7222.**

# WILLIAM HEFFERNAN

# UNHOLY ORDER

## A PAUL DEVLIN MYSTERY

**AVON BOOKS**

*An Imprint of HarperCollinsPublishers*

*For my brother, Terry*

This is a work of fiction. Names, characters, places, and incidents are products of the author's imagination or are used fictitiously and are not to be construed as real. Any resemblance to actual events, locales, organizations, or persons, living or dead, is entirely coincidental.

AVON BOOKS
*An Imprint of* HarperCollins*Publishers*
10 East 53rd Street
New York, New York 10022-5299

Copyright © 2002 by Daisychain Productions, Inc.
ISBN: 0-380-81882-5
www.avonmystery.com

All rights reserved. No part of this book may be used or reproduced in any manner whatsoever without written permission, except in the case of brief quotations embodied in critical articles and reviews. For information address Avon Books, an Imprint of HarperCollins Publishers.

First Avon Books paperback printing: December 2002
First William Morrow hardcover printing: February 2002

Avon Trademark Reg. U.S. Pat. Off. and in Other Countries, Marca Registrada, Hecho en U.S.A.
HarperCollins ® is a trademark of HarperCollins Publishers Inc.

Printed in the U.S.A.

10  9  8  7  6  5  4  3  2

If you purchased this book without a cover, you should be aware that this book is stolen property. It was reported as "unsold and destroyed" to the publisher, and neither the author nor the publisher has received any payment for this "stripped book."

## Chapter One

*T*hey followed the vested priest in long lines, two abreast, first the men, then the women, all of them young, all looking as though they had just stepped from steaming baths—every one so clean and fresh and seemingly innocent. Next came the nuns, also young, each one dressed in the black-and-white habits you seldom see anymore, large rosary beads wrapped around their waists, the crucifixes at the ends hanging to their knees. Brothers followed in black suits, each distinguishable from the handful of priests who brought up the rear only by the black neckties they wore in place of clerical collars.

Paul Devlin watched as the coffin was placed over the open grave. Watched as the young men and women divided, each sex moving to opposite sides of the bier, the nuns then stepping in front, closest to the coffin, the brothers and priests forming a rank at its foot.

Sharon Levy leaned in to Devlin and whispered, "God, all those kids. They look so freshly scrubbed. It's scary."

Devlin glanced at his tall redheaded sergeant. "You have something against clean?" he asked.

"I love clean," Sharon said. "It's uniformed clean that makes me nervous."

She was right, of course. Devlin had noticed it too. All those pink-cheeked kids, all in their late teens or early twenties, all with faces that looked almost angelic. Every bit of it so out of place, considering the corpse.

The mutilated body of the young nun they were burying had been found three days ago, gutted and stuffed in the

trunk of a car at Kennedy airport. It was late summer, still op-
pressively warm, and the car had been abandoned in the
long-term parking lot. There hadn't been much left by the
time the nun was found—at least for forensic purposes. But
there was enough to tell she had been carrying heroin in her
body. A lot of heroin, packed in condoms she had swallowed.

The detectives who first caught the case initially specu-
lated that the young woman had only been posing as a nun
when she came through customs. It had proven a false as-
sumption. The woman, Maria Escavera, was a naturalized
U.S. citizen whose parents had emigrated from Colombia.
She was also a postulant in The Holy Order of Opus Christi,
where she had chosen the religious name of Sister Manuela.

So far the media hadn't tumbled to the drugs. That part of
the forensic report had been buried. They only knew that a
nun had been viciously murdered, and that was how Mayor
Howie Silver wanted it to remain.

We don't need a goddamn media circus, he had said,
when he had handed Devlin the case.

Devlin looked down the long winding cemetery road all
the way to the main gate. Uniformed cops were there now,
holding back the newspaper reporters and television crews.

It was already a circus, and it would be an even bigger
one once the newshounds got wind of the drug angle. Then
it would become a full-scale three-ringer. Of that Devlin had
no doubt. There was no way to avoid it. Sooner or later word
would leak out—a cop hoping to curry favor, someone in the
ME's office. He only hoped it came after they had found the
killer. If it came before . . . ? He didn't even want to think
about it. He shook his head, annoyed by his thoughts. Stop
whining, he told himself. It's part of the job, the one you
wanted, the one you agreed to do.

Devlin was inspector of detectives, a rank that had lain
dormant for many years until the mayor had cajoled him into
returning to the force from an early disability retirement.
The promotion that went with the job gave him unusual
power in the New York Police Department, a fact that he enjoyed more often than not. He worked directly for the
mayor, with the right to supersede even senior commanders,

under Howie Silver's umbrella of protection. It was Silver's way of escaping the political intrigue that permeated One Police Plaza, the headquarters building better known to working cops as the Puzzle Palace. It allowed the mayor to put Devlin in charge of the high-profile, politically danger-ous cases that so often battered, and occasionally broke, any man foolish enough to become mayor of New York.

But the power of the mayor might not be needed for this case. The NYPD brass seemed more than willing to step aside.

Devlin considered the gathering again. Everyone present was a member of Opus Christi: The Holy Order, as it was known to its members. It was one of the most influential fac-tions within the Catholic Church—some said the most influ-ential, even surpassing the Jesuits. The mayor had made his position clear. Devlin was to find the killer and keep the press at bay—not only to cover Hizzoner but also to avoid any em-barrassment for the Archdiocese of New York. Devlin under-stood. He had already clashed with the archdiocese on an earlier case, and the mayor had borne the brunt of its wrath. It was with good reason that New York's Catholic prelature was known as the Powerhouse to the city's politicians, a dis-tinction not lost on NYPD's senior commanders.

The priest began the final prayers, driving away Devlin's thoughts. The prayers were in Latin, something he had not heard since childhood, when he spent every Sunday morn-ing sitting with his sister and his parents at Saint Joseph's Church in Queens. During the intervening years, the long-dead language had been abandoned by all but a few Catholic sects. Hearing it now, he recalled how mysterious it had seemed to him all those years ago, a tongue known only to those initiated in the sacred rituals of Holy Mother, the church. A faint smile flickered on his lips as he thought of that term and how the Dominican nuns who had ruled his earliest years of school had used it over and over again to el-evate those in Rome who ruled the lives of every Catholic.

Again, he studied the gathering of young men and women as they recited the Latin responses to the priest's prayers. He wondered if they understood the meaning of the words they mouthed, something he had never achieved himself. Perhaps they did. They seemed so intent. Many had their eyes closed; others had raised them to the heavens, all emulating a "Christlike" attitude of devoutness that his own nuns had struggled but failed to achieve with their ragtag collection of New York street kids.

Devlin's gaze stopped on one young nun. Tears streamed down her cheeks and her entire body seemed to tremble. He leaned in close to Sharon Levy. "That nun in the first row, the one who's crying and shaking like a leaf . . ."

"Yeah, I already spotted her," Sharon whispered back. "Looks like somebody we should talk to. Find out what's got her so scared."

Devlin felt eyes burning into his back. He turned and found that two suits had slipped in behind the priest. The older of the pair—a man who appeared close to Devlin's own age of thirty-eight—was staring at him intently.

The man started toward him immediately, stopping only a foot away. His voice was low and hushed to avoid disturbing the service, his words blunt to the point of rudeness.

"If you're with the press, you don't belong here," he said.

Devlin reached into his jacket pocket and withdrew his badge and ID wallet. He opened it, flashing the tin. The man studied it intently. "And who are you?" Devlin asked.

The man ignored the question. "Are you investigating Sister Manuela's death, officer?" he asked instead. He was a few inches shorter than Devlin's six feet and painfully slender, except for a slight paunch. His eyes were a soft pale brown, like his hair, and he had a long thin nose and tight narrow lips. His pale-gray suit hung on him like a sack.

The man's tone had remained overbearing, and Devlin decided to put a quick end to it. "The rank is inspector, not officer," he said. He nodded toward Sharon. "And this is *Sergeant* Levy." He paused a beat. "I asked who you were?" He held the man's eyes, defying him to continue his self-important game.

The man broke eye contact and forced a smile. "I'm Matthew."

Devlin waited for more, but nothing came. It was like pulling teeth. "Matthew what?"

The insincere smile came again. "My last name is Moriarty. In Opus Christi we tend to use only our Christian names." He held the smile. "As the apostles of Our Lord did."

"You're here in some official capacity?" Devlin asked.

"Well, of course I'm here to celebrate Sister's life in Christ and her reunion with Our Lord and Savior. But otherwise, yes, I'm also here for a more official purpose." Matthew appeared ready to stop with that, then seemed to realize that further reticence might be unwise. "I'm director of public information for The Holy Order," he said. "I'm here to deal with the media."

Or not deal with them, Devlin thought. "Good. Then maybe you can also expedite some interviews for us."

"Interviews? Whom could you possibly want to interview?" Matthew waved his hand, dismissing the foolishness of his words. "What I mean is, I can give you whatever information you need."

Devlin offered up his own insincere smile. "That's not how it works, Matthew. *We* decide who we want to talk to, and we talk to *them*."

"But the members of our order don't know anything about this tragic business."

Sharon Levy stepped forward, moving closer to Matthew. She was a tall willowy redhead, strikingly beautiful. She also was an out-of-the-closet lesbian who had little tolerance for self-important male bullshit.

She patted Matthew's arm, instantly unnerving him. "Matthew, Matthew, Matthew. Let me explain. People in your holy order knew the victim, right?"

"Well, of course."

"Good. We need to talk to them." She hurried on before Matthew could object. "And if I'm right, nuns never travel alone—sort of a custom to go at least in pairs. Am I right there too?"

"Well, yes, but—"

Sharon cut him off. "So when Sister Manuela flew into Kennedy, there were probably one or more other nuns with her. Am I still on target here, Matthew?"

"Yes." Matthew's eyes had grown severe and suspicious.

"Then for starters we need to talk to whoever was with her. Then we need to talk to anyone who knew her."

Sharon gave him a bright smile that almost made Devlin laugh.

"So, you see, even though you can probably tell us a great deal, there are still a lot of people we need to talk to. And since some lowlife scumbag viciously murdered one of your sisters, I'm sure you want to do everything you can to help us do that. Am I right again?"

Matthew had seemed jolted by Sharon's choice of words, the term *lowlife scumbag* making him take an involuntary step back. But Sharon had achieved what she was after. Matthew's little game of Who's Running the Show had come to a screeching halt.

He began tentatively. "You must . . . understand . . . that life within The Holy Order is very insular . . . very protected. This is done for the benefit of our members' immortal souls. Contact with the outside world is . . . limited."

Again, Sharon cut him off. "Hey, we understand. And I promise we'll be as gentle as possible."

Matthew eyed her suspiciously, clearly not believing a word she had said.

"Certainly you don't expect to have free run of our complex and all its members."

Now it was Devlin's turn. Sharon had set the tone. He was definitely *bad cop* to her *good*. "That's exactly what we expect," he said. "We can't find a killer if we're told who we can talk to and who we can't."

Matthew shook his head. "I'll have to consult my superiors."

"You do that," Devlin said. "And you explain that we're looking for their cooperation. If we don't get cooperation voluntarily, we'll have to do it with a court order." He hurried on before Matthew could speak. "Now, I'm running this investigation at the request of Mayor Silver. And the mayor has asked me to do everything in my power to keep the press deaf, dumb, and blind about certain particulars of the case—namely, the heroin that was found in Sister Manuela's body, and the facts that she was smuggling it in condoms she had obviously swallowed and that somebody gutted her to get the heroin back." Matthew's eyes had widened in horror. "Now, I'll do my best to do what the mayor wants and keep your group and the archdiocese from being embarrassed by all this." Devlin shook *his* head, imitating Matthew's earlier reaction. "But if I have to start getting court orders and hauling people downtown to talk to them, it's going to make that part of the job very hard. The press isn't stupid. And they find out about court orders very quickly. You make sure your superiors understand that, okay?"

Matthew seemed stunned. "I'll do what I can," he said. He reached into his jacket pocket and withdrew a business card. "Call me at this number later."

"I'll do that," Devlin said. "By the way, what was Sister Manuela doing in Colombia?"

Matthew seemed momentarily flustered. "I'm told she was visiting her family," he said.

Devlin watched Matthew walk away, a slight slump to his shoulders. Then he turned back to the gathering around the grave, taking in the nuns who stood closest to the coffin, wondering which of them had been with the murdered nun on her family visit. It was a hot steamy day, and Devlin noticed that despite the humidity the nuns seemed crisp and fresh. In all the years he had dealt with nuns, going back to his childhood, he had never seen one perspire. He wondered now, as he had many times, how they managed to do that.

*B*ack in the office, two rooms in a city-owned building two blocks from city hall, Devlin sat behind his desk; Sharon Levy perched on its edge. Devlin only used his office for private conversations, preferring a vacant desk in the outer bullpen where he could work more closely with his team of five detectives.

"How do you want to handle this?" Sharon asked.

"With speed." Devlin raised his hands and let them fall back to his desk. "There's no way we're going to keep the press in the dark, no matter what the mayor thinks. They're already circling the carcass, and sooner or later they're going to be all over our collective ass. So first I want two people handling the interviews at Opus Christi. Get as much as we can, as fast as we can. You head that up. I think those kids, especially the young women, might talk more openly to you." He grinned. "Besides, I think Matthew likes you."

Sharon rolled her eyes. "Who should I take with me?"

"Ollie Pitts."

"Oh, Christ."

"Exactly. But I think a dose of Ollie will keep Matthew and everybody else in line."

"Do I get combat pay?"

Devlin laughed. "Because of sweet, lovable Ollie? How can you even suggest such a thing?"

The telephone interrupted them. It was the mayor. Devlin had been expecting the call. He listened for several long minutes as an unusually nervous Howie Silver rattled on. Sharon watched him. There was a scar on Devlin's cheek, a gift from an earlier case, and it whitened whenever he became angry. His team of detectives had learned to watch for it—a sign they had pushed the boss too far. Now, as Devlin listened to the mayor, Sharon saw the scar grow whiter with each passing second.

The mayor paused for breath and Devlin jumped in. "Howie, here's the bottom line. I can't promise you the press won't find out about the drugs, or that this nun was gutted to retrieve them. My people and I will do the best we can, but there are too many mouths, too many people who know what happened. Second, our best shot is to get this killer *before* they find out, and we sure as hell can't do that if you're telling me we have to tiptoe around these Opus Christi clowns. And finally, limiting our ability to investigate this case the way it *has* to be investigated defeats the whole purpose of having this squad. If you insist on it, you have to accept the fact that it's a prescription for failure—"

Sharon could tell the mayor had cut him off. She watched as Devlin listened and stewed. But he wouldn't have it any other way, she thought. She had worked for this man for two years now, and she had learned he was a truly complex character. First he was a detective, deep down into his personal core. He loved the challenge of finding the answers to something that seemed unsolvable. But even that wasn't enough. He seemed to need more. He reveled when obstacles were thrown in his path by outside forces. She hadn't been with him on his last case in Cuba, where a combination of the Castro government, Afro-Cuban voodoo cults, and a faction of the U.S. Mafia had been aligned against him. Ollie Pitts had been there and told her about it. It was the type of case that brought out Devlin's best, just like the Roland Winter case. She had been at his side throughout *that* bit of madness, as the city's most powerful real estate magnate had tried to end Devlin's career and, when that had failed, his life.

Devlin's voice roared back as the mayor paused again. "Look, Howie, you've got plenty of people at the Puzzle Palace who can handle this case. Pick one and give them the scenario you're giving me. Then sit back and watch the walls come tumbling down. Because their chances of finding this killer are just about nil if they can't interview everyone they *need* to interview."

Devlin listened again. When he resumed his own side of the conversation, there was an even sharper edge in his voice. "It won't work. It's that simple. You have to start by investigating the nun and everybody who knew her. There is no other way. And when the press discovers what happened—and they will—and when they find out we don't have a killer in custody because we've run a half-assed investigation—and they'll find that out too—then I can promise you that *all* our butts are going to be hung out to dry."

Again, Devlin listened. When he spoke his voice was smoother, softer, but just barely. "What I need is for you to tell those Opus Christi people to cooperate with us. And I need you to tell them that if they don't there is no way you can keep the press deaf, dumb, and blind. You also have to tell them that I *will* get a court order if I have to, because if you take that ability away from me I can't do the job. It's obstruction, pure and simple, and we can't work that way. So, boss, I hate to say it, but if you insist on that, you might as well give the case to someone else right from the start. Because my people and I won't be able to do you a damn bit of good."

Again Devlin sat and listened. Finally, a small smile flickered across his lips. "We'll do our best," he said.

Sharon grinned at him as he hung up the phone. "So?" she asked.

"The mayor says find the killer before the press and the archdiocese have him for lunch."

"Do we have to tiptoe around everybody?"

Devlin shook his head. "But the mayor doesn't want us to break too many chops, either. These people like to make phone calls, and that gets Hizzoner jumpy."

"So Ollie's out?"

Devlin grinned at her. "Not a chance. Ollie's in."

Sharon rolled her eyes again. "Well, I tried. What about a court order if we need it?"

"Not a problem, but we should try to avoid it."

Sharon raised her eyebrows, feigning surprise. "So you got what you wanted."

Devlin stared up at her. "We'll see. The mayor's been known to change his mind when things get unpleasant. I do know that we better deliver. We better catch this guy *before* the press starts chewing on Hizzoner and these holy rollers. Otherwise we might find ourselves working out of a squad room on Staten Island."

Sharon shrugged. "Hey, there's always a chance we'll get a nice view of the harbor," she said.

**W**hen Sharon and Ollie Pitts had left for Opus Christi's Manhattan headquarters, Devlin joined his remaining three detectives in the bullpen and handed out assignments.

Stan Samuels was a tall, thin, ascetic-looking forty-year-old, who looked more like an accountant than a first-grade detective. He was known as "the mole" to his fellow cops because of his passion for digging through old records. Devlin told him to search every record he could ferret out, to learn everything he could about The Holy Order of Opus Christi, from the time the group was founded through the opening of their new headquarters in New York.

Red Cunningham was a three-hundred-pound baby-faced behemoth who could plant a bug anywhere. He also had close contacts with NYPD's wire experts in narcotics and intelligence. Devlin told him to call in any favors he had in those divisions and get whatever they had on major drug dealers who were importing heroin into the city from South America. He also told Red to check city records for architectural drawings of the Opus Christi headquarters and figure out where best to plant wires if that proved necessary.

Ramon "Boom Boom" Rivera—the group's self-proclaimed Latin lover and the squad's computer whiz—was assigned a complete computer search of everything dealing with Opus Christi. He also was to find out the type of computer system the group used and to determine if and how that system could be hacked.

"Sounds like you think maybe this group might be involved in this drug deal," Boom Boom said, when Devlin finished.

"Not necessarily the group itself," Devlin said, "but maybe somebody who's *part* of the group." He leaned back in his chair and glanced at each of the three detectives. "I just don't buy a young nun getting tied up in a drug deal all by herself."

"I read the DD-Fives those homicide detectives filed. Said her parents were from Colombia," Boom Boom said. "Could have been a family thing. Maybe I should run a check on them."

"You do that," Devlin said. "I talked on the phone with the homicide dicks who caught the case. Now I want to talk to them in person. Get things they might not have put in their DD-Fives and work back from there." He pushed himself up from the chair. "We don't have a lot of time. The mayor didn't hand us this case until it was two days old, and that's very old for a homicide, so get cracking. One other thing. No comments to the press. You refer all questions to the deputy commissioner for public information. No exceptions."

# Chapter Two

*F*ather Patrick Donovan hummed a show tune as he removed a starched white surplice from the sacristy's vestment drawer. He wasn't sure about the lyrics, or even the title, only that it was a lesser song from the Broadway musical he had seen the previous week. Still, the melody had hidden itself in his brain, and he had found himself humming it off and on ever since.

The priest laid the surplice on a small table and smoothed it with his hands. His frail wrists stuck out of the sleeves of his cassock. He looked at them and frowned.

You're wasting away, he told himself. He ran a hand through his thinning hair. He had lost so much of it in recent months. It was the medication, he was certain of it.

The priest did not hear the man enter the sacristy door behind him. Only the sound of the door clicking shut alerted him. He turned, smiling, thinking one of the boys from the choir had arrived early.

Ten feet away a slight, swarthy man returned his smile.

"May I help you?" Donovan asked.

"I came to see about joining the choir," the man said.

Donovan tilted his head to the side, a sign of regret. "I'm afraid it's a boys' choir," he said. "We do have adult men join in on special occasions: Christmas, for instance. We need them to sing the *basso* in more complex pieces." He studied the man's slight frame. "You don't sing bass, do you? You look more like a tenor."

The man shrugged. "I can try." There was a hint of an accent in his voice that the priest could not place. The man offered up another smile that did not carry to his eyes. There a hard, cold glint resided that made the priest uneasy.

"Well, if you wait in the church proper I'll give you a brief audition when the boys arrive. It shouldn't be more than fifteen minutes."

The man nodded and started for the door, and the priest turned back to his surplice. Then the man was behind him, so quickly and quietly the priest never heard or sensed the movement.

One hand covered the priest's mouth and the other flashed a double-edged blade before his eyes. The priest's head was pulled back until his ear was against the man's mouth.

"A gift, *maricón*," the man whispered.

The last thing the priest sensed was the smell of spices on the man's breath.

*O*pus Christi's Manhattan headquarters was located on Second Avenue, between 44th and 45th Streets, a twelve-story tower set amid some of the city's pricier residential and commercial real estate.

From the sidewalk, Ollie Pitts eyed the building with distaste. He ran a hand over his buzzed hair, then placed both hands on his hips.

"What's wrong?" Sharon Levy asked.

"There used to be a great little Irish gin mill right here," Pitts said. "Christ, this city's turning to shit. First Disney destroys 'the deuce'; now a bunch of Bible thumpers are tearing down bars. What the fuck is next?"

Sharon gave a snort of laughter and glanced up Second Avenue. A few blocks north was a notorious sex shop that claimed to have the city's largest selection of sex toys. The shop was also known for its outrageous holiday window displays, with Easter especially causing major angst among the city's more spiritually inclined. Then the shop windows were decorated with Easter baskets, each holding multicolored vibrators, dildos, and vaginal eggs. She smiled to herself, wondering how Matthew—"as the apostle"—would react if any of the Holy Order's female members were caught window-shopping.

She grabbed Ollie by the elbow. "Come on, let's get this done," she said. "We'll commiserate on the decline of Irish bars later."

*M*atthew met them in the lobby. The light-gray suit he had worn at the funeral was still in place, hanging on his scarecrow frame like an expensive sack. Standing next to Ollie he looked even more emaciated. He extended a hand and Ollie swallowed it with the ham that protruded from his coat sleeve.

There was a second man with Matthew, younger and huskier but still no match for Ollie's two hundred and forty pounds. Matthew introduced him as John.

Ollie gave them a flat smile from his bulldog's face. "Matthew and John. Huh. You got Mark and Luke stashed someplace upstairs?"

Matthew blinked at the remark. John frowned.

Sharon fought off a smile. So it begins, she thought. The irrepressible charm of Ollie Pitts.

Matthew held up a manila folder to Sharon. "This is all the information the order has on Sister Manuela," he said.

Sharon took it and gave him a broad smile. "I'd also like a list of all the members of the order," she said. A look of shock erupted on Matthew's face, and she hurried on. "It would be helpful if they were divided by sex. Detective Pitts will be interviewing the men and I'll handle the women. It will let us know we've talked to everyone."

"You don't . . . seem to understand," Matthew sputtered. "We are a worldwide organization."

Sharon's smile became patently patient. "The New York members will do," she said.

"But our membership and our files are confidential."

"I understand that," Sharon said, still smiling. "And we'll *keep* them confidential. But we need the list to make sure we're not missing anyone when we interview these people." She gave him a seemingly regretful shrug. "Inspector Devlin explained all this to you. One way or another we're going to have that list, Matthew." She softened the implied threat of a court order by flashing the smile again. "Just try and remember that we're the good guys; we're on *your* side. Now, if you'll get that list together and give us two rooms where we can interview the men and the women, we'll get started."

"I don't . . . see the point. I mean . . . you have the folder."

Sharon raised the hand that held the folder. "This is nice. But it's *bubkes*, Matthew. Now listen to me. We're going to interview each member of the order. And we're going to do it today. Any delay will impede this investigation and reduce our chances of catching the animal who killed Sister Manuela. And we can't allow that to happen. Do we understand each other?" Sharon's smile was gone now, replaced by a toothy grin spread across Ollie Pitts's face.

Matthew was certain that Pitts was hoping he would say no. He felt a shiver move along his spine. "I'll have to get approval from my superiors," he said. "It will take about fifteen minutes."

*T*he two homicide detectives who caught the Sister Manuela case worked out of the Queens precinct that covered Kennedy International Airport. They were old hands, both nearing the end of thirty-year careers and the pensions that awaited them. Consequently, neither objected to handing over this high-profile case to Devlin's team.

"It's like I told you on the phone," Detective Harry Hannigan said. "There was no way I believed this was a nun when we found the body."

They were gathered around Hannigan's desk in the precinct squad room. Hannigan resembled a side of beef, right down to his red face. His size reminded Devlin of Ollie Pitts, but all similarities ended there. Hannigan was in his early fifties with a full head of gray hair and the demeanor of a cop who has seen more than his share of police work.

His partner, Murray Cohen, was half Hannigan's size and two or three years younger. He had a drab everyman look that probably made him a natural running a tail, someone you could see every day and never notice.

"There was no question about it being a drug-related

murder," Cohen said. "There was white powder residue on her habit." He drew a long breath. "The perp who did this was an animal. The ME said he didn't even put her out of her misery before he sliced her open. Cut her throat *after* he opened her belly. We figure she started screaming, so he didn't have a choice."

"He didn't do it first because he didn't wanna risk losing more of the drugs," Hannigan said. He tightened his lips and shook his head, again the man who had seen more of life than he cared to. He raised his chin toward the calendar on his desk. "Three months from today I'll have my thirty years in, and my papers will hit personnel an hour later. . . . I can't fucking wait," he added for emphasis.

"The way this is starting out I may want to join you," Devlin said. They were words of mollification and camaraderie. He wanted—no, he needed—the cooperation of these men if he was going to make up the time already lost. He leaned forward. "I've read your initial DD-Fives. Tell me what else you've come up with."

"Squat," Hannigan said. His face became defensive. "Look, Inspector, we ran a clean crime scene. Everything by the book. What the ME and the criminologists ended up with was as good as they could get. But you gotta remember that this little nun baked in that car for a couple of days. So . . ." He ended the sentence with a shrug. "We're hoping we'll end up with some hair or fibers from her habit, but those results haven't come back yet."

"I understand," Devlin said. He glanced at Cohen. "You get background on the nun?"

"Only that she and her family came here from Colombia ten years ago." Cohen shrugged. "We hit a stone wall with those Opus Christi characters. We even sicced our lieutenant on them, and they told him to talk to the archdiocese, he didn't like their answers." Cohen laughed. "You can imagine how far he got with *those* guys."

"Hell, we couldn't even find out where her parents live, or if they're even still alive," Hannigan said.

"The nun's parents weren't at the funeral," Devlin said. "Or anyone we could identify as a relative."

"Guy I talked to at Opus Christi headquarters said their members cut all family ties when they join up." He shook his head again. "Maybe they weren't invited. Wouldn't that be a helluva thing."

"Or they could be dead or back in Colombia," Cohen said.

"What else?" Devlin asked.

"We took down the license plates of every car parked within a hundred yards of the crime scene," Hannigan said. "Then we ran all the plates through the DMV computer." He laughed. "Came up with four stolen cars. So far we've contacted about a third of the people whose cars were parked there but came up with zilch. Nobody saw anything suspicious. You want, we'll finish the list for you."

"That would be a big help. It would free my people for other things."

"You got it," Hannigan said. "It'll take us a day and a half, tops."

The telephone interrupted them. Hannigan answered it, then handed the receiver to Devlin. "For you, Inspector," he said. He raised his eyebrows. "Mayor's office."

Devlin listened and made some quick notes as one of Howie Silver's aides babbled excitedly. "Tell the mayor we'll handle it. It's probably not related, but he's right; the press will treat it as though it is." He listened again. "Okay. Tell him I'll call as soon as I know what we've got."

Devlin handed the receiver back to Hannigan, who raised his eyebrows again, this time as a question.

"Somebody killed a priest in Greenwich Village," Devlin said. "Cut his throat from ear to ear in the church sacristy."

"Just like the nun," Cohen said. "Still, it's gotta be a coincidence. But you're right, the press won't think so." He scratched his chin. "No indication of drugs?"

Devlin shook his head.

"Jesus, what the fuck's *with* this city?" It was Hannigan this time. He blew out a long stream of air. "I guess my sainted mother was wrong. Old girl tried to talk me into a seminary when I told her I signed up for the cops. Said the priesthood was safer work."

"What do you mean they'll be sitting in on our interviews!" Sharon demanded.

The two men who were the cause of Sharon's anger stood behind Matthew. They were in their early thirties, at best, and like Matthew both wore bland suits and neckties.

"These gentlemen are attorneys," Matthew said. "They are also numerarier in our order and are well acquainted with our members. I'm sure they'll be a help to you. Of course, they'll also be there to protect the rights of the people you're questioning."

"These are interviews, not interrogations," Sharon snapped. "These people are not suspects. We're simply looking for information."

"I believe they are within their rights to have an attorney present," Matthew said. "We are not denying your request. We're cooperating fully. But we are also offering this protection to our members."

"Sounds like you wanna find out what we find out," Pitts said. "Have your own boys there to—"

Sharon raised a hand, cutting him off. "We'll ask each person if they want these gentlemen present," Sharon said. "That's their right, too."

Matthew gave her a thin smile. "I'm certain they'll say that they do," he said.

The priest's body lay in a pool of blood that had spread over much of the tile floor. From the broad, uninterrupted arterial spray that covered a nearby wall, Devlin could tell that the killer had stood behind the priest as he cut. A blood-soaked vestment lay next to the body, part of it still clutched in the priest's hand.

Devlin glanced at the two detectives who had caught the case. "The victim was getting ready for some service?" he asked.

"Choir practice," one detective said. His name was Rourke. He was tall and slender, with a wispy mustache, about thirty-five, Devlin guessed. His partner, about the same age, had an identical drooping mustache, typical of so many younger cops. But he was shorter and rounder. His name was Costa. Mutt and Jeff, Devlin thought.

Rourke nodded toward the body. "He ran the choir. The pastor said he liked the choir kids to wear their white robes when they practiced. Thought it cut down on the fooling around. Said the father always wore his, too." He glanced down at the blood-soaked garment, which was now mostly brown. "I guess that used to be white," he added.

"What was his name?" Devlin asked.

"Patrick Donovan." It was Costa, reading from his notebook. "He's been curate here for seven years."

"Are the priests here part of any order?"

Costa shook his head. "They're diocesan priests, according to the pastor."

Devlin glanced around the sacristy. The crime scene appeared well established. The patrolmen who had responded to the initial call had closed off all entrances to the church. They had gathered information from the choirboys who had found the body and from the pastor, to whom the boys had gone first. Then they had isolated all of them under guard in the church proper and taken statements.

When Rourke and Costa arrived, the patrolmen had passed on all information gathered, along with their initial observations. Then, under the detectives' direction, the area had been secured with crime-scene tape, while additional units were brought in to guard the exterior of the church.

"Did the kids notice anything or anyone?" Devlin asked.

Rourke shook his head. "They were scared shitless. Wouldn't have seen Christ himself, he floated down from the altar." He tilted his head to one side. "Good thing, though. Kept them from walking through the crime scene and contaminating everything. They just ran like hell for the pastor when they saw the body."

Devlin nodded. "I'd like you both to canvass the area. Stores, people living near the church, anyone who might have been passing by. Tell one of the uniforms to wait with the body. I'm going to talk to the pastor."

*M*onsignor Anthony Fucci was a short round man with a thick shock of white hair. His face was as round as his body and bore webs of broken capillaries that spoke of someone who liked his wine a bit more than he should.

Devlin smiled at the boys still gathered around the priest, then identified himself to the pastor and explained that he had a few questions.

"Could we move away from the children?" Fucci asked.

Devlin nodded and followed the priest to a pew at the rear of the church.

"Was it a robbery?" the priest asked.

"There's no indication of that, but we'll want you to check the sacristy and the rest of the church when our forensics people finish." Devlin inclined his head toward the sacristy. "Was any money, or anything of value, kept back there or out here?"

"No. At least nothing that should interest a thief, nothing that could be easily sold." The pastor looked down into his lap and shook his head. "Money is removed each day to the rectory. It's deposited into the parish bank account almost immediately."

"Was Father Donovan in the habit of carrying much money on his person?"

Again, Monsignor Fucci shook his head. "Just walking-around money. Our incomes aren't very substantial, and to my knowledge Patrick didn't have money of his own."

"Did he have any enemies, anyone he'd had difficulty with who might hold a grudge?"

"No. Everyone loved Patrick. He was a gentle soul, not at all confrontational. In fact, he abhorred confrontations of any kind."

"What can you tell me about him? His friends? People he worked with?"

"Nothing that would lead to this. *Oh, God.*" Fucci closed his eyes. "Maybe it was God's mercy."

"Why do you say that?"

The pastor drew a long breath. "Patrick was dying. He was very ill, and the condition was going to worsen, according to his doctors. He had only a year, perhaps less."

"What was wrong with him?" Devlin asked.

Fucci placed his hands over his face and rubbed softly. "He had AIDS. It was in a very advanced stage. And the medication he was taking wasn't working."

Devlin kept his eyes on the pastor's face, watching for any hint of something hidden. "Was it from a blood transfusion?" he asked.

Fucci rubbed his face again, shook his head. "No," he said. "And he wasn't a drug user to my knowledge."

The pastor had fallen silent. Devlin waited, and when nothing more came, he laid a hand on the priest's shoulder.

"Monsignor, I have to know all of it if we're going to find the person who did this."

The priest nodded. "I know, I know. But I was also his confessor. So I can only tell you things I knew outside of that."

Devlin waited again, then finally asked, "Was Father Donovan gay?"

Fucci let out a long breath. "Yes. He made no secret of it. In fact, he served as an advocate for the gays of the parish." He looked toward the altar and smiled sadly. "It's not something that finds favor uptown." He turned back to Devlin and offered his sad smile again. "There are certain elements in the archdiocese who prefer to live life with blinders on."

"Did the archdiocese know about his illness?"

"Yes, of course. There was even talk about transferring him to another parish." He smiled again. "To get him out of Greenwich Village. Away from the occasion of sin, so to speak." Tears came to his eyes. "I opposed it. God, I wish now that I hadn't."

Devlin knew he had to keep the priest talking before his grief got in the way. "Monsignor, now comes the hard part," he began. "It's possible this was done by someone Father Donovan knew as a gay man. I'll need names of anyone he was especially close to or was possibly involved with."

The pastor shook his head. "If I knew that it would be

from the confessional. But I honestly don't. I never asked for names. I only dealt with the sin and counseled him on how he might avoid it." He drew another breath. "Patrick was well known throughout the gay community. I'm certain others can help you with names."

Devlin glanced toward the choirboys seated toward the front of the church. "It's an ugly question, but was there any involvement with young boys?" He saw anger flash in the monsignor's eyes and hurried on. "It's been known to happen, Monsignor. And sometimes relatives of a child become vengeful."

"No, definitely not. He would have told me that, and he never did."

"You understand that the boys will have to be questioned. We have officers who specialize in that sort of thing. I assure you it will be done discreetly and in a way that won't be harmful to the kids."

The priest let out a long breath. His jaw tightened. "Do what you have to do," he said.

*D*evlin waited for the forensics team and the medical examiner to finish with the crime scene and then contacted Rourke on his cell phone and told the two detectives to meet him back at the church, forthwith.

"So the priest was gay," Rourke said, when Devlin had explained. "Seems to be a lot of that goin' around."

There was a grin on the detective's face that caused the scar on Devlin's cheek to whiten. "That is *not* to go outside the investigation," he said.

Rourke raised his hands, immediately contrite. "Hey, it won't come from us. But you gotta understand. Some newsie starts nosing around down here, we can't control what the local poofs might say. Christ, they find out a priest who was one of their own got iced, they might even have some kinda protest parade."

Devlin knew he was right but kept the warning in his voice. "Just remember, this gets out, some people in the archdiocese will be very unhappy. That will make city hall unhappy, and when city hall's unhappy the bosses at the

Puzzle Palace get downright miserable. So unless you fancy wearing the blue bag again, make sure nothing comes from you." Rourke started to speak, but Devlin waved him off. "Let it rest. We don't have time. I want you out in the neighborhood right away. Find out who this priest was close to . . . in a romantic way. Then I want that person or persons run through the grinder. I want to know what they did and where they were every second of the day. Are we clear?"

"You got it, Inspector," Rourke said.

# *Chapter Three*

*I*t was seven o'clock when Devlin got back to the SoHo loft he shared with his lover, Adrianna Mendez, and his ten-year-old daughter, Phillipa. As he opened the door he saw Phillipa sprawled on a sofa, stereo earphones clamped to her head, feet dangling over the sofa's arms, toes dancing in the air. He let out a sigh. She had been a toddler when his wife was killed in an automobile accident, and he had raised her alone until she was eight, his delight in the child growing each day. Then Adrianna had come into his life, and Phillipa had accepted her eagerly, as though she had been yearning for a mother figure. Now it was Adrianna to whom Phillipa turned when "things" had to be discussed. He once had asked her why she bypassed him in these discussions. Phillipa had rolled her eyes and tolerantly explained that there were things *women had to talk about with other women.*

The statement, precociously naïve though it was, had hit him like a brick. There was no question it held an element of truth. Adrianna seemed to understand the child far better than he. She even understood Phillipa's taste in music, which had blossomed over the past year. To Devlin it was cacophony mixed with sexual innuendo, uttered by emaciated young men, distinguishable only by their bizarre taste in clothing or lack thereof. Had he seen them gathered on a street corner he would have watched and waited for the inevitable drug transaction to take place.

He had tried to overcome this growing gulf between himself and his child, had even visited a music store, boned up on the names of some of the supposedly popular groups, and then raised them in discussion with Phillipa. She had smiled—again, tolerantly—and explained that he was talking ancient history.

Later, Adrianna had commiserated. Then she had explained that today's preteen music icons rose and fell within days. Just listen, she had advised. Let her tell you about them. Don't try to make her think you understand any of it yourself, because you probably never will.

So he had surrendered, lost one more point of contact with the child he adored. There were days when he wondered if he'd ever get any of them back.

Adrianna came out of the portion of the loft she used as a studio, looking paint-splattered and beautiful. She was a highly successful artist, whose paintings sold for more money than Devlin made in several years, and it provided their family with a lifestyle—and him, in particular, with an independence—that few honest cops ever enjoy.

"You're late, and you look exhausted," she said, as she raised herself on tiptoe and kissed his cheek.

To Devlin she was incredibly beautiful, yet far from classically so. In truth, her nose was just a touch too large, her mouth a bit too wide, and her light-brown eyes too great a contrast with her raven-black hair. Yet in combination it all came together to make her one of the most striking women he had ever seen. And her sensual Cuban disposition only added to that delightful mix.

"I'm afraid my day isn't over yet."

Adrianna raised her eyebrows, and Devlin explained how his one new case had suddenly become two. She grimaced when he told her about the priest, glancing quickly at Phillipa to make sure the earphones were still in place.

"I left a message for Sharon and Ollie to stop by here before they head home," Devlin added. "I need them to fill me in on *their* day. Howie's going to want an update on both cases before he goes to bed."

Adrianna rolled her eyes at the mention of the mayor, and Devlin smiled, wondering if that was where Phillipa had picked up the gesture. No, he decided, it was definitely something inbred in the female of the species.

"We had Chinese takeout for dinner," Adrianna said. "I'll warm a plate so you can eat before Sharon and Ollie show up."

He went to the sofa and squeezed in next to Phillipa's supine body. He lifted the earphones from her head, kissed her nose, and said, "Hi, kiddo." From the earphones the strains of young male voices filtered through a heavy bass beat. "Who you listening to?" he asked.

Phillipa grinned at him, a bit too knowingly, he thought. "Backstreet Boys."

The name was lost on him. He smiled. "How was school today?" he asked, changing the subject.

Her grin widened (knowingly?). "Easy, like always," she said. "You must have a new case for the mayor," she added.

"How do you know that?"

"You're home late. You're always home late when you have a new case."

"Very good detective work," he said.

"Tell me about it."

"Uh-uh."

"Mmm. Must be a good grisly one," she said. "You never want to tell me about those. Who got killed?"

He knew she would read about it in the paper the next day, making a point of it just to show him she could find out. "A Catholic priest and a nun," he said.

"Yikes. Sounds like a religious nut," she said.

Devlin shook his head. Where did it come from? He had to cut down on her television time. "They're separate cases, far as we can tell," he said.

"Double yikes." She gave him a knowing look. "Definitely a religious nut, Dad. I guarantee it. And the two cases *have* to be connected. Don't waste time on any other theories."

Devlin fought back a laugh. "Thank you, Inspector. When I talk to the mayor I'll pass along your theory."

Phillipa raised her chin a bit haughtily. "Wait and see," she said.

Devlin bent down and kissed her nose again. God, he loved this kid—precocious and lovely and innocent, and ten years old going on thirty. He ran a hand against her blond hair, noted how the once-prominent freckles were disappearing from her nose and cheeks. Every day she looked more like her mother. The thought sent a pang through him. How he wished Mary could be here to see her child blossom into a young woman. He was certain she would handle *things* just as Adrianna did. She would probably understand her daughter's music as well.

**S**haron arrived an hour later, minus Ollie Pitts. "I sent him home," she explained. "He was still snarling over our little encounter with those Opus Christi clowns."

"What happened?" Devlin asked. "They try and stonewall you?"

"Not in the least," Sharon said. "They gave us everything we wanted. Access to all their members who were at the headquarters. Separate rooms to interrogate the men and the women."

"So?"

Sharon told him about the two "numerarier" lawyers. She shook her head. "Every time I asked a question, the person I was interviewing would look at this numerarier—which by the way is some kind of muck-a-muck in their order. If he nodded they would answer. If he didn't, they would say they didn't know. It was the same with all of Ollie's interviews. There were a lot of 'I don't know' answers. We might as well have just interviewed these numerarier guys and called it quits."

They were seated at the kitchen table. Devlin leaned back in his chair and shook his head. "What's with these people? One of their nuns gets murdered in an obvious drug deal. Embarrassing, sure, but the mayor and the department have promised to cover them with the media as best we can. And they still throw one roadblock after another in front of us. With the press waiting in the wings, these people are nailing their own asses to the wall. It doesn't make sense."

"Unless they're involved in the drug thing themselves," Sharon said.

"A religious order of the Catholic Church? What for? That makes even less sense."

"Maybe somebody inside the group."

"That's a possible, sure. But when you think about it, it doesn't make a lot of sense either. It would have to be someone with enough authority to make a young nun work as a drug mule. I just can't imagine that happening."

Sharon let out a weary breath. "I can't either. But, dammit, something is going on there. And until we find out more about these people, we're not going to have a chance in hell of finding out what it is."

Devlin tapped a finger against his lips. "I know a Jesuit who teaches philosophy and religious history at Fordham. I'll make an appointment to see him tomorrow. Maybe he can shed some light on these people. What about that young nun, the one who seemed so shaken at the funeral?"

"She wasn't there. According to Matthew she was out doing missionary work." Sharon made quotation marks in the air around the last two words and added, "Whatever the hell that means."

"Let's keep after her."

"I will." Sharon paused a beat. "I heard about the new case, the murdered priest. Any possible connection?"

Devlin smiled at her. "My daughter thinks so. But the evidence doesn't point that way."

Sharon returned the smile. She was aware of Phillipa's penchant for offering up theories on their cases. Then she listened as Devlin filled her in on what they had found at the murder scene.

"Gay. Dying of AIDS." Sharon gave him a pained look. "You think it was an old lover the priest gave it to? Or maybe the person who gave it to the priest, afraid he might out him as a carrier?"

"We're checking both angles. The priest was also the church choirmaster. We're interviewing the parents of all the kids too."

Again, Sharon grimaced. "God, I hope it's not that. Not more kids sexually abused by a gay priest. If it is, I'll start rooting for the killer." She shook her head. "Listen to me. Do I sound homophobic, or do I sound homophobic?"

"You sound homophobic," Devlin said. "Nothing stirs up homophobia like a sexually abused kid. Even for gay police sergeants."

## Chapter Four

*F*ather William Martin's office was on the top floor of the faculty building on Fordham's Lincoln Center campus. Martin was very much the aesthete, and every inch of his tall, lean body exuded his Jesuit training. Devlin had first met the priest years ago when Martin taught ethics to new trainees at the police academy, and he had formed a friendship with the scholarly priest that had lasted over the intervening years.

Devlin smiled. Martin sat behind a desk so cluttered with papers no wood showed on the surface. "If the Dead Sea Scrolls had been hidden on that desk they never would have been found," he said.

Martin tapped the pile with a long bony finger. "I know exactly where every scrap is," he said. "Unfortunately, some of those scraps are so old, I don't recall why I put them there."

Martin had disheveled, wispy white hair that marked his sixty-three years, but everything else about him save his desk seemed ordered and purposeful. The broad smile he offered Devlin made him seem ten years younger.

"So how are the lovely Adrianna and the equally lovely Phillipa?" he asked.

"Both still the joy of my life," Devlin said. "Although Phillipa has reached an age that I find mystifying."

"How old is she now?" Martin asked.

"Ten. She'll be eleven in a few months." Devlin let out a breath.

"And you don't understand her at all, I take it."

"Less each day."

Martin brought his hands together in a clap. "Good. It will keep you on your toes. Children need parents who are on their toes, watching and struggling to understand. They may think their parents are hopeless fools, but deep down they know they're loved, and that's what counts." Martin raised his hands as if giving a benediction. "As you can see, I enjoy offering advice about children from the safety of my celibacy." He leaned back in his chair and steepled his fingers before his face. "So, you said on the telephone that you had some questions about Opus Christi. That is truly a fascinating subject. Why are you interested?"

Devlin filled him in on the murder of the young nun and on the problems they had in getting even minimal cooperation from the order.

"The death, or at least the nature of it, of course, surprises me," he said, when Devlin had finished. "The lack of cooperation does not surprise me at all."

"Why is that?"

The priest spread his hands and then brought them back to a steeple. "First, let me point out that you are asking a Jesuit about Opus Christi, a group the Society of Jesus is said to vehemently oppose—primarily, as current church wisdom holds, because Opus Christi is said to have replaced the Jesuits as Catholicism's most influential religious order, especially among the powers in Rome."

"Is that true?" Devlin asked.

"Oh, yes, it's quite true. Opus Christi has more power and more influence with the present pope and those surrounding him than the Jesuits ever hoped to have."

"Why is that?"

Martin raised a hand. "Let me get to that later. First, let me tell you bluntly that I consider Opus Christi to be nothing more than a very dangerous cult, dangerous to both its members and to the church itself. That said, I'll give you a brief history of the order and a summary of its practices."

Martin rose and began walking behind his desk, hands

clasped behind his back. It was the pose of a lecturer, and it brought another smile to Devlin's lips.

"Opus Christi was founded some seventy years ago by an obscure Colombian priest by the name of José Chavarría de Mata. He was only thirty-one at the time and was already working in the Colombian prelature at Bogotá. By all accounts he was a brilliant young man, and had caught the eye of Colombia's cardinal, who himself was highly regarded by Rome. Chavarría claimed to have had a vision in which God directed him to found a lay religious order, exclusively for men, that would lead them to lives of holiness by following the message of Christ in their daily endeavors. Under supposedly divine inspiration, Chavarría wrote a book—a catechism of sorts—called *The Way,* in which he detailed in broad brushstrokes the principles that should be followed to achieve this Christlike way of life. Those principles, that message of Christ, is, of course, subject to interpretation by those who run The Holy Order."

"And that's the problem as you see it?" Devlin asked.

Father Martin raised a lecturing finger. "The devil's always in the details, isn't it?" He tapped the finger against his nose. "Opus Christi, translated from the Latin, means work of Christ. But to the order the meaning of those words is not that they are *doing* the work of Christ but rather that they *are* the work of Christ. Ergo, there is an assumed infallibility in all their pronouncements and in their very interpretation of how a good Christian life should be lived." He clasped his hands and gestured with them. "Unfortunately, no matter how great one's piety, no matter how devoutly one strives to live a good life, none of it guarantees that one's beliefs are correct. Neither does it guarantee that one's actions are not misguided."

Devlin considered that, stored it away, and went on to something that was bothering him. "You said the order was exclusively for men. But we found women as members— and nuns."

Martin let out a small chuckle. "There was a second vision about ten years after Opus Christi was formed. Chavarría claimed the Holy Ghost appeared to him again and told him to include women among the order's members. There were strict caveats, however. Men and women were to be kept isolated from each other. This was to ensure there were no romantic contacts. Celibacy was to remain inviolate. Female emancipation was also to be avoided. Women were to be confined to cleaning and cooking, with male and female members not even allowed to see each other at those times." The priest laughed again. "I suspect those who first ran the order found that their accommodations were not quite tidy enough, their meals not quite satisfying enough, and decided a second visitation by the Holy Ghost might cure that initial planning error providing there were strict rules that would not compromise purity."

Martin sighed. "I know that sounds terribly snide, but for those of us who have steeped ourselves in the sometimes shameful history of the church, it is frustrating to see the relatively few advances we have made in women's suffrage trampled underfoot with the blessing of Rome. It's just one more of the practices and pronouncements that are driving people away from the church. And if we want to bring people back, want to see the church prosper and grow, a return to medieval thinking and cultist practices is not the path we should follow."

"You've used the term *cult* twice now, but you haven't explained it," Devlin said.

Martin took his chair, clasped his hands again, and rested his forearms on the desk. "Like all elitist organizations, Opus Christi puts most of its energy into recruiting new members. Its education methods, though quite bizarre to most people, are not all that unusual for the type of organization it is. The Holy Order employs iron discipline, brainwashing, and insistence on absolute obedience. It demands a spartan lifestyle, constant self-accusation, complete subordination to authority, and a missionary attitude that can only be described as arrogant. These are characteristics that have always been employed by elitist organizations, be they the boarding schools of Britain—in certain instances, even some Jesuit schools—in the Prussian or Soviet cadet academies, and in the educational practices of the Third Reich."

"Whoa," Devlin said.

"I know, I know," Martin said, "I sound rabid on the subject. But I assure you those feelings are well founded." He leaned back in his chair and gave his head a sad shake. "As I'm explaining my reasoning, I want you to keep in mind other cults you've become familiar with, be they Jim Jones, the Reverend Moon, the Branch Davidians, or a host of others."

"Are you telling me this group is run by either madmen or charlatans?" Devlin asked.

"No, I am not. I don't question that these people are devout believers, and the good Lord knows we have few enough of those today. But like the others I mentioned it's a religious piety that operates in an atmosphere of secrecy and zealotry and fanaticism, and from those positions, I'm afraid, it's only a small step over the brink.

"First and foremost, The Holy Order is based on absolute secrecy—even secrecy from those it hopes to recruit." He looked at Devlin soberly. "They target young, religiously motivated people, often those who seem somewhat lost and uncertain of themselves. Hence, recruits are usually in their late teens or early twenties. But here's the important point. Those slated for recruitment never know *who* is recruiting them until they are considered emotionally dependent and safely in the fold. And when they do find out it's too late. They're dependent. They've come to believe they *need* the order for their very salvation. In short, they've become victims of psychological entrapment.

"To do this, The Holy Order operates youth centers and clubs, offering things they know will attract young Catholic men and women. They offer camping and cycling trips, very closely chaperoned social gatherings, excursions to various places—all of it free, of course—and, later, discussion groups, some say to pinpoint areas of weakness to be worked on by those operating the centers. But throughout it all, those who have been targeted for membership are never allowed to know who really operates the center or club—not until they are considered safe and ready for recruitment.

"Right now, Opus Christi opens approximately forty new clubs and centers each year worldwide and has eighty thousand members. They're relatively new to this country, only about three thousand, but they are growing quickly. In Europe and South America they're already quite a formidable force, with well-placed members in the media, medicine, the judiciary, universities, and, above all, in finance and politics."

"How do you know all this?" Devlin asked. "It sounds as if there are some big holes in their so-called penchant for secrecy."

Martin smiled. "We Jesuits have been keeping watch." He gave Devlin a small shrug. "What we know about the organization's inner workings we've learned from those who have fled."

"Fled? As in *escaped*?"

"In some cases members have even been kidnapped and deprogrammed."

"Deprogrammed by professionals?" Devlin asked.

"In some cases, yes. In others the individuals simply left on their own and told their families or parish priests what they experienced."

"I'd be more inclined to believe the latter," Devlin said. "Professional deprogrammers and the results they end up with bother me. Deprogramming can be a form of brainwashing in itself."

"I agree completely," Martin said, "except for one troubling fact. In almost every instance the stories told were frighteningly similar."

"How?"

The priest tapped the tips of his fingers together. "First, recruitment appears to concentrate on students, intellectuals, professionals, and those who are wealthy. The reasons for this, of course, are obvious: vulnerability, influence, and financial gain. Next, all new members are required to turn their incomes and assets over to the order and are given a modest stipend to live on. They are also required to make the order the sole beneficiary of their wills."

"You're kidding," Devlin said. "And this is completely voluntary?"

"Oh, yes. There is no force or coercion." Martin laughed.

"Other than fear of eternal damnation if they refuse. And, at that point, those recruited appear to believe that result will inevitably occur if they disobey."

The priest raised a hand and grasped two fingers. "Next, members must forsake all contact with their families. The Holy Order *becomes* their family. Each member is assigned to an older ranking member of the order, who becomes their spiritual guide—in effect, their new father or mother—and they must submit to that guide's discipline without question. And the discipline is strict. Their mail is read before they receive it. They must confess all their thoughts and lose all sense of self. They are taught that if they are not happy all the time, it is because they are not connected with God; that such unhappiness is a sin and must be confessed to their spiritual guide."

Martin had run out of fingers and let his hands fall back to the desk. "Members must fall on their knees during spiritual discussions and confess their unhappiness. They must also perform acts of mortification every day. These start out simply at first. Taking a cold shower in the morning, denying oneself sugar or cream in one's coffee if one prefers it that way, putting it in if one does not. Later, more painful acts of mortification are required. Members must wear a repentance belt for two hours each day. This is a metal wire that is tightened around one's leg, a wire with sharp spikes inside that actually pierce the skin. Then there is scourging, beating one's bare buttocks with a cord that has knots tied in it. This is required once every week for the duration of a Credo or a Salve Regina, or some similar prayer. And their bodies are checked regularly to make sure these acts are being done . . . adequately."

"And they actually get people to do this?" Devlin's voice was filled with incredulity.

"Oh, yes. The people in charge are quite persuasive, very powerful personalities. And they demand and receive total obedience." Again, Martin shrugged. "Except from those who wake up one morning and realize what's happening to them. Those are the ones who leave."

Devlin shook his head. "It's hard to believe this is happening in the church I knew as a kid. But then I never expected to hear about the sexual and psychological abuse that priests and nuns inflicted on kids in Catholic orphanages either."

The priest swiveled his chair to stare out the office window, as if looking away from that ugly truth. "Evil doesn't stop at the church's door," he said at length.

Devlin nodded. "Or at the precinct door. Tell me about the organizational structure and the people who run the order."

Martin turned back and smiled. "Now you get a Jesuit's subjective—perhaps even jaded—interpretation. Be forewarned."

"I'm so warned," Devlin said.

The priest leaned back in his chair and stared at the ceiling, looked back at Devlin, and inclined his head to one side. "Very little is known about the organizational structure, other than that it is very rigid. Other facts are well guarded from public view. We do know that a German named Reinhard Holtz now heads the order. Up until five years ago he was a very successful banker in Frankfurt, but apparently he had been a member of the order most of his adult life. He is now an ordained priest—ordained by the order itself under its prelature status—and works out of Rome, where the order maintains its world headquarters."

"From banker to head of the order in five years? Isn't that a bit unusual?"

The priest shook his head. "You must understand how the order operates. First there are regular members, who function as soldiers in the field, so to speak. They do the religious work of the order, primarily working in areas that seek to advance 'family values.' " Farther Martin used his fingers to place quotation marks around his final words. "Essentially that means vigorous opposition to divorce, abortion, homosexuality, the ordination of women, and any other efforts that propose equality for women. They also work in Opus Christi business enterprises. The public, by the way, is never allowed to know that the order operates these businesses. That fact is always kept hidden.

"Next we move up the ladder to the numerarier. These are

trusted, established members, usually ordained priests within the order, who supervise the regular members. In actuality they control the lives of those members from morning until night, enforcing all discipline and ensuring that the directives of the order are followed exactly.

"Above them are the supernumerarier." Martin smiled. "This is where the secrecy of the order hits its zenith. Supernumerarier are known only at the highest levels of the order. In most cases even trusted numerarier don't know who these people are, or exactly what their positions are within the hierarchy. But these supernumerarier are always prominent people—men at the top of their fields in business, banking, higher education, journalism, medicine, politics, or simply *wealth*—people who can act on behalf of the order without anyone's knowing of their personal involvement. Ergo, they are powerful assets who can be used behind the scenes." His smile returned. "Imagine if the entire College of Cardinals were known only to a select few, that instead of acting as bishops, they held high positions in the very institutions that governed and regulated every facet of modern society; and that they moved among us, doing the church's work, without anyone's knowing the true purpose of their actions."

"You're scaring me," Devlin said.

Martin nodded. "Indeed." He extended his hands at his sides, the long, bony fingers spread apart. "What you have in that instance, my friend, are tentacles that reach everywhere, secret untraceable power—all of it without accountability. And when you have that, the opportunity for abuse is limitless."

"How did the Jesuits breach this secrecy?"

"With great effort," Martin said. "And when the Society of Jesus applies great effort, it usually succeeds." He rocked back in his chair. "Actually, when Reinhard Holtz became head of Opus Christi five years ago, we realized what was happening. He came out of the blue, so to speak—already an ordained priest, who had been a major world-banking figure for more than two decades. From there we began to look for others in Europe, and we found them in every facet of business and government, education and the media. All highly placed, and, to a man, dedicated above all else to the work of the order."

"What about here in the States?" Devlin asked.

"The order is too new here. At present, we haven't a clue. But I assure you, we are working on it."

Devlin stood and paced the small office, shaking his head. "How in hell did they get this kind of power within the Catholic church?"

Martin let out a soft laugh. "Well, first, they fully agree with the present pope's program on sexuality and reproductive health. This was not a widespread attitude when John Paul II received the white hat in 1978, so they quickly became a favorite of that new and somewhat embattled pontiff. But the real basis of their power came four years later with the Vatican banking scandal. That, if you recall, began with the 1982 failure of Banco Ambrosiano, one of Europe's most influential banks. And since the Vatican Bank was inextricably linked with Ambrosiano, it too faced a financial crisis of immense proportions." Martin raised his right hand in a dramatic gesture. "Enter Opus Christi, stage right, with an offer to pick up thirty percent of the Vatican's annual expenditures—an offer the pope quickly and eagerly accepted. And suddenly, within months, Opus Christi was granted a personal prelature, and since that time its growth within the church has known no bounds."

Devlin shook his head and laughed. "The order has that kind of money?"

"Oh, yes."

"And the chutzpah to bribe the pope?"

Martin grimaced. "Let us just say they found a way to touch upon the pragmatism for which our current pope is famous."

Again, Devlin shook his head and laughed. "Given all that, what chance do I have of cracking their shell?"

Martin raised a finger. "Only one chance, my friend."

"Which is?"

"An obscure Franciscan brother who works with street kids in Hell's Kitchen. It seems he too has concerns about

Opus Christi, especially its treatment of easily influenced kids. Presently he's working with several who would like to escape the order but are afraid to try. I'm also told he's working with a numerarier who has begun to doubt the holiness of The Holy Order."

"Can you put me in touch?"

"I can do better," Martin said. "I'll call Brother Michael and arrange a meeting. It will have to be in the evening. Most of his work is done at night."

"Please set it up," Devlin said. "I'll be there any time he can see me."

---

## *Chapter Five*

*H*e moved down the sidewalk with a smile creasing his round, cherubic face. Father Peter Falco believed the smile should remain a constant part of his demeanor. As someone who was "one with Christ," he felt it an obligation imposed on him by his priesthood. There was nothing more dispiriting to those seeking God's grace than a gloomy priest.

Today the smile was difficult. Every part of his body ached. He knew it was the medication. The doctor had warned him that the treatment might prove more debilitating than the illness . . . at least for a time. It was all part of God's punishment—at least that was what the bigots said. He shook his head. There was nothing to be done about either the illness or the bigots, except to endure both.

An old woman stopped in front of him, ending the thought. Without preamble she began telling him about her grandson. He was becoming a hoodlum, hanging out with other hoodlums, refusing to get out of bed on Sunday to attend mass, she said. The priest nodded and told her to bring the boy to see him. He would talk to him, try to get him involved in the CYO.

He continued down the street, a slight waddle to his short, round body. A greengrocer, sweeping his sidewalk, stopped him and began putting together a small bag of fruit. The priest took it gratefully, although the thought of eating anything at all nauseated him. Even the weight of the small bag made his arm feel leaden. He was like a man in his late sixties, he thought, rather than his true age of thirty-seven.

Another man watched from across the street, his eyes never leaving the fat little figure. He wasn't certain it was the right one, the priest who was second on his list, but he would find out. If it was, he would be even easier than the first.

He crossed the street to the greengrocer's, as the priest moved away, and began filling a small bag with oranges. The greengrocer approached, nodding approval at his choice.

"Clementines," he said. "As sweet as a good woman."

The small swarthy man smiled at him with crooked teeth. "Nothing is as sweet as a woman," he said.

"You're right." The greengrocer pointed at the oranges. "But this is close."

The man inclined his head down the sidewalk in the direction the priest had gone. "Did you give some to the priest?" he asked. "I saw you giving him fruit."

"Father Pete? Yeah, sure. I always give him the best. The best for the neighborhood's best priest, that's what I say."

"He's that good, huh?" The man smiled again, his narrow, pinched features so feral the smile seemed more like a grimace. "I just moved into the neighborhood," he said. "Haven't had a chance to check out the church yet."

The greengrocer nodded. "You go see him. He'll set you up. Father Peter Falco. You'll like him. Every day he's out visiting the seniors and the sick people. Always got time for anybody who needs him. You don't find many priests who do that no more. Most of them sit around on their fat asses all day." He looked at the stranger more closely. "You Spanish?" he asked.

"Yeah. Why?" There was an edge in the man's voice.

The greengrocer ignored it. "It's just that you'll like the church, then. Lotta Spanish people belong now. Used to be all Italians, a few Irish. Now there's just as many Spanish as everybody else, just like the rest of Brooklyn. Pretty soon we'll probably have a mass in Spanish, just like we used to have one in Italian in the old days."

There was a hint of disapproval in the greengrocer's voice, only a hint, but it made the swarthy man bristle. He wanted to reach out and grab him; make him say what he really meant. But that couldn't be. The greengrocer was an old man, late fifties, maybe older. Still, he had a set of arms and shoulders on him from years of lifting crates of fruits and vegetables. Messing with him would raise the level of risk, and that was something he had been told to avoid.

The man paid for his fruit and started back toward the subway that would return him to Manhattan. He had a meeting with the person who had given him this job, and he had to report that he had located the second priest.

When he reached the subway entrance, he threw the bag of clementines into the gutter. Fuck the old man and his fruit, he told himself. Maybe when the job was finished he'd come back and pay him a little visit.

**D**evlin studied the DD-Fives that had just been faxed to him by Rourke and Costa, the two Greenwich Village detectives who had caught the murder of Father Patrick Donovan. The report indicated that their investigation into the priest's background had turned up no specific lover to date. There had also been no involvement with any of the children who attended his church. Donovan, however, was known to frequent one of the area's gay bathhouses. The report stated that the two detectives were now attempting to determine "what persons, if any, the priest may have had sexual liaisons with at that location."

Devlin handed the report to Sharon Levy and waited while she read it.

Levy snickered. "Nice phraseology," she said. "*What persons he may have had sexual liaisons with.* I love it."

"It *is* sensitive," Devlin said.

"Oh, yeah. I can just hear them discussing it in the squad room." She dropped the report on Devlin's desk. "Anyway, fat chance they'll get somebody to admit to a bathhouse tryst. Not with the priest getting offed."

"It's still our best shot," Devlin said.

"You think AIDS was the motive—that he infected someone and this was payback?"

"It's the only motive we have . . . so far. Everything else about this priest has come up clean."

"You should let me handle it then," Levy said. "At least I talk their language."

Devlin shook his head. "I need you to stay with Opus Christi. You've got a better chance of getting through to the young women there. Which brings us to some overtime you'll have to work. I've got a meeting tonight with a Franciscan brother who might be able to help, and I'll need you there."

Sharon raised her eyebrows, and Devlin explained what his friend at Fordham had arranged.

"That's beautiful," she said. "It's exactly what we need—one of their numerarier in our pocket. It's the only way we'll find out what's really going on in that place. So who's gonna handle the dead priest?"

"I want Ollie on that." Devlin smiled at the groan that came from Levy. "I'll be working it too. But I want Ollie to work with the Greenwich Village detectives. He's good on the street, and who knows, maybe somebody will fall in love with him and tell him everything they know."

Sharon let out a snort. "That's fat chance number two," she said.

"You don't think Ollie's lovable?"

She rolled her eyes and ignored the question. "What time do we meet this Franciscan brother?"

"Ten, tonight." Devlin handed her a slip of paper. "That's the address. I'll meet you outside at ten, sharp."

*"T*his time it must look like an accident." The man stopped and raised a finger. "Or perhaps a suicide. Yes, suicide would be an excellent choice. Then that filth could not be buried in consecrated ground."

The swarthy man, whose name was Emilio, shook his head. "Makes it harder," he said. "And more dangerous."

The man stared at him. He was tall and fit, despite the gray that ran through his finely barbered hair, and the blue pinstriped suit he wore looked handmade, an easy two grand, Emilio decided. He did not know the man's name. He had been told it wasn't necessary. They were seated on a bench just inside Central Park a short distance from Grand Army Plaza. It was where they always met. The man would call and give a time, and he would be there to receive his instructions.

"How is it harder and more dangerous?" the man asked.

Emilio shrugged as if the answer were obvious. "It takes time to fake a suicide. And more time makes it more dangerous." He raised his hands and let them fall back to his lap. "It's also hard to fool the cops."

"Why?" There was a demanding edge to the man's voice.

"It's best if the person's unconscious when you set it up. If they're not, they usually fight, and that always leaves marks that can give it away. Then there's the question of how—for a priest, I mean. I don't see him shooting himself. Like, where would he get a gun? That's the first thing the cops would want to know."

"A drug overdose. Sleeping pills, perhaps," the man said, and immediately shook his head. "No, the church would insist it was accidental, and I don't want that. I want him disgraced, just as he's disgraced his priesthood."

"See?" Emilio shrugged again. "It's hard. He falls in front of a bus or a subway, the church is gonna say it's an accident. Unless there's witnesses. And that ain't good for me. He slashes his wrists, I've got to get him someplace quiet: his own bathroom or a hotel, maybe. Same thing with taking a dive out a window. So, how do I get him there?" Emilio shook his head. "It's best I just do him, just like the other one."

The man stroked his chin and thought. "No," he said at length. "There is a way." He explained what he wanted.

Emilio grimaced. "That's hard too. I still gotta get him someplace."

The man stared at him. "Try." His voice was emphatic. "He runs the CYO—the Catholic Youth Organization—at his parish." He shook his head in disgust. "Imagine, a homosexual in charge of those children. Teaching them the way to lead a good Catholic life."

"Hey, I understand how you feel. But that don't make it easier."

The man's eyes hardened. "Listen. I am providing excellent service to your people. They are getting *exactly* what they want. I expect no less in return. If you need me to telephone your boss to confirm that, I shall."

Emilio thought about that phone call and what it might mean to him. He raised a hand and showed his crooked teeth in a smile. "Hey, I'll try. I just want you to understand if it don't fool the cops."

The man took out a crisp handkerchief and patted his forehead against the heat. He gave Emilio a patient smile. "The police aren't as clever as you think they are," he said.

*B*rother Michael took Devlin by surprise. He was younger than Devlin had expected, no more than thirty. He was also bigger, six-foot-four and built like a middle linebacker. And he was black.

"Let me start by telling you my bottom line," Brother Michael began. "I want to help two young women I'm working with, help them find the courage to escape from these people. I also want to help the young man—their numerarier—help him see that he can escape too. Anything you want them to do that interferes with that, I will oppose. Vigorously."

Brother Michael was seated behind a battered wooden desk cluttered with paper. He dwarfed both the desk and his closet-sized office, located at the rear of the Hell's Kitchen Way Station on Eighth Avenue. It was a one-man counseling center, run for the past ten years on donations and augmented by youthful volunteers. He worked with the runaways, prostitutes, and drug addicts who inhabited the area. Outside, the great mix of New York wandered by, seldom noticing the small storefront office. There were commuters headed to the nearby Port Authority bus terminal for a ride home to the suburbs, mostly sports fans who had just left Madison Square Garden. There were bums seeking out doorways in which to spend the night, and the occasional street kid moving aimlessly, in search of something, often not certain what it was. Inside, Brother Michael's office was utilitarian. Aside from a crucifix on the wall behind his desk, there was little sign of religious affiliation. Brother Michael himself was dressed in jeans and a T-shirt, rather than the brown robes of the Franciscan order. Only his head gave him away. It remained shaved with the Franciscan's trademark tonsure.

"We'll work with you to make sure that's not a problem," Devlin said. "Even pass any requests through you, if you want." He gave the brother a small shrug. "It's not good police procedure, but we're the ones with our hands out. And, frankly, we've hit a stone wall with these people."

He watched a small smile come to the brother's face. It softened the man, made him seem boyish, his brute size less intimidating. Devlin thought about Ollie Pitts, equally brutish but minus the softening smile. Who would walk out if the two met in a dark alley? Right now, he'd lay odds on Ollie.

"That's a generous offer that I accept," Brother Michael said. "When I'm sure I can trust your intentions, I'll get out of your way." He brought his large hands together. "So where do we start?"

Devlin leaned forward. "First, tell me about this numerarier. I've been told that members of Opus Christi are never allowed contact with people outside the order. Did he come to you? And, if so, how and why?"

Brother Michael hesitated, as if thinking over what he could reveal and what should be held back. "Several years ago—six, to be exact—I was working with this man's sister. She was fifteen at the time. A runaway." He shook his head. "Just like so many others." He leaned back in his chair, ignoring its creak of protest. "She was 'all grown up,' 'knew all the answers' "—he used his fingers to place quotation marks around each phrase. "Except she decided to prove it by running away from her family in New Jersey and coming here. Within weeks the vermin who prey on these kids had her all wrapped up. She was well on her way to drug dependence and was peddling herself on the streets for some child-molesting pimp." He raised his large arms as if taking in the room. "And this was a kid from a good Catholic family, someone who had attended Catholic schools all her life and had never once missed Sunday mass."

"An old story," Sharon said.

Brother Michael seemed to flinch at the words before he surrendered to them. "Yes, it is. But this time it had one of our few happy endings." He let out a long breath. "I can't count the number of parents I've taken to the medical examiner's office to identify the bodies of their children." Brother Michael leaned back again. "But not this time. And all because of her brother."

"The numerarier," Sharon said.

"Yes, but he wasn't a member of the order then, although I've since learned that he was in the process of being recruited at the time. It seems I helped save one while the other was falling into something almost as bad." He shook his head. "I never even asked what was going on in *his* life. And I should have, you see. I know better. I know if a home is troubled, it usually doesn't stop with just one kid."

"So that's how he came to you this time? Because he knew you from the past."

Brother Michael gave Sharon an absent nod, as if still dwelling on his perceived failure. "When he came to the city looking for his sister, some neighborhood people sent him to me. Together we found her, got her away from her pimp and into drug rehab."

"That's a neat trick—getting her away from her pimp, I mean," Sharon said. "They usually don't give up that easily."

"Oh, this one didn't give up easily. He threatened the young man. And it was a threat he was ready to make good on. But the kid was a rock. He wasn't about to let his sister stay in that sewer."

"And the pimp backed off?" There was surprise in Sharon's voice.

A smile flickered briefly on Brother Michael's lips. "Let's say I helped a little. I made that little street rat an offer he decided to accept."

Devlin nodded. The odds on Ollie in the dark alley had just gone down.

"When can we meet him?" Devlin asked.

Brother Michael glanced at the Timex that barely made it around his wrist. "He's working on a recruitment tonight—a new victim for the order. He said he'd stop by on his way back to their headquarters. It should be any time now."

The numerarier arrived twenty minutes later. Again, Devlin was surprised. The young man was small and slight, with owlish glasses that made him look like a kid who had grown up in a library. Brother Michael had said he was twenty-five, but he looked no more than eighteen. Devlin doubted a razor passed across the young man's cheeks more than once a week.

He introduced himself as Peter, no last name, in keeping with Opus Christi practice. He was nervous, his fingers dancing in his lap as he took the third visitor's chair in Brother Michael's office.

"I want you to know that this goes against everything I've been taught to believe," he said. He looked down at his hands and clenched his fists to stop the dancing fingers. "It goes against the life I've lived for the past five years," he added, as he looked up again.

"I understand that," Devlin said. "Can you tell me why you've decided to do this?"

The question seemed to throw Peter off stride. His eyes blinked rapidly, and he let out a long breath. "I guess because something's wrong there. At the order, I mean."

"Can you give us an example?" It was Sharon this time.

Peter shook his head, as if saying he could not. It was his way of fighting to get the words out. "Okay. The order is very big on religious artifacts: pictures, statues, even relics, all for use in the future when we open new centers. Right now they're being stored in warehouses, but they're not shipped there. They come to headquarters, and then numerarier are used to deliver them. We're told they have to be checked first, to make sure they haven't been damaged. But I've never seen any evidence that they've been opened after they arrive."

"Do they all go to the same place?" Devlin asked.

"I don't think so." Peter's fingers were dancing again. "I

made three deliveries to a warehouse in Greenpoint. It was in a pretty seedy section, and it made me kind of nervous, you know? Well, I knew two other numerarier who were making deliveries, and I asked one of them how he liked going there—just making conversation, really. But he told me that wasn't where he went. He was going to a place in lower Manhattan—I don't know where; we're not supposed to tell each other things like that. Well, anyway, I asked the third numerarier the same thing, and I found out *he* was going to a place on the Lower West Side, near the docks. We were all going to different places, you see, and that didn't make sense to me. Then, on my last delivery, I passed by this trash container. And it was open, and I happened to look inside." He stopped, drew a breath, and shook his head. "Inside were some broken religious statues and some picture frames that had been broken apart, and I could see they were hollow inside." He stopped again, clenched his fists again. "I went back there about a week ago, on my own. I wanted to look in the container again, but the container was gone, and the warehouse was locked up. I looked in a window and it was empty. Like, everything had been moved out."

Peter hesitated and Devlin urged him on.

"Well, then this thing happened with Sister Manuela, and we heard rumors. . . ." Again he stopped, as if the next words were too painful, too unbelievable.

"You heard about drugs," Sharon said.

Peter nodded. "Yeah." He looked at her, his eyes pleading. "But that can't be right. It just can't."

"Where do these religious artifacts come from?" Devlin asked.

Peter shook his head. "I don't know about the first two deliveries. I never looked. But I did with the last one. It came from Bogotá."

Devlin looked at Brother Michael. His face was as cold as stone. "You think it's possible?" he asked.

"That the order is involved in shipping drugs?" He shook his head. "But I think it's possible that someone inside the order may be. The order is rife with fanatics. And fanatics often become quite Machiavellian to further their goals."

"It fits," Sharon said. "Drug warehouses don't stay open for very long. They move around. They also don't operate from just one location. They spread out, spread the risk."

"Oh, God." It was Peter. His trembling fingers had gone to his face, hiding it.

"How can we get inside your headquarters?" Devlin asked. "It's the only way we'll ever find out what *is* going on."

Peter shook his head. "You can't. Not unless you're a member. And then you'd have to live there."

"Can we get somebody in—as a member?" It was Sharon. She threw a quick glance at Brother Michael to see if she was stepping over boundaries that he had created.

"Could you recruit someone?" Brother Michael asked. He inclined his head toward Devlin and Sharon. "Someone they picked?"

"I'm not sure." Peter hesitated. "I suppose I could. I'm ready to recommend the person I've been working with. No one else in the order has met him. They only know him by the number that's been assigned to the reports I've submitted. It's a way we have of keeping others in the order from knowing who we're recruiting." He shrugged. "Sometimes people get nosy, even though it's frowned on." He paused and thought about it. "I suppose I could substitute someone you picked, propose him as this probationary member. But to get inside headquarters, to live there right off, he'd have to be sort of special—someone they thought they could use right away."

Sharon leaned forward. "Do they have any special needs right now?"

Peter mulled that over. "Well, the computer system's a mess. It's new, and the operating system keeps crashing. It's causing all kinds of havoc, and the order won't let anyone from outside in to work on it. And the people we have . . . well, they just don't seem to be able to solve the problem."

Sharon glanced at Devlin. "You thinking what I'm thinking?"

"Yeah, I believe I am," Devlin said. "I'm thinking Detective Boom Boom Rivera."

# Chapter Six

*T*he telephone roused Devlin at six-thirty the next morning, the frantic voice of the mayor's top aide driving away any lingering drowsiness. He grabbed a pad and pen he kept on the nightstand.

"Slow down and give me the address again." He jotted down the address. "All right, tell the mayor I'm leaving forthwith." Devlin listened. "What? What do you mean he's not up yet? How is he assigning this case to me if he doesn't even know about it yet?" Devlin listened again, shaking his head. "Okay, when he does wake up, tell him I'm already there."

He put the phone down and stretched his shoulders. Adrianna's hand reached out, her fingers running along his back. He turned and looked down at her sleepy, sexy eyes.

"What is it?" she asked.

"We've got another dead priest. This one's out in Brooklyn. I've gotta get out there."

"I thought I heard you say the mayor was still asleep. How . . . ?"

"He left standing orders. A priest, a nun, a rabbi, whatever—one of them gets so much as a hangnail, the case is mine. Apparently Howie is very close to the panic button."

Adrianna's fingers ran along his back again. "That's too bad," she said. "I had some very definite plans for you this morning."

Devlin looked down at her. Adrianna's hair was tousled with sleep, her eyes clearly alluring; one very lovely breast peeked out from the covers. "You really know how to hurt a guy," he said.

"Go ahead," she said. "Go play cops and robbers. I'll just have to call the plumber or that cute new delivery boy at the pizza place."

"You just be sure and be here when I get home." He reached out, deliberately pulled the bedsheet up to her chin, and turned back to the phone. He called Ollie Pitts, filled him in, and told him to swing by the loft to pick him up.

Adrianna's voice stopped him as he headed for the bathroom. "If it was another woman I could understand—*maybe*. But Ollie Pitts?"

Devlin turned back to her, grinning. "Please do me a favor. Call Sharon at home before she leaves for work and tell her what happened. We were supposed to meet two young women at a counseling center this morning. Tell her I may not be able to get there and she should see them alone."

Adrianna gave him a fake pout. "Now I'm not only rejected as a sex object, I'm relegated to playing secretary."

Devlin winked at her. "And you're terrific at both jobs," he said.

Adrianna sat up in bed, allowing the sheet to fall away. "You be careful, buster. Or the plumber really will get the surprise of his life."

Saint Donato's Church was in the Red Hook section of Brooklyn, once home to Joey Gallo, a Mafia wannabe who headed a gang of improbable gangsters that a New York newspaper columnist once novelized in *The Gang That Couldn't Shoot Straight*. Now Gallo was long dead, and the old-line neighborhood of Italian longshoremen that once lionized him was largely gone, replaced first by middle-class gentry, then by the encroachment of poor Hispanics who laid claim to the neighborhood's fringe.

Devlin thought about those days of mob mayhem as he walked around the priest's body. Corpses hanging from longshoremen's hooks had not been uncommon. But never a priest. Especially not one hanging by his neck in the basement of his own church.

He stepped back and looked up into the priest's face, avoiding any physical contact that might contaminate the crime scene. Still, he could tell the body had been there a considerable time. The neck had begun to stretch grotesquely. The face had turned almost black from lividity above the ligature and in the visible parts of the priest's extremities. And as the body slowly rotated on the rope around its neck, it appeared as stiff as the proverbial piece of lumber.

Ollie Pitts came up beside Devlin and followed his gaze upward. "Well, we know he's been dead at least twelve hours, because we got us full rigor here," he offered. "But with the level of lividity, and the way the neck has begun to stretch, I'd guess it's been longer. Maybe sixteen hours, maybe more."

"He was a heavy guy—two hundred and twenty, two hundred and thirty pounds," Devlin countered. "And all of it packed on a short frame. That could have added to the stretching." He considered the body again. "You're right about full rigor, but lividity can be tricky in a hanging. I'd stick with twelve hours, at least for now."

"You figure suicide?" Pitts asked.

Devlin shook his head.

Pitts seemed surprised. "Why not?" He began to look for something he had missed. He glanced at the overturned chair lying next to the priest's body, moved his eyes along the length of the body and along the rope that had been looped over a ceiling rafter before being tied off on a pipe that ran along one wall, and finally to the silent oil burner a few feet away. He shook his head. "I don't get it. We got the chair, the rope, and all the privacy he wanted. Shit. I can't think of a better place to bump yourself off in early September than the boiler room of a fucking church. Not much chance somebody might come along and stop you."

Devlin nodded. "All true. But also very hard to do if your feet don't reach the chair."

Pitts eyed the overturned chair, visually measuring it, then did the same with the distance between the floor and the priest's feet. "Son of a bitch," he said. He took a small tape measure from his pocket and measured the length of one leg of the chair, then again from the floor to the bottom of the priest's feet. He barked out a laugh. "He's a good three inches too high, even with his neck stretched like a fucking giraffe." He turned and grinned at Devlin. "I guess that's why they pay inspectors the big bucks."

Devlin kept staring at the priest. "Look at the section of rope between the rafter and where it's tied off on the pipe. A good four feet of it is chafed where it rubbed against the wood. Somebody hauled him up manually. And that was a helluva lot of work." He shook his head. "What I can't figure is why the perp went to so much trouble to make it look like a suicide. If you want to hide a murder, why fake a suicide when it's easier to make a death look accidental?"

"Hey, perps ain't always the sharpest tacks in the box."

Devlin shook his head again. "Were you raised a Catholic, Ollie?"

"No. I wasn't raised as nothin'."

Devlin stepped back several paces to get a longer view of the corpse. "Suicide is a big deal with Catholics. It's an unforgivable sin. It's an act of despair, a rejection of God's forgiveness, and according to the church it guarantees you a one-way ticket to hell. Because of that, suicides can't be buried in consecrated ground. And for a priest that would be the ultimate disgrace."

"You think that's maybe what the perp wanted?"

"It's something to look at."

"You think there's a connection with the other priest? Maybe a copycat? Somebody saw how the first priest got offed, had some kind of grudge against this one, and decided he'd do it too?"

"That's the best-case scenario," Devlin said.

This time Ollie shook his head. "Naw, they can't be connected more than that. The first one, there was no attempt to hide what it was. A straight slice job." He drew his thumb across his throat. "No, I don't buy it. The MO we got here, it's too far out of whack."

"Unless somebody was trying to hide the fact that they

were connected." Devlin glanced at Ollie and shrugged. "But maybe you're right. It's pretty damned Byzantine."

Ollie raised his eyebrows at the word. "Yeah, whatever you say, boss." He grinned at Devlin. "Hey, you spotted that business with the chair. So maybe I should just shut up and listen. I'll ask around, find out if this priest was a left footer like the first one. Just in case."

Devlin returned the smile. "I'll start it off when I talk to the pastor. You stay with the body until forensics and the ME are through with it."

*F*ather Enrico Giuliani glared at him, his sallow complexion suddenly flushed with anger. The priest was in his early sixties, with thinning gray hair and a pinched face. He reminded Devlin of a long-dead pope, Pius XII, the one who had turned his back on the Jews during World War II. The priest's angry eyes continued to bore into Devlin. He had already explained that he had been pastor of Saint Donato's for twenty-five years. There was little question about the proprietary feelings the man had for his parish.

"Father, I'm not trying to suggest anything," Devlin said. "Or in any way denigrate Father Falco or his priesthood. I'm trying to get at the truth."

The pastor's dark-brown eyes still blazed. He was seated behind his desk in the small rectory office. Behind him a portrait of Jesus stared into the room, almost as if it were a party to all that was said there. "You don't think it's bad enough when a priest takes his own life? That's not enough disgrace for you? Maybe you'd like to explain it to our parishioners."

"Father Falco didn't commit suicide, Father. He was murdered." Devlin let the statement sit there and watched as varying emotions moved across the old priest's face. First came shock, then a slight but very clear sense of relief, and finally disbelief.

He shook his body, as if trying to fight off all the conflicting emotions. "You're certain?" he finally asked.

"Yes, Father, I am. The question now is why?" Devlin leaned forward as though preparing to impart some secret that only they would share. "You read about the priest who was murdered in the Village?"

Father Giuliani nodded numbly.

"Well, that priest had been diagnosed with AIDS, Father. My concern here is the possibility of some connection between the two crimes. That's one—only one—possibility. But it's something I have to check."

The pastor's face had visibly whitened. "Dear God," he said. He folded his hands before his chest, prayerlike, and began to move them forward and back in a rocking gesture. "I was Father Peter's confessor, so I cannot discuss this with you." His eyes snapped up to Devlin. "I want to. Believe me, I very much want to. But it's impossible." The hands kept rocking. "I can tell you that he was seeing a physician, but that's all I can say."

Devlin nodded, showing that he understood. "The autopsy will tell us whether or not he was infected with any disease. But you could save us some time if you know the doctor's name."

The pastor nodded, still visibly shaken. "Of course. I hadn't thought about the autopsy. And I do know the name of the doctor. Serious illnesses must be reported to the archdiocese for personnel purposes." He hesitated, thinking about what he had just said. "I'm not sure the archdiocese would want me to give out that information. I should check with them first."

"I wish you wouldn't do that, Father." The priest seemed shocked by the suggestion, and Devlin hurried on. "If they refuse to give you permission, I'll be forced to subpoena your records, and if I do that it will be very hard to keep it out of the newspapers. I think we would both like to see this kept as quiet as possible."

The priest jumped at the statement as though it were a lifeline. "Oh, yes! Yes, of course. And they might, you know. The archdiocese, I mean. They can become very secretive where scandal is concerned, and sometimes their secrecy only makes it worse in the end." A pleading look came to his eyes. "Do you think it's possible? To keep this matter out of public view?" He shook his head, as if imagining what might happen. "Our parishioners loved Father Peter, and this would be very hard for them to understand."

"We can try," Devlin said. "Not the murder, of course." He hesitated, thinking he could lie to the man, deciding it would be foolish in the long run. "A lot will depend on what comes out at a trial, but I'm sure the district attorney would be sensitive to the wishes of the archdiocese." He smiled, trying to soften his words, and added, "But we're still a long way from that. And keep in mind that many murder cases never go to trial. So I think there's a fair chance none of the . . . difficult matters . . . will ever come out."

The priest closed his eyes. "Dear God, let it be so." He drew a long breath and then stood abruptly, went to a file cabinet in the corner, and withdrew a small folder. Finding what he wanted, he wrote a name and address on a slip of paper. He handed it to Devlin with a weak smile. "Please keep this between us," he said. "I would very much like to finish out my days in this parish."

"No one will know, Father. I give you my word."

*T*hey stood on the steps of the church, just outside the massive front doors. Devlin filled Ollie in on what the pastor had told him, and when he had finished Pitts let out a long low whistle. "You must of done something really bad in your life."

"Why's that?" Devlin asked.

"Well, first off you got these Opus Christi clowns in a possible drug scam. The archdiocese is gonna love that. Next you maybe got somebody running around bumping off gay priests, which, of course, don't really exist, according to the black suits at Saint Patrick's." He shook his head and grinned. "If you're really lucky, maybe we'll find out the pope's been diddling teenage girls, and you'll have a hat trick."

Devlin laughed in spite of himself. "How about you sit down with the mayor and explain it all to him?"

Ollie shook his head. "Uh-uh. It's like I said. This is why inspectors get the big bucks."

"Not big enough. I'll have to make sure the mayor's got a cardiologist standing by when I tell him."

"Hey, the guy's gotta have a sense of humor, right?"

"I'll tell him you said so. In the meantime, get what you can from the priest's doctor and run a thorough—and I mean *thorough*—canvass of this neighborhood."

Rain suddenly began to fall in large heavy drops that bounced back off the sidewalk a good three inches, one of those late-summer/early-autumn storms that seem to come from nowhere. They stepped back under the arch of the church doors.

"Why's it always gotta rain when I gotta canvass a neighborhood?" Pitts groused.

"Get help if you need it. Use Brooklyn detectives if you have to. Their commander gives you grief, refer him to me. Just make sure I know everything this priest did yesterday, anybody he saw, anybody who showed any interest in him, everything. And I want it by the end of the day. And find out if these two dead priests knew each other too. It's only a short subway ride between Red Hook and the Village."

"You think maybe they were having it off with the same guy?"

"It's a long shot, but I don't want to overlook any possibilities. Get those Greenwich Village dicks we've got working the Father Donovan homicide to check that angle."

"You got it, boss." Pitts grinned at him again. "And let me know where to send all the reports . . . after you tell the mayor about all this shit."

**D**evlin took a subway to Hell's Kitchen in time to make the tail end of Sharon's meeting with the two young women from Opus Christi. The rain had stopped by the time he reached Brother Michael's storefront counseling center, and he found everyone gathered in the cramped back office. The two young women were in their late teens or early twenties, each freshly scrubbed, each more demurely dressed and innocent-looking than 99 percent of the women walking the city's streets. Sharon introduced them as Claudia and Joan, no last names, in keeping with Opus Christi practice. Brother Michael sat next to them like some two-hundred-and-forty-pound guardian angel.

Both young women moved nervously in their chairs, clearly troubled by the appearance of yet another detective. They looked remarkably alike: both blond and blue-eyed, both dressed in skirts that hung well below their knees, and clean white blouses, a size too large, to hide any hint of a figure beneath. Devlin smiled to himself. When he was a kid in Catholic school the nuns referred to the style of dress as *Mary-like.*

When Sharon had finished the introductions Devlin leaned forward, keeping his tone as gentle as possible. "I'm sure Sergeant Levy has explained that we're investigating the death of Sister Manuela. I'm sorry if I'm making you repeat things you've already told her, but it will save me time if I hear it directly from each of you. First off, did either of you know her?"

Both young women nodded, but it was Claudia who spoke. She had freckles on her nose and cheeks, and her complexion flushed slightly. Devlin wasn't sure if it came from speaking to a man or the subject he had raised.

"She lived on our floor before she took the veil," Claudia said. "She was very devout and very . . . happy. Very one with our Lord."

"Did either of you consider becoming nuns?"

Devlin threw out the question as part of his interrogation technique—to come at them from different angles to see what that might draw out. It didn't seem to faze either woman. Claudia shook her head, but Joan picked up on the question. She seemed to squint a bit, as though she needed glasses and was struggling to get Devlin's face in focus.

"I considered it," she said. "But I'm not good enough yet."

Devlin was surprised by the response. "What do you mean?"

Joan seemed flustered this time and stammered a bit as she began to speak. "I-I get depressed sometimes. And I find myself wishing for things I shouldn't."

"Like what?" Devlin asked, surprised again.

Joan stared at her hands. "Going out . . . alone. Or with young men. Maybe going to a movie or out to dinner."

"Is that wrong?"

Her head snapped up. "For us it is. We've been called to Christ . . . to do his work. Sister Manuela never thought those things. She *believed.* She did *everything* she was told to do. I just can't. My faith is too weak."

"I want to leave the order." It was Claudia again; the words just blurted out. "I think Joan does too, but she's afraid to admit it, afraid it's wrong to even think it."

"No," Joan said. "No, I haven't decided that. I think I just miss my family and my friends . . . from before."

"When was the last time you saw your family?" Devlin asked.

Joan lowered her eyes again. "Two years ago. My mother and father came to see me."

"And they haven't been back since?"

"Yes, but I wouldn't see them. I wrote to them, asking them not to come again, but they did. My spiritual guide said it was best if I didn't encourage them. That it would distract me from the work of Christ." Tears had come to her eyes.

Devlin thought about his own daughter, Phillipa, and about what he would do if someone convinced her not to see him again. There would be something just short of murder, he decided. "Maybe your parents miss you too," he said.

The tears came now. Claudia slipped an arm around Joan's shoulders.

"I've been trying to explain to them that Christ taught the commandments," Brother Michael said. "That he would never suggest not honoring one's parents."

Joan answered through sobs. "But these . . . are holy people . . . people who've been . . . chosen by Christ. They . . . can't . . . be . . . wrong."

Brother Michael let out a long breath. Devlin could tell he'd been here before with these women.

"Don't you think it's possible to be devout and also to be wrong?" Brother Michael asked. "Think of the Inquisition, the Crusades, the Salem witch trials in Massachusetts, the slaughter of people in modern-day Islam—all of it done by deeply religious men and women. I'm not saying the men and women who are telling you to reject your family aren't devout. I'm telling you that they're wrong, that what they're saying goes against the teaching of Christ when he told us to obey the commandments God gave to Moses."

They were moving away from Sister Manuela, where Devlin needed to be. "Do you know if Sister Manuela ever questioned her superiors about things she was asked to do?"

Claudia looked at him, surprised by the question. "Not that I know of. I can't imagine she ever would. I always thought she was very, very devout."

Devlin realized he was running into the same wall as Brother Michael. He tried another approach. "Did she ever seem upset?"

"What do you mean?"

"Did she seem nervous or concerned about anything in the last days you saw her?"

"Yes." It was Joan this time, the question seeming to bring her back from her own miseries. "One of my jobs is cleaning the chapel every day. I do it very early in the morning so it's clean when everyone comes down for morning prayers. That last week Sister Manuela was always there, always well before the regular time."

"Did you ever ask her why?" It was Sharon now, easing into the questioning.

Joan nodded. "One day, while I was cleaning, I noticed there were tears in her eyes, and I went over to make sure she wasn't sick or something. I asked if she was all right, and she told me she was just upset about something and was praying for guidance. It was the day before she left for Colombia. I knew her parents had moved back and thought she must have been told not to see them while she was there."

Sharon leaned forward. "We were told she was visiting her parents."

Joan seemed confused. "I don't think so. I don't think anyone is allowed to do that."

Sharon made a mental note to check again. "Would the order know whether she did or not?" she asked.

"Oh, yes," Joan said. "They always know where we are. We never go anywhere alone."

"Where do they think each of you are now?" Devlin asked.

"We have part-time jobs at a pro-life center," Claudia said. "But it's not run by the order, and the people who run it don't keep very good track of when we get there and when we leave, since they don't pay us."

"So how does the order keep track of you during that time?" Devlin asked.

"We're each questioned about it—separately. But we're just asked where we went and if we were together the whole time." Claudia looked down at her hands, which were demurely folded in her lap. "We don't tell them about any side trips we might have made, and we always make sure they're not very long ones."

A lie of omission, Devlin thought. Something the nuns in school had repeatedly warned against. He smiled at the memory. Like all forms of totalitarian authority, holes always seemed to appear in its self-protective armor. He was glad to see Opus Christi wasn't an exception.

"Who would have been with Sister Manuela during her workday?" Devlin asked.

"Sister Margaret," Claudia said. "They were always together."

"And it would be Sister Margaret's job to report on what Sister Manuela did or didn't do?"

"Yes," Claudia said. "It's the way it's done." She hesitated over the next words, as if searching out a way to make Devlin understand. "It's for our spiritual protection," she finally added.

Devlin studied the floor for a moment before looking up at the two women. "I hope you'll keep *our* meeting confidential," he said. "It would be best for the investigation and probably best for you."

Claudia stared at him, almost defiantly, he thought. It was as if she were trying to recapture something she had lost in their conversation. "If our spiritual guide asks us specifically if we talked to you, we'll have to tell him we did. But if he doesn't ask—"

*W*hen the two women had gone, Devlin turned to Brother Michael and shook his head. "You've got your hands full trying to help those two. I've heard about these spiritual guides from Father Martin. What's *your* take on it?"

Anger flashed in the brother's eyes. "It's the ultimate hold they have on these kids," he said. He leaned forward, his massive forearms resting on his equally massive thighs. "Each member has a spiritual guide, someone who has been assigned to direct their lives on the path of Christ. It's always a numerarier, someone who's been tested and has proven loyal. According to their teachings, lying to a spiritual guide is one of several unforgivable sins that will damn you to hell for all eternity." He shook his head. "There are quite a few of those unforgivable sins. Masturbation is another one, or any form of sexual activity, although they don't worry very much about sex between two consenting parties, since they make sure that opportunity never exists."

"What are some of the other unforgivable sins?" Sharon asked.

"Basically, anything that goes against their agenda. Birth control is considered an intrinsic evil, as is any nontraditional, nonmatrimonial relationship. Abortion, for any reason, is viewed as murder. In vitro fertilization is an unnatural act against God's will. Homosexuality is a curable disease, something willfully performed in denial of God's instruction to man, an act that results in divine punishment through AIDS."

"How the hell do they get kids—*especially* kids—to believe all this stuff?"

Brother Michael sat back and smiled at her. "You don't spend a lot of time working with kids, do you?" He waited while Sharon shook her head. "Young people today, especially those in their teens and early twenties, are desperately searching for something to believe in. You might think that kids who end up in religious cults grow up in homes where religion is a big part of daily life, but that's not the case. Most of them have grown up in homes where their parents didn't believe in anything other than making money and acquiring *things*. Oh, religion may have been a part of their lives, but if it was, it was a small part. Maybe something their parents thought they should do for any number of reasons and did halfheartedly, if at all.

"In some ways these kids are similar to ones who grow up poor. Poor kids *want* something. Usually something material, the stuff they've grown up without. But these other kids have grown up with enough money so it isn't something they think about a great deal. And they've had plenty of *things* all their lives, so that's not a driving force." He gave a broad shrug. "It's why some middle-class kids end up piercing and tattooing themselves, or living on the streets, or getting into drugs, or becoming groupies to rock bands. They're looking for something they can *put* into their lives that they think will give them meaning. Religion can become one of those things. Some are born again and find some degree of fulfillment, at least for a time. But, unfortunately, when the need is great the cults beckon and the sheer vulnerability of these kids make them easy meat: ripe and ready to be manipulated." He raised his hands in a helpless gesture. "Now, some grow out of it and see these cults for what they are, as I'm hoping will be the case with these two young women. But others never do. Their lives become irreversibly tied to these 'truths' they've been taught to believe in. And some of them never escape those beliefs. Some end up in places like Waco and Jonestown."

"But don't you, as a Catholic brother, believe in some of the same things that Opus Christi teaches?" Sharon softened the words with a smile.

Brother Michael returned it. "I came to my vocation out of a love of God and a very strong need to serve him. It was a hard choice, something I desperately tried to avoid for a long time." He smiled again, at the memory of that decision. "You see, the things one gives up are very substantial, especially for a healthy young adult." He waved his hand as though dismissing his own sacrifice. "The Franciscan order also made it difficult to join. They wanted to be sure my vocation was a true calling, that I was coming to them for the right reason. And the correct reason is not to put meaning *into* one's life. The correct reason is to give meaning *to* one's life through service to God." He glanced from Sharon to Devlin to see if they understood. "It's a subtle difference but a very important one. Now, the answer to your question is Yes, I believe in many of the same things Opus Christi espouses. Not all, but many. But I also believe in redemption, and there's a subtle difference there as well. I believe that all sin, all wrongdoing, is forgivable. The people who run Opus Christi don't offer that belief. They can't, you see. If they did they would lose control."

Devlin studied the man for several seconds and nodded. "I hope we can help you with these young women," he said. "Seeing them here, and listening to them spout what they've been force-fed, makes me twitchy about my own daughter."

"Just stay close to her," Brother Michael said. "The one common factor I find with all troubled kids is an absence of closeness to their parents."

Devlin nodded again, privately hoping he was already doing that. "I've got to ask you for one more favor," he said.

A large smile filled Brother Michael's chocolate-colored face. "As our Lord said, 'Ask and you shall receive.' " The smile had suddenly turned a bit impish. Devlin realized he had truly come to like the man.

"I want to arrange another meeting with this numerarier, Peter—but this time with the police officer I'd like him to recruit for Opus Christi."

Brother Michael scratched his chin. "This young officer you're proposing, he'll have to appear quite religious, you know . . . and quite needy. Do you think he'll be able to pull that off?"

"I hope so," Devlin said. "It looks like our only hope of getting inside." He thought about Boom Boom Rivera. He certainly had the chutzpah to pull it off. And he was definitely an actor. Now, all Devlin had to do was convince him that he'd just experienced a religious epiphany.

On the way back to the office, he filled Sharon in on the murder of Father Peter Falco.

"You think somebody's killing priests because they're gay?"

"It's a possibility. We should know more by the end of the day."

"You have to put me on that case." Sharon was driving but had turned to face Devlin as the car raced down Broadway.

"Watch the damned road," Devlin snapped.

Sharon turned back to the traffic, but her voice became even more determined. "Paul, this should be my case. It makes sense. I understand these people. I know how to talk to them. Christ, they'll take one look at Ollie and think some tyrannosaur just came stumbling out of the bushes."

The small scar on Devlin's cheek whitened, indicating he was fast reaching his limit. The last thing he needed was more grief. "You're Ollie's sergeant," he snapped. "You'll be supervising him. But that's *all* you'll be doing on that case. I need you where you are. I need you following up with this other nun who partnered with Sister Manuela. You saw those two women at Brother Michael's center. I haven't got anyone else who has a chance in hell of reaching them. And if this other nun is cut from the same mold, you'll have a better chance with her than anyone else. Besides, I'll need you to run Boom Boom once we convince him to go in there undercover."

Sharon glanced at him, noted the now-white scar, and decided to back off. She let out a breath to let him understand her reluctance. "Okay. You're the boss. But I think you're wrong." She forced a smile, then found it growing naturally. "God, Boom Boom Rivera in a religious cult! I can just hear him telling all those celibate kids how Hispanics have dicks that never get soft." She snorted. "Before he goes in there we better start filling his tacos with saltpeter."

Devlin glanced out the window, his irritation seeping away. "I was thinking more along the lines of having him neutered," he said. He watched the lunch-hour chaos that filled the sidewalks as their car sped through the garment district. Boom Boom wouldn't be the only candidate for castration, he thought. Not when the mayor heard how his two pet cases were going.

*T*hey met at six o'clock in the squad bullpen, and the reports from the other detectives offered little encouragement. Everyone seemed to be hitting one solid wall after another.

Ollie Pitts flipped through his notebook with thick, angry fingers, almost as if the book itself had frustrated his efforts.

"It's the same story with both murdered priests," he said. "If they had any regular or full-time boyfriends, they've either left town or are still hiding in their closets."

Sharon glared at him but said nothing. Pitts ignored her stare.

"Both of these guys were favorites among their parishioners." There was a Who-can-tell-about-people? tone in his voice. "In both parishes, everybody I talked to described these guys as the person they'd go to if they had a problem." He gave a slight shake of his head. "Now, Donovan, the first victim, he worked openly with gays. But, hell, in the Village, what choice did he have, right? But nobody, outside of the people he saw at the gay bathhouse, had a clue he was part of the fruit brigade himself."

"All right, Ollie," Sharon snapped. "Enough!"

Pitts looked up, feigning shock at the rebuke. Devlin saw a small smile creep to the corners of his mouth.

"Let's not try to get a rise out of Sharon," Devlin warned. "Just make the report . . . minus the editorial comments."

Pitts went back to his notebook, the grin growing slightly. "Okay. As far as any connection between the two priests, we got zip. If they ever met each other, even they probably didn't remember. So we're drawing a blank on suspects we can tie to both of them. Neither one had been threatened. Neither one had any arguments with anybody we know about. The only connection is that they both had AIDS, and both of them were diagnosed over the last six months. But they even went to different doctors, and to different hospitals for their tests, so we got no connection there either."

He raised his eyes, shrugged, and flipped through his notebook again.

"Right now it looks as if AIDS was only a coincidence. The ME confirmed that they both had it, but I can't find a way that any one perp could have identified each of them as a carrier. Forensics came up with all kinds of stuff that we're checking through now. I got fingerprints up the wazoo, but nothing the computer picked up any matches on. We got some especially good prints on the second priest. They were on the pipe where the rope was tied off. But again, zip from the computer. Right now, we're having everyone who had any access to the church basement printed so we can eliminate any legit matches, but that's gonna take some time. Right now I'm stuck, so I got the dicks who caught the cases going back over the same ground to make sure we didn't miss anything." He looked at Devlin. "If it was the same perp, boss, it was a pro. This guy didn't make any of the usual mistakes."

Devlin shifted his gaze to Stan Samuels. "All right, tell me what you found out about Opus Christi."

Samuels shook his head. "This is quite a group, boss. Even their money has money. They operate—at least behind the scenes—a handful of pretty successful businesses. They got an advertising agency, a PR firm, even a group of political consultants who work mainly with antiabortion and pro-family candidates. They all bring in some heavy bucks. But they're all privately held companies, so there isn't a helluva lot I can get on them. The order itself also holds a lot of stock, mostly financial—banks, insurance companies, even a couple of brokerage houses. Their financing on this new office and housing complex they built on Second Avenue is like walking through a maze. It comes from a series of loans made to corporations they control. The money is borrowed by one corporation, then that company lends money to another company, then in at least one case to a third company. Finally it gets lent to Opus Christi to finance their project. The interesting thing is that none of it comes from the Catholic church. It's all private, and it's all washed from one company to another. It's like they don't want anybody to know where it all comes from. But it's all legit, so it doesn't make any sense to do it that way. I'll tell you one thing. They spent a lot more money on their building than they had to spend, and most of it went into security. And some of that security seems to be run against themselves."

"What do you mean?" Devlin asked.

"Well, the building is divided into offices and dormitories, right? Men and women. But even the dormitories are sealed off from each other, based on sex. Separate staircases and elevators for the men and the women. It's like the building is physically divided in half. Even the ductwork is separate, like they were afraid somebody was gonna crawl through from one side to the other. I showed the building plans to an architect I know, and he said he never saw anything like it. He said it boosted the cost by a good twenty percent. The same thing's true about the section where all the offices are. Separate access, separate ventilating systems, plus a security system the Pentagon wished it had. It's like they don't trust anybody, not even themselves."

Devlin turned to Red Cunningham, whose three-hundred-pound bulk overflowed his chair. "What does that do for a chance at phone taps—assuming we can eventually get a court order?"

Cunningham ran a hand through his red buzz cut. "It'll be tough. All the phone lines are tied into a very sophisticated computer system. The only shot we'd have is if I could get inside and get access to that system. Then it'd be a piece of cake. But getting inside's the trick."

That brought Devlin to Ramon Rivera—Boom Boom to his fellow cops, who had given him the nickname owing to his endless claims of sexual prowess. He leaned back in his chair and studied the short slender Hispanic cop.

"You feeling particularly religious these days?" he asked.

Boom Boom blinked at the question. Then he grinned nervously. "Hey, boss. God is love."

"Yeah, I know." Devlin smirked. "And love is your middle name, right?" He paused a beat. "The reason I ask is that I've got this feeling you're about to have a religious crisis and a sudden overpowering need to reach out to the Lord."

Boom Boom blinked again, and his eyes filled with suspicion. "I am?"

"You are. At least I think you are, providing you volunteer."

"Uh-oh, watch yourself, Boom Boom," Ollie warned. "The last time I volunteered for something, I ended up in Cuba using my vacation time."

Rivera shifted in his chair. "What's this all about? I mean, like, you're gonna tell me, right? Like, before I say yes or no, right?"

A smirk came to Devlin's lips. "No. First you volunteer, then I tell you. Just like always." Devlin steepled his fingers in front of his face. "Of course, if you don't like the idea, you have the option of requesting a transfer to another unit." Devlin leaned back in his chair and waited. Like all the other members of the team, Boom Boom was regarded as a misfit in the NYPD, an unconventional cop in a department that despised the unconventional. Any of them, if returned to normal police duties, would find themselves working one of the many shit assignments that no cop wanted.

"Okay, okay, I get the point," Boom Boom said. "I volunteer. You happy?"

Devlin smiled at him. "I'm happy." He turned to Sharon. "Since you'll be running this little undercover job, you explain it to our little Spanish Romeo."

Sharon did, her words punctuated by snickers and guffaws from the others. As she concluded, she leaned forward, bringing herself as close to Rivera as possible. "The important thing here, *Boom Boom*," she said, emphasizing the nickname, "is that you keep your pecker in your pants. As far as anyone in Opus Christi is concerned, sex is the last thing on your mind. You don't even know what your little ding-a-ling is used for. Got it?"

Boom Boom's eyes took on a look of someone deeply offended. "Hey, first, it ain't little, and second, you're asking for a fucking miracle here."

"Yeah? Well, from now on, we call you Saint Ramon. You got it? Once you're inside you don't even look at any of the women, let alone give any of them your line of

Latin bullshit. So, first off, lose the tight pants and the open-neck shirt and the gold chain." She glanced at Devlin. "I also wanna get those curly locks sheared before we send him in."

"Hey, hold on there. I ain't gonna go that far," Boom Boom threatened.

Sharon ignored him. "Maybe get him fitted to a pair of phony glasses, too."

"Sounds about right," Devlin said. "You're the boss on this. You do what you think is best."

"Hey, come on."

Sharon turned back to Rivera. She was enjoying herself fully now. Over the past two years, ever since she had joined the squad, Rivera had repeatedly suggested that she could be "cured" of her lesbian tendencies if she'd only put herself in his hands. She smiled at the memory. "Yes, indeed. We are gonna have us a new Boom Boom," she said.

"Hey, Sha-ron, wait a minute."

"Shut up. We've got a meeting tomorrow morning with the guy who's gonna get you inside." She paused. "You ever go to Catholic school?" she asked.

"Yeah," Boom Boom said. "Grammar school. In Queens."

"You have nuns teaching you there?"

"Yeah, of course."

"Who was your favorite?"

Rivera eyed her. "Whaddaya mean?"

"It's simple. Which nun did you like best?"

He shrugged. "I dunno. Sister Mary Elizabeth, maybe. Why?"

"Because by the time we have our meeting tomorrow, I promise you one thing. You are gonna look and act just like Sister Mary Elizabeth's class pet. You got that, *Boom Boom*?"

"Hey, Sha-ron. This ain't fair."

"Shut up. Right now you and me gotta find us a barbershop that's still open. It's crew-cut time."

Boom Boom glanced at Red Cunningham, who was grinning back at him and rubbing his buzz cut.

"Oh, Christ." Rivera's eyes fled to Devlin. "Hey, boss, this ain't right."

Devlin shrugged. "Hey, Ramon, what can I do?" He fought down a smile. "You have to talk to your sergeant on this. I just want you to get us into that computer. You do that, hell, you can take a week off and let your hair grow back."

Rivera stared at him. He shook his head, his face filled with disbelief. "Aw, shit, man. Aw, shit."

## Chapter Seven

*E*milio stared at the front page of the *Post*. The man had handed it to him as soon as he seated himself on the Central Park bench that had become their meeting place. The headline read: SECOND PRIEST MURDERED.

He carefully placed the paper on the bench and turned. "I warned you it might not fool them," he said.

The man stared at him, eyes like ice. He was such a demanding bastard, Emilio thought. The people he worked for were just as bad, but at least they were capable of doing the work themselves. This one didn't know shit. This one never had blood on his shoes when he put someone away. He did it with his fucking checkbook, nice and clean and neat.

"I expected better," the man said. "I thought the medical tests might reveal the truth after a day, perhaps even two. This didn't fool them for an hour."

Emilio felt his anger rise. "Hey, you know you're changing the rules here. You want these people put away; they're put away. Then you want it so it looks like they did it themselves. I tell you it's tricky, but I try; now you tell me it's not good enough. Hey, listen up here. The cops, they find themselves one murdered priest. Then they got another, and they think, Hey, what's this we got going on here? It's only natural. They're not stupid, even if you want them to be stupid, right?"

The man continued to stare at him and then looked away, disgusted.

Emilio wanted to reach out and grab him, put a knife under his chin, let him feel how close he was. He didn't even know the bastard's name, didn't know anything about him. But this shit he was handing out now changed all that. Now he would find out about him. And maybe later, when he was finished with this job and his own boss was satisfied, maybe then, in a month or two, he'd come back and pay him a little visit.

"Have you found the third one?" the man asked.

This time Emilio looked away. "I found him." He jerked his chin, indicating some unspecified area behind him. "It's not far from here. A church over on Columbus Avenue."

When he turned back the man was staring at him again, his face expressionless. "Today," he said. "I want it done today."

"If I can," Emilio said. "It depends on what's happening with him. It's gotta be safe." He jabbed a finger into his own chest. "Safe for me." A small thin smile came to his lips. "You don't want me caught, right?" He had almost made up his mind. This man here, this big *patrón,* if he said he didn't care, he'd cut his throat right there, right now.

"Of course not. But I want it done quickly, and I want it done well."

Emilio sneered at him. "If they're dead, *compadre,* and if I get away, it's done well. I can't give you any better than dead." He looked down at a pigeon scuttling near his feet. "How many more will there be?"

"That doesn't concern you," the man said. He seemed to think better of his words. "Not that many—not here in the city, at least."

Emilio's head snapped around. "Hey, you expect me to do this other places too?"

The man glared at him. "Your employer and I are discussing that now. I don't know if it will involve you or someone else. That hasn't been determined. You needn't worry yourself about it. Just do the job here."

Emilio looked back at the pigeon. There were two now. He kicked out at them halfheartedly, making them scatter a few feet away.

"You don't seem very pleased with the work," the man said. "Does it offend you?"

"It bothers me I don't get respect for the work." He looked back at the man, held his eyes.

"You're doing the Lord's work. Be satisfied with that."

Emilio's eyes widened. God wanted priests put away? He smiled for the first time. The man was loco. Or he was on something. He looked at his eyes more closely. Nothing. Just crazy.

"Tell me. Why are we doing this to these priests? I'm just curious."

The man seemed to think about his answer, then dismissed it. "It's irrelevant. The important thing is to get the work done quickly." He paused a moment. "I have special instructions for you with this one. I want you to follow them exactly."

"Again?"

The man shook his head. "It's not what you think. Faking a suicide is pointless now. The police will be looking for that. But I want a message sent, so listen closely."

*E*milio left first, as he always did. But this time he ducked behind a portable bookstall on Fifth Avenue, where he could watch the man still seated on the bench. Five minutes later the man rose and followed the same path out of the park. He exited on Grand Army Plaza, crossed the avenue, and headed east on 60th Street.

Emilio let him go and dropped in about fifty yards behind him. The man was tall, and his silver-tinged hair stood out above the other pedestrians, making him easy to follow. He continued across Madison Avenue to Park, where he turned south.

Foot traffic was heavier now, and Emilio shortened the distance between them until he was only twenty yards back. The man turned into a large glass-fronted office building, and Emilio watched him as he strode past the security desk unchallenged and went straight to a bank of elevators. Another rare smile came to his thin lips. Now I know where to find you, he thought. The sun broke through the clouds, and the sudden warmth on his shoulders soothed his entire body. He stood quietly for a moment, enjoying it. He hadn't decided yet whether or not he would kill this man. It was enough for now to know that he could.

"You have no idea how hard the press is coming down on me."

Howie Silver paced behind his desk. The morning sun filtered through the bulletproof glass in his office windows, giving his sallow complexion a sickly green tint. Devlin sat in a leather club chair well away from the desk. He watched as Silver stopped to jab a finger in his direction.

"Maybe I should let you find out. Maybe I should put you up there next to me when I have to face those bastards an hour from now."

Devlin looked down at the tips of his shoes and then raised his eyes slowly back to the mayor. "I'll go if you want me to, but I think it's a bad idea."

Silver's jaw tightened. "They'll ask to talk to you, you know that. They'll even bitch that you always refuse."

Devlin shrugged. "It's the way we've set it up. Just refer them to the public information office. I can't do the job if I spend half the day fielding questions from the media."

Silver sneered. "But you think I can, right?" The sneer grew. "Those bastards. I'll spend the rest of the morning listening to them. First at the press conference, then on the phone with their goddamn editors." He stared at the blank expression on Devlin's face. "Don't say it," he warned.

"I wasn't going to say anything."

"Yeah, but you're thinking it. You're thinking that I asked for it. That I love every goddamn minute of it." He turned around and went to his chair but didn't sit. "The whole idea of this special squad you run is to keep me out of this shit." He turned back to Devlin as if challenging a response.

Devlin shook his head. "No, it's not, Howie. You formed the squad so you wouldn't sit here holding the bag every time a high-profile case hit the papers; so you could keep those humps who run the Puzzle Palace from playing political games behind your back." He shook his head. "That's all the squad gives you. It lets you know what's really going on and keeps the brass at One Police Plaza from sticking it to you every time you bend over to tie your shoes. It gives you that, it gives you me, and it gives you my people. All of us working directly for you. But that's all it does."

Silver's jaw tightened again. "Well, it's not enough. Not this time. Sure, I love to keep those simpering chiefs in line. I love it even more when I hear them bitching that *they're* being kept in the dark. But I had the goddamn archdiocese on my ass at seven this morning. I didn't even get a goddamn cup of coffee before I had the cardinal's secretary on the line asking me what we're doing to keep his priests from getting knocked off." He held his hands out at his side in wonderment. "Can you imagine? What am I doing to keep every goddamn priest in this city from getting killed? Why not all the rabbis? Why not all the ministers? Why not every store-front scam artist with a clerical collar around his goddamn neck?"

"Did you ask him that?" Devlin fought off a smile.

Silver sneered at him. "Yeah, I asked him. I want every priest in every pulpit next Sunday telling every Catholic voter that I'm a putz."

Devlin crossed one knee. It was time to drop the bomb that would send the mayor into orbit. "Next time he calls, tell him we think only gay priests are being targeted."

Silver's eyes widened. His mouth worked for several seconds before he was able to form the words. "Don't tell me that. Don't tell me somebody's knocking off gay priests."

Devlin clasped his hands in front of him. "We're not positive yet. It could be a coincidence. Or it could be one guy getting back at priests he was sexually involved with." He paused, then continued. "But my gut tells me it's more than that." He paused again. "One other thing. Even worse. Both priests had AIDS."

Now Silver did sit in his chair—collapsed would be a better description, Devlin thought. He seemed to be looking at the news from all directions, his mind snapping like a political calculator.

"So we have to cover it up somehow." It wasn't a question, it was a political judgment.

"That won't be your choice. Not yours alone, anyway.

And I'm not sure it can be pulled off, even if you want it."
Devlin watched Silver's eyes narrow. "I'm not talking
about me, I'm talking about the DA. We clear this case, it
all falls into his lap. How much of it he lets come out is up
to him."

Silver shook his head. "Jesus Christ." His lips tightened
into a straight line. "What's the matter with these goddamn
priests? They're supposed to keep their goddamn peckers in
their pants. I mean, I don't give a rat's ass if they're gay. I
got half a dozen fruits working for me, for chrissake. But I
expect them to be discreet about it."

He was becoming irrational now. Devlin had seen it before and knew he just had to ride it out.

The political calculator started snapping away again.
"Can we keep this AIDS business under wraps?" Silver
asked at length.

"I've got the ME's word. But you know what a sieve that
place is. Half the people who work there are media stoolies."

Silver thought about it and waved his hand, dismissing
that concern. "I'll tip off the archdiocese," he said. "They'll
get on the ass of every TV executive and newspaper editor
in this city. There'll be more threats flying around than you
can count. They don't call them the Powerhouse just to be
cute."

"I think they already know the priests were gay," Devlin
said. "The pastor at one of the churches told me they have to
report all illnesses to the archdiocese. He said it's some kind
of personnel thing. I guess they have to know ahead of time
if they're going to have to replace somebody."

Silver nodded. "Yeah, but they don't know that *we* know.
And they sure as hell don't know that the media may blow it
all to hell." He thought again. "And they'll be grateful for the
tip-off." He considered his words and seemed to come to a
decision. "I'll tell them at the news conference that it's a del-
icate matter, that there are things about the investigation we
just can't discuss. That'll cover me at that end, too. Maybe
I'll even call a couple of editors. No, they're all pricks.
Maybe a couple of publishers. They always like to know
things their editors don't." He nodded to himself. "Yeah, and

they'll keep their mouths shut if they think the archdiocese might go to their advertisers."

He looked at Devlin and grinned. "They've done it before, you know." His eyes glittered with pleasure. "This one time I know about personally the *Daily News* was going to run this piece about the foster-care agencies that Catholic Charities runs." He let out a cackle. "Their foster-care operation was being run on city money, just like all of them are, and the archdiocese had nuns and brothers running these agencies, all of them pulling down nice fat salaries. Except the nuns and brothers had taken vows of poverty, so they had to kick back the salaries. Then the archdiocese used that money to sign up every nun and brother they had in the Social Security system, whether they ever worked for the agencies or not." He let out another cackle. "It was beautiful. They hustled the city, gave all the loot to the feds, then got it all back, and solved all their retirement problems at the same time. And none of it ever cost them a dime."

"So the story never ran?"

"You bet your ass it never ran. The archdiocese had a little meeting with the editors and let it be known that there might be a boycott of any stores that advertised in their paper." He gave Devlin a wide grin. "That story disappeared so fast the ink never had a chance to dry."

"And the city never got its money back." Devlin just threw it in for the hell of it.

Silver gave him a long look. "Hey, my friend. This is the real world we're talking about here."

Devlin let out a long breath. "Just be careful what you tell the press. For my sake. You tell them too much, we might tip off the guy we're after."

Silver stared at him, unmoved. "Like I said, it's the real world here. You just catch the bastard. The one who killed the nun, too. And what's happening with *that?*"

"The same big stone wall," Devlin said. "But I'm working my way around it."

"How?"

Devlin shook his head. "You don't want to know."

Silver closed his eyes momentarily. "Just do it," he said. "And do it fast."

**D**evlin met Sharon in a small coffee shop across the street from Opus Christi headquarters. Despite its excessive cost, the building seemed nondescript, its only outward sign a large crucifix hanging above the main entrance—that and the periodic flow of freshly scrubbed men and women who moved through its doors.

He raised his chin, indicating the entrance. "It's just like those two kids said, isn't it? They always go in pairs." He took a sip of his coffee. "If Boom Boom has somebody hanging on his shoulder every minute it's going to be hard. How are you going to get around that?"

Sharon drummed her fingers on the table, clearly worried about the same thing. "He says it won't be a problem. He says once he figures out their codes and passwords, he can work from anywhere."

Devlin shook his head. "We still can't pull him out. He leaves and they change the passwords, we're screwed."

"I already told him that. I'm more worried he'll get his ass thrown out of there for propositioning some virgin."

Devlin continued to stare at the building. Two young women were just leaving, both as fresh and clean-looking as any he had ever seen. He thought about his daughter, that she too could fall into something like this. Sharon tore the thought away.

"You should have seen him. His cute little haircut, his polo shirt, his nice crisp baggy khaki pants. He looked about fifteen." She let out a laugh.

"Is he armed?"

Sharon nodded. "I gave him this small automatic I had at home. Fits into a little garter holster."

"He's wearing a garter holster?"

"Oh, yeah. I told the little prick he ever comes on to me again, I'd let Ollie know about it." She shook her head. "I'm not sure he gives a shit. I had to help him get it on, and the little bastard asked to move it up a bit—closer to his dick."

Devlin laughed. "That's our Boom Boom. How'd he get on with this numerarier, Peter?"

"He was good. He played it straight, none of his usual macho bullshit." She gave a small shrug. "He'll do okay. For all his crap, he's a good cop."

"I'll tell him you said so."

Sharon's eyes snapped to him. "Don't you dare. I like him thinking I hate his guts."

Devlin ran a hand over his mouth to hide his smile. "You're a softhearted broad, Sharon Levy."

"Bullshit. You wanna try me in a dark alley, I'll show you." She glanced at him. "I mean, I'll show you, *sir*."

"I'll take a pass," Devlin said. "But I'm glad you're showing a little respect for my lofty rank." Two years ago Sharon had saved his life. As far as Devlin was concerned, there was little she couldn't get away with. He thought she probably knew that, too.

"I'm more worried about this Peter guy," she said. "He was like a cat in a dog pound when they went in there."

"You think there's someone in there he's afraid of?"

Sharon shook her head. "I think it's more of an identity crisis. He's been with them for five years, a true believer. I told Boom Boom he sees this guy doing a meltdown, he should get his ass out of there." She toyed with her coffee cup. "That may be the hardest part of the job. Boom Boom keeping the kid straight, I mean."

Devlin thought that over. "In a couple of days, after we're sure they're comfortable with our guy, I want Cunningham to fit him with a wire. We'll put Red on it with you, so he can monitor him."

Sharon turned to him, surprised by the statement. "You think these Bible thumpers could be dangerous?"

Devlin inclined his head, indicating his own doubts. "I don't know. I just want to play it safe. *If* somebody in there is dealing drugs—and that's a big *if* right now—then that somebody's dangerous in my book. Right now I've got two dead priests and a dead nun on my plate. I sure as hell don't want to add a dead cop. Especially not one of my own."

*E*milio watched Father Walter Hall as he concluded the Friday evening rosary service. He stood at the foot of the altar, a crisp white surplice covering two thirds of his black cassock. He was young, younger than the others, with unruly blond hair that fell across his forehead. He also seemed more physically fit than the others had been. More so than Emilio would prefer.

There were about two dozen people at the service, and all but two were older women. Just like at home, he thought. The old women go to pray their way into heaven, the old men too macho to do so, counting on luck to get them there.

The priest went to the back of the church to shake hands with the people as they left. Emilio remained in the back pew he had chosen, then stood after everyone had gone and the priest had started back to the altar.

"Father, forgive me, but I was wondering if you could hear my confession?" He spoke the words as the priest moved past him.

Father Hall stopped and offered a regretful smile. "Confessions are normally on Saturdays," he said. "Two to four in the afternoon, and seven to nine in the evenings."

Emilio nodded, lowering his head contritely. "I know, Father. It's just . . ." He let the words fall away, as though he couldn't bear to finish them.

"Is it a special need, my son?" the priest asked.

Emilio nodded. "Yes, Father. Very special. If you only could." Emilio slipped his hand into his jacket pocket, feeling the ice pick he had placed there. He glanced toward the door. If the priest refused, he would do it here quickly and take the body where the man wanted it, so he could follow the instructions he'd been given.

The priest smiled at him. "Of course," he said. "If you'll follow me, I'll take you to the small room we use for confessions."

He started to turn away but Emilio reached out, stopping him with a gentle touch of his arm. He inclined his head toward one of the old, now-unused confessionals that lined the rear walls of the church.

"If we could use one of those, I'd be grateful, Father."

Father Hall glanced at the old-fashioned confessionals.

"We don't use those anymore," he said. "Now we just sit at a table across from each other."

"I know. I know." Emilio looked down as if embarrassed. "I come from South America, Father. From Colombia. And there we still use the old confessionals. I've never gotten used to the new way here." He smiled sheepishly. "The new way makes me nervous. It's why I haven't been to confession in a long time."

The priest glanced at the confessional, then back. He smiled again. "And I've never used one of the old confessionals," he said. "But we'll do it, if it makes you more comfortable. My pastor is always telling me how easy it is now; how I don't have to sit for hours in a dark, cramped little closet, listening to people's sins." Again, he smiled. "After tonight I can tell him that I have."

The priest led the way to the confessional. It consisted of three doors, each opening onto a small space. The center space was the largest. It held a built-in padded chair for the priest, with enough room to stretch out his legs. The spaces to either side were equipped with solitary kneelers and room enough for one person. A sliding partition provided access to the priest.

Father Hall extended his hand to one of the side doors, then opened the center one and started inside. Emilio stepped in behind, spun the priest roughly around and pushed him into the chair. The ice pick was in his hand now. He closed the door and placed the point of the pick under the priest's eye.

The priest stared up at him, his face a horrified mask. "I have no money," he said, his voice little more than a croak. "It's all back at the rectory. If that's what you want. . . ."

"I don't want your money, *maricón*." The final word came out as a curse, as Emilio pressed the ice pick forward, pushing it though the eye and into the young priest's brain.

Father Hall's body convulsed wildly for almost five seconds. Emilio fought it, holding tight to the weapon, keeping the priest's head pressed against the wall until all muscle control fled the body. Then came the part Emilio always hated, the small space suddenly filling with a heavy stench as the priest's bowels gave way, sending up their final offering to life.

Emilio grimaced as he fought off the smell. It was worse than usual in the confined area. He worked quickly, afraid the stench might make him ill. He pulled the ice pick free, wiped it clean on the priest's surplice, and tucked it away in his jacket pocket. Then, still holding his breath, he went about arranging the body as the man had instructed.

**D**evlin stood next to Ollie Pitts as they stared down at the priest. Father Walter Hall was still seated inside the old confessional, head thrown back against the wall, a stream of blood and fluid already dried on his cheek, his one remaining eye staring straight ahead, dull and blank and dead.

But that wasn't the worst. Devlin stared at the priest's right hand. It was closed into a fist around his penis—as though the priest were masturbating his way into the afterlife.

"This is one sick perp we got here," Ollie said. "I mean, to do this to a priest, right in his own fucking church."

"Ease up on the language," Devlin warned. "We got the pastor sitting behind us in one of the pews."

The pastor had found the body. He had gone looking for Father Hall when he failed to return to the rectory after the evening rosary service. The smell coming from the old confessional had led him to his dead curate.

"You talked to the pastor. Did this one have it too?" Pitts asked.

"Yeah, he had it too," Devlin said.

Pitts let out a long breath. "I guess there ain't no question about a coincidence now. But, hey, they couldn't all have been having it off with the same guy, right? That just don't figure. So how's our perp finding out about these guys? It ain't like it's a club. AIDS Anonymous, or something like that."

"Check counseling," Devlin said. "From what I've read about this, there are counseling services that help these people prepare for what's going to happen to them. There are also support groups. Check those out too. If we're lucky we'll find all three were going to the same counselor or group."

"Hey, I'm ready to try anything," Pitts said. "I just keep hitting one brick wall after another. It's starting to piss me off."

Devlin thought about Howie Silver and the call he would soon have to make. "You think *you're* pissed off," he whispered.

Ollie glanced at him. "You mean Hizzoner, huh?"

"I do."

"Have you told him yet?"

"No. That pleasure awaits me."

"Can I listen?"

"You can like hell."

"Jeez. You take all the fun out of this job."

Devlin looked down at the priest's body. "What fun?" he asked.

# Chapter Eight

Charles Meyerson stood before the wide windows that overlooked Central Park. It was a pleasing view, one he never tired of. Fourteen floors above the street, everything seemed small and inconsequential. It always made him feel elevated—in far more than just his physical proximity. As he looked down, he watched the people who meandered through the park, the ones who scurried along sidewalks, and he felt as though God's hand had raised him up above all others.

Meyerson knew he was toying with the sin of pride, but it was difficult, given all he had accomplished, not to feel that way. He atoned in other ways. His lavish Central Park West apartment was necessary for business reasons, but he did the best he could to humble his personal accommodations. His own room, the smallest of the eight he occupied, was a former maid's quarters off the kitchen. Now it was even more spartan, fitted out like a monk's cell with a hard narrow bed and a solitary nightstand, the only ornaments the simple crucifix that hung above the door and a bedside photograph of his mother that he had placed before a statue of the Virgin Mary. His business clothing was kept in the master bedroom, which he used only when he had guests. The lone piece of clothing in his cell was a plain black cassock, which he wore when he was there alone or on the rare occasions when special guests visited his home. This Saturday morning he was dressed in a crisply starched white shirt and a regimental necktie in preparation for the visit he would make later that morning.

Behind him he heard the door to the master bedroom open. Moments later a young woman entered the living room still dressed in the flimsy nightgown she had worn to bed.

"Is there any coffee, Charlie?" she asked.

Months ago, when she had first started visiting him, he had asked her not to use that abbreviation of his name. "It's Charles," he had told her. "Please try to remember." She had tried, but it was useless. Her mental powers simply couldn't sustain the thought.

He looked at her now, enjoying what he saw yet feeling a prick of guilt. She was tall and lean and beautiful, with blond hair that hung to her shoulders, vivid blue eyes, and lips that were suggestively full. There was nothing vulgar about her body, nothing excessive. Her breasts were almost nonexistent, something he found completely alluring. It wasn't the common perception of physical beauty, but that was inconsequential. The attraction was what she did for him, and he felt himself begin to harden as he studied her from across the room and thought about her skills.

"Yes, there's a fresh pot in the kitchen," he said. "You can bring me a cup as well."

The young woman, whose working name was Ginger, turned and moved away, the thong underwear she wore beneath the short nightgown revealing the subtle sway of small, almost childlike buttocks. He stared at her, then turned away, willing denial on his growing passion.

Ginger, of course, was his other sin, his other failing, he told himself. She was a professional call girl, who came to him one night each week for a fee of five hundred dollars. It was something he prayed that God would understand. Other than Ginger, he lived a life of complete celibacy. Her visits helped him do so. They kept him from the other temptations that might make him unworthy of the path God had chosen for him.

Ginger returned with two cups of coffee and placed them on the large glass table that stood before a long sectional sofa. Then she came to him slowly and reached up to run her fingers through his graying hair. Despite her own

height, she had to rise on tiptoe to accommodate his six foot
four inches. She kissed his lips, her tongue moving gently
against them. Then she smiled and slowly began to move
down the length of his body until she was kneeling in front
of him.

"What are you doing?" he asked, his voice catching
slightly.

She smiled up at him as she began to unzip his trousers.
"You always ask me the same question," she said, her own
voice husky now, "and I always tell you the same thing. I'm
doing what you like me to do in the morning, Charlie."

He felt her hand slip around him and let out a small gasp
of pleasure.

"Do you want me to stop, Charlie?" she asked. There was
a hint of laughter in her voice that he found disturbing but
chose to ignore.

"No. No, I want you to do what you always do," he said.

*B*oom Boom Rivera sat before the computer terminal, his
fingers flying across the keyboard. He was working in DOS,
trying to ferret out a problem that had been giving the Opus
Christi computer operators fits for the past week. It was a
simple glitch, one he could have solved within half an
hour—one that any competent technical support person
could have fixed just as easily. But the people who ran the
order were unwilling to allow outsiders near their machines.
That paranoia had now put him precisely where he wanted
to be.

He had diagnosed the problem quickly and had decided
to make it seem more difficult than it was. He wanted to
make himself appear indispensable, or at least as close to it
as these people allowed anyone to be. He also wanted as
much time on the system as possible. Sooner or later they'd
look the other way. Then it would be game time.

Peter had brought him to the center the previous day for
a series of interviews, and he had played his part just as it
had been laid out for him. He was still Ramon Rivera, but
now he was twenty, instead of twenty-eight. He was a computer technician for the city, part of a group that kept the

city's entire system up and running. It was a cover story Devlin had arranged, one that would stand up to any checks that Opus Christi made.

The first interview had dealt with religious questions, and he had followed the script laid out by Peter. His life, he said, had become increasingly meaningless, and he had found himself drawn more and more to the church. But it was difficult. His friends at work mocked him for his faith, and even the few good Catholics he knew had tainted their own beliefs with a worldliness he could not accept. Until he met Peter at one of Opus Christi's social gatherings, he had begun to question whether his own faith was demanding more of him than people could accept.

The second interview had been harder. It was conducted by a numerarier named Thomas. He was older than the others, well into his thirties, and he seemed to have all the skills of a good police interrogator. Even the look in his eyes— hard and cold and penetrating—made Boom Boom wonder if he had once been a cop.

Thomas had concentrated on sex. He had grilled Boom Boom about his past experiences, his attitudes, and his beliefs on what constituted sexual sin. Again, he had followed Peter's advice, almost choking on the words, silently praying that members of the squad would never find out what he had said.

He had told Thomas that sex had never been a force in his life. It had frightened him when he was younger, because it seemed so overpowering at times, seemed to occupy so many of his thoughts, even when he did not want it to. Because of this he had decided on personal celibacy, at least until he met someone he wanted to marry. But he had not found any woman who attracted him in anything but a lustful way, and he had just about given up hope of finding someone who valued the same things he did. Lately, he explained, he had even considered the possibility of a religious vocation.

Thomas had jumped on that, asking why he thought he might make a good priest or brother. Again, he had followed Peter's advice. He had told Thomas it was that very question that had stopped him from pursuing his interest. He wasn't good enough. Not yet, at least, and perhaps he never could be. He simply wasn't close enough to the Lord, not strong enough to live the life he knew Christ wanted. The answers seemed to satisfy Thomas, although his eyes had continued to bore into Boom Boom's face as if he knew some lie might be found there.

The final interview had been purely business. It was just as Peter had promised. The order was in desperate need of computer expertise. While it had many experienced computer operators, it completely lacked any technical support staff and had been left with the choice of outside contractors, something its leadership wanted to avoid if at all possible. The third interviewer, whose name was William, had put the best possible spin on that stringent need for privacy.

"We are a self-contained celibate order, and we try to avoid any outside influences that might jeopardize our spiritual well-being," he had said.

Boom Boom had interpreted that as making sure nobody got laid in the computer room.

When the inquiries ended, Peter and the three interviewers met privately for almost an hour. Peter explained later that he, too, had been thoroughly questioned before the others had agreed on a trial residency, during which Boom Boom would be more completely evaluated. For the present, he would live at the center but would go to his job each day. After a month, if all went well, he would be given the opportunity to become a full-time resident and would work solely for the order. They asked that in the meantime he spend his free hours—those not devoted to religious needs—solving the order's computer problems under Peter's supervision.

Peter remained at his side that Saturday as he worked out the first problem. The computer room was just off the main entrance and was filled with state-of-the-art equipment. Boom Boom wished the NYPD had invested half as much on its own hardware.

"How long will it take?" Peter whispered, as he looked over Boom Boom's shoulder.

"Another half hour or so," Boom Boom whispered back. He had decided to keep Peter in the dark as well. The guy was already a bag of nerves and would only be worse if he knew about this little scam.

The room was oddly divided. A high partition ran down the center, cutting the room in two. There was no access to the other section from his side, but cables ran through holes in the partition, and he could hear more than one person tapping away on keyboards. He inclined his head in the direction of the clatter. "Are there more computers over there?" he asked.

"Yes. Female operators work on that side. They have a separate entrance. If you have to work there, you can only go inside after they're finished working."

"Why?"

Peter bit his lip. "We don't have any contact. Men and women, I mean. It's for our spiritual protection."

"You mean I won't see any of the women while I'm here?"

Peter shook his head. "You may see someone accidentally, but we don't have any regular interaction. The women live separately. If they have work to do on our side of the building, they do it when we're not there. They cook and clean down here before seven in the morning. We leave our rooms at seven, and then they clean upstairs. All business areas they work in have separate entrances." Peter hesitated, as if embarrassed by what he had just revealed. "It's just the way things are done here."

Boom Boom shook his head. "A guy could get lonely for female companionship," he whispered.

Peter's jaw tightened. "It's not what we're here for," he whispered back. "And I wouldn't talk too freely. Some people believe there are listening devices in some parts of the building."

Boom Boom nodded, then raised a thumb in acknowledgment. He kicked himself mentally for not suspecting as much himself. These fruitcakes were as paranoid as anyone he had ever met. He decided to solve the problem at hand quickly, just in case his work was being monitored.

"I think I've got it now," he said. "Just a few more minutes."

*J*ust as Boom Boom put the final touches on his fix, a short, round, balding man entered the room. Peter stood immediately, almost snapping to attention. Boom Boom followed his example.

"Good morning, Father George."

The heavyset man was dressed in a gray pinstriped business suit, making the term *father* seem out of place. He smiled at Peter and turned to Boom Boom. "Is this the new computer wizard I was told about?" he asked.

Father George waited while Peter made the introductions. His smile widened as he shook Boom Boom's hand. "Well, Ramon Rivera, you may be the answer to my prayers. We were beginning to think our computers were possessed."

"Sometimes I think they all are," Boom Boom answered. He returned the smile. "At least some of them seem to suffer from personality disorders."

Father George clapped him on the shoulder. "Well, then, you be our resident psychologist and save us from their deviant personalities. The Lord will bless you if you can."

Movement behind him made Father George turn. Through the doorway to the computer center, a tall graying man could be seen walking through the lobby.

"Charles. Just a moment." Father George turned back to the two younger men. "My next appointment," he explained, and moved quickly toward the lobby, throwing a "Keep up the good work" over his shoulder as he left.

Boom Boom watched him. He had the hunched, lumbering gait of many overweight men, almost a waddle. The other man, in contrast, seemed erect and limber. He was well past forty but still had the movements of a younger, more athletic man.

"Who are they?" Boom Boom asked.

Peter kept his voice hushed, almost reverently so. "Father George runs the center," he said. "Father Charles only comes here occasionally. Mostly, he works with the religious—the other priests and the nuns."

"They're both priests?"

Peter nodded. His thin boyish face had taken on a guilty look. "Father Charles is a supernumerarier. I'm not supposed to know that. The identities of the supernumerarier are kept secret. I found out accidentally when I was working in the business office."

"Tell me about these guys, these supernumerarier." They were both speaking in hushed tones, each still concerned they might be overheard.

"The supernumerarier are the highest members of our order. Almost all of them are ordained priests. But almost all work outside the order in influential positions. Father Charles is a senior vice president for one of the city's largest banks. He's in charge of all their foreign investments."

Boom Boom shook his head, struggling to make sense of what he was being told. "So they're priests who joined your order, then got jobs in outside businesses?"

Peter shook his head. "It's the other way around. All of the supernumerarier were successful businessmen *before* they were brought into the order. They were all deeply religious men, devout Catholics, and they all came to see that the order was the only salvation for the church. Then, later, those who proved themselves worthy were ordained as priests. But they continued working in their professions as well. It's why no one is supposed to know who they are. It might affect their ability to do the work of the Lord."

Again, Boom Boom shook his head. "So they took time off from their jobs and entered a seminary?"

"No, their instruction for the priesthood was conducted privately. Opus Christi has its own religious order within the overall order itself. Years ago, the pope granted us a personal prelature, which entitles us to ordain our own priests. It's the same as the Jesuits or the Franciscans or the Dominicans. We operate our own seminaries. They're not traditional institutions, but I'm sure the fundamental instruction is the same."

Boom Boom blew out a long breath. He had a sudden vision of tentacles reaching out everywhere. Hidden priests, ordained privately, who were also influential businessmen.

Maybe even doing things they shouldn't. "That's quite a setup," he said. "Quite a nice little setup."

*F*ather George's face was grim. "The police are hounding us, Charles, and we can't seem to discourage them or even deflect them."

Charles Meyerson studied Father George's eyes. The eyes were where one found weakness, he believed. That simple hint of uncertainty gave it away. Years of negotiation had taught him to look for it, and he thought he saw it now in George.

They were seated in George's office. It was large, befitting his position in the order, and it was furnished in a starkly modern decor not unlike Charles's own office at the bank, which he particularly liked. Yet it seemed to have neither the substance of his own office nor the sense of grandeur he had always associated with the church.

"What is it they're pestering you about?" he asked.

"Sister Margaret," George said. "The nun who accompanied Sister Manuela to Colombia." He shook his head. "I still don't understand any of this. How it all could have happened."

"Has Sister Margaret been able to offer any explanation?" Charles asked.

George shook his head, his fleshy cheeks and jowls quivering with the movement. "She has no idea what happened. She told me personally that Sister Manuela just disappeared one morning for several hours. When she returned she told Sister Margaret that she had wanted to walk around the city where she had grown up. She said Margaret was still asleep when she left, and she hadn't wanted to disturb her, so she had gone alone. Sister Margaret assumed she had gone off to visit her family, despite our instructions that she not do so." He raised his hands in frustration. "But no matter what she was doing, it was a complete violation of our rules. And then . . . then to disappear the way she did after clearing customs, and to have narcotics found in her body! I don't understand how it could have happened."

Charles crossed one leg over the other, taking care that

the crease in his trousers would not be damaged. "She obviously went to see her parents or someone in her family. I understand they returned to Colombia a number of years ago. It seems clear they gave her the drugs she attempted to smuggle into the country." Charles raised his hands, imitating George's earlier gesture. "I understand it's quite common in that country, even among the middle class. Narcotics have become almost a currency of choice, I'm told."

He shifted in his seat. "It would appear that a family member arranged to smuggle this vile substance to New York and somehow convinced Sister Manuela to help them. Perhaps it was a spur-of-the-moment decision. Perhaps the person they had planned to use was simply not available." He waved a dismissive hand. "It's all speculation, of course, but it's obvious Sister Manuela became ill, and whoever was receiving the narcotics took extreme measures to make sure they weren't lost."

"But she was working for *you,* on assignment to *you.*"

There was a hint of accusation in George's voice that caused Charles's jaw to tighten. "Obviously I picked the wrong person. She was simply to oversee the shipment of the artifacts we were moving into the country. I thought her familiarity with the country and its customs made her a wise choice. Apparently I was wrong."

Charles decided to turn the table a bit.

"I'm surprised this tendency toward disobedience hadn't come to light before this. Usually the order is quite adept at spotting these things."

George stared at him. There was little doubt Charles intended to spread the blame, if it came to that. "Obviously, we failed too." He spoke in a conciliatory tone, still making it clear that while he might share the blame, he would not do so alone.

A small smile flickered on Charles's lips. He had gotten the message and actually admired George for having the grit to offer it up. "Where is Sister Margaret now?" he asked.

"She remained with the artifacts you were bringing into the country. When they reached the New York warehouse you shipped them to, she continued on to our monastery in Bedford. She's still there, at my direction."

"I think she should remain there," Charles said.

"But what about the police?" George insisted. "We certainly can't tell them we don't know where she is."

Charles stared at him coldly. "I don't want the police speaking with her. Not yet. The religious artifacts we brought into the country are the problem. Several of those items were not supposed to leave Colombia. It was a violation of their laws when we moved them. We also had to . . . *compensate* . . . some Colombian officials for looking the other way. In addition, the items were far more valuable than we indicated to U.S. Customs. If any of that comes out . . . well, it would be embarrassing at the least."

"But there's no reason for them to find out," George insisted.

Charles was becoming irritated. The man was an idiot. "George, the police have been told that Sister Manuela was visiting her family—that's how we've explained her presence there—and that Sister Margaret merely accompanied her. If Sister Margaret now tells them that a shipment of artifacts was the real reason they were there, the police will certainly become suspicious. God, drugs were involved in this nun's death! When the police learn about the shipment, they will want to see those artifacts. And I do not want that to happen."

George seemed thoroughly exasperated. "Then what am I to do with this police sergeant who keeps hounding me? She called again this morning, saying she wanted to see Sister Margaret *forthwith*. Her exact words, mind you. *Forthwith*, of all things."

"Just keep stalling her," Charles said. "I'll send someone to Bedford and make it clear to Sister Margaret that she has to remain quiet about the artifacts. Then we can let this sergeant see her."

George seemed to ponder that idea. "I'm not sure that's wise," he said at length. "This woman sergeant is somewhat of a bully. I'm not sure Sister Margaret is up to dealing with her." He hesitated for a moment. "Frankly, I get the impression she's one of those deviants the police department seems willing to tolerate these days."

Charles stiffened in his chair. "A homosexual?"

"I suspect as much," George said. "Matthew spoke with her earlier, and he had the same impression."

"What's her name?" Charles asked.

"Detective Sergeant Sharon Levy," George said.

"A Jew," Charles added, as though that too held some significance. He had begun tapping his fingers against his trousers. "I'll look into the matter," he said. "I'll look into it very thoroughly."

*T*he squad gathered for a late-afternoon briefing. An oversized bulletin board had been set up in the squad room with a morgue photo of each victim pinned to it. Beneath each photo, written on index cards, was every scrap of information the squad had gathered. To Devlin the large board seemed obscenely bare.

"All right. It's Saturday. It's getting late in the day. I know all of you are anxious to get out of here, see your families, get your weekend started. Well, it's the old good news, bad news gag. Good news: I only need you for about half an hour. Bad news: Everybody works tomorrow."

Not one groan, not even a grimace. It surprised Devlin. It was very unlike a group of cops. He wondered if the frustration they were facing at every turn had begun to attack their sense of professionalism, if it had begun to piss everyone off.

"Okay. Ollie, Stan, and Red. Tomorrow morning I want you at each of the churches where a priest was murdered. Each of you take one. I don't care who goes where; decide among yourselves. I want you at every mass, talking to every person you can. Contact the pastors before you leave today and get a handle on their Sunday schedules. Also, ask each of them to announce from the pulpit that you're there and to urge their parishioners to go to you with any information they might have."

He turned to Sharon. "Okay. You don't have to spend all morning in church, but I do want you at Opus Christi headquarters. Part of that job will be to loosely monitor Boom Boom. If he comes out, and he's alone, get to him and find out what he's been doing. He said he'd send us e-mails if he could, but so far nothing's come in.

"Second, you're still being stonewalled about this Sister Margaret, right?" He waited while Sharon nodded. "Then I want you to stop and question every woman who comes out of there. Anybody knows anything about Sister Manuela or the whereabouts of Sister Margaret, you bring them down to the office and contact me on my cell phone."

Devlin turned to the bulletin board and shook his head. It was a sorry display for all the work they'd put in. "Ollie, tell us what's new on the priests," he said.

Pitts leaned back in his chair, the irritation in his eyes almost palpable. "I checked on any counseling or group therapy each of them might have gotten. It was another big zero." He shook his large head. "From what I'm told, the archdiocese provides any counseling that's needed. But it's all in-house. All of it done by other priests who get trained in that sort of thing. None of our priests took advantage of it. One of the pastors told me it's not a pleasant experience. Ends up dealing more with their sins than their problems. But the archdiocese did know about all three of them. Any claims a parish makes for insurance gets reported back."

"What about the insurance company?" Sharon asked.

Pitts shook his head. "Each parish has its own policy. It's more expensive that way, but it also keeps the cost in the parish. That way the archdiocese doesn't have to cover the nut for all of them. The reports the parishes file are really just a check on what money is coming into the parishes, and what the health of the priests are, stuff like that. It's supposed to help the archdiocese figure out where replacements might be needed so they can plan for it."

Sharon leaned forward. "Wait a minute. I read somewhere that there's a computer network that keeps track of any insurance claim that gets filed. There was a lot of controversy about it. HMOs were requiring doctors to report any illnesses they treated to this network so all insurance companies could get access to that central information. The problem was, the network was also selling that information to private corporations and banks and just about anyone who wanted it, even though medical information was supposed to be confidential. The upshot was that people were getting turned down for loans and jobs and credit cards based on medical problems that had turned up on the computer."

Devlin turned to Pitts. "Check it out, Ollie. See if anyone has asked for information about these priests." He turned back to the bulletin board and jabbed his finger at the morgue photos of the three dead priests. Their names were printed on cards pinned above the photos. "Anybody notice anything about our victims, about the order in which they were killed?"

All eyes went to the bulletin board. Pitts was the one to see it first. "Shit," he said. "Donovan, Falco, Hall. They're in fucking alphabetical order."

"Bingo," Devlin said. "I just noticed it when I got back here today and put Father Hall's picture up." He turned back to Ollie. "That suggests a list, my friend. So first, find out if there's a central list of all people treated for AIDS. If there is, see if anybody's checked out all the people on that list by profession. If not, let's get a list of every priest working in the archdiocese and then check this computer network and find out if anybody has asked for medical information on all the priests working in the archdiocese. It's a big job, but unless this is just one big coincidence, somebody just may have found a way to put together a hit list on gay priests."

"What about the archdiocese itself?" Sharon asked.

"I'll handle that part," Devlin said. "I doubt a list would have come out of there. Knowing the archdiocese, I think that information would be very closely held. But I want it. I intend to ask them for the name of every priest they know about who's infected with AIDS."

Pitts grinned at him. "We're gonna stake out the one whose last name comes next in the alphabet."

Devlin tapped the side of his nose. "You bet your ass we are."

# Chapter Nine

"A cop? You know the kinda heat comes down when somebody puts away a cop?"

"I don't think the police department will be terribly saddened this time. This particular police officer is a lesbian. I had that confirmed through a source I have. I also obtained her home address and her description. She's tall and she has red hair. She shouldn't be hard to identify." He handed Emilio a slip of paper.

Emilio stared at the address and shook his head. "What if this source you got remembers you asked about this cop when she turns up dead?"

Charles stared at him. "I assure you it can never come back to me. Do you think I'm a fool?"

Emilio looked away, as if not wanting to answer that last question. "I dunno. This thing we got going here is getting out of hand," he said.

They were seated on their regular bench in Central Park. Charles's entire body stiffened under Emilio's rebuke.

"This detective is investigating a murder, and in doing so she's poised to discover the work I've done for the people you work for," he snapped. "She's trying to locate the nun who was with Sister Manuela. This whole problem would not exist if Sister Manuela had not been killed."

Charles glared at Emilio. The man had been in Bogotá when the shipment of artifacts was prepared. He had then followed the two nuns and the shipment to the United States. There was no question in Charles's mind that he had somehow coerced Sister Manuela into carrying a separate cache of drugs for him and then had brutally killed her when she became ill. Emilio denied it, of course. He insisted she was transporting the drugs for someone else. His boss didn't seem to care, as long as the deal Charles had set up with him was not affected. Sister Manuela had become nothing more than an unfortunate casualty.

"If you're worried about the cop getting to this nun, why don't we just put away the nun?" Emilio asked. "It would be easy and a lot safer."

The man seemed angered by the suggestion, and the reaction brought something close to a smile to Emilio's lips. This man could order the death of priests without even blinking his eyes, but the idea of killing some little nun offended him.

"Sister Margaret has done nothing to deserve punishment," Charles snapped. "Therefore, nothing will be done to her unless it proves absolutely necessary. Do we understand each other?"

"Hey, you just give me the names, and I do the work."

"I've given you a name," Charles snapped. "And an address." He paused a moment. "I will also compensate you for this extra job, since it wasn't part of the original arrangement. It will be something private between us, something your boss doesn't have to know about."

Emilio's eyebrows rose with pleasure. "How much?" he asked.

"How does five thousand dollars sound?"

Emilio let out a barking laugh. "Hey, man, that's pretty cheap. This is a cop we're talking about here."

"What, then?"

"Ten sounds fairer to me."

Charles's jaw tightened. It wasn't the money. It was the question of negotiating from a position of weakness. It was something he had never allowed himself to do—until now, and with this cretin. "Consider it done," he snapped. "Cash on delivery."

Emilio looked away, trying to hide how much he enjoyed playing with this man. "Usually, it's half up front," he said. "But since we know each other—"

"Cash on delivery." Charles's hands began to tremble with rage.

"You drive a hard bargain, man," Emilio said.

There was laughter in Emilio's voice. It seemed to strike at every nerve in Charles's body.

*D*evlin came up behind her and slipped his arms around her waist. The scent of Adrianna's hair—sweet and clean and fresh—filled him as he bent to kiss her cheek. His hands ran lightly along her stomach. What he really wanted was to take her back to bed. Spend the next hour lost in her warmth. Then a leisurely Sunday breakfast, with the rest of the day devoted to some much-needed time with Phillipa. The idea filled him like her scent had. It would all be possible if he handed in his shield and returned to the disability pension he had given up when he took over the squad. Howie Silver had lured him back with the promise that he could pack it in whenever he decided it was time. The pension was there, waiting for him. It would work. The drop in income would never be noticed. Adrianna's success as an artist had removed financial concerns from the equation. They could spend their weekdays at the beach house they owned in the Hamptons. Phillipa could go to a civilized country school, and they could all come into Manhattan for the weekends. It would be an idyllic life.

Adrianna leaned back against him, almost as if reading his thoughts. He knew she wanted the very same things he did. They talked about it from time to time—the hours and the days and the weeks his job took away from their lives; how good it would be to have that time together before Phillipa was grown and off finding her own life. Each time they spoke of it, it seemed to reinforce his thoughts. So why not just give in? He closed his eyes and pushed it all away. He knew the answer. This was just a game he played with himself: retirement, the idea that reared up whenever he acknowledged how much time he was losing with the people he loved. The game assuaged his guilt. Someday he'd surrender to it, and within two weeks he'd be climbing the walls. You love the damn job too much, he told himself. You feed on it like a starving animal.

So none of what he needed would happen today. Instead, he'd be headed up to Saint Patrick's to deal with the cardinal's secretary.

Adrianna's head leaned back against his shoulder. "How late will you be today?" she asked.

"I'll be back by lunch. We can go out to eat. You and Phillipa pick the place and we'll go. Then we'll do whatever you guys want for the rest of the day." Guilt, he thought. It was so easy to soothe.

"And you'll leave your cell phone at home?" Adrianna asked.

"Um. . . ." He began searching for an answer.

Adrianna turned and took his face in her hands. "I'm only teasing you." She rose up on her toes and kissed his lips.

"Mmmm. Love in the kitchen. I'll have to write this in my journal for future reference."

Devlin turned and found his daughter grinning at them. She loved catching them at anything. He was sure she kept a scorecard somewhere in her precocious little mind. *Walked in on them kissing.* Two points for Phillipa.

"I have to go out this morning, but we're planning a big afternoon. You and Adrianna get to choose." He feigned a hard look. "But no rock concerts."

Phillipa rolled her eyes. "Rock concerts happen at night, Dad. Maybe in olden days, when *you* were a kid, *before* they had electricity, they had rock concerts in daylight." She shook her head. "Now it happens when the sun goes down."

"You think I don't know from rock concerts?" He narrowed one eye, playing with her. "You ever hear of Woodstock?"

Phillipa fought off a smile. "I've heard about Christopher Columbus too, Dad."

He looked back at Adrianna in mock horror. "She thinks I'm old," he said. "I'm thirty-eight. Just thirty-eight."

Adrianna put a finger against his lips. "You sound like Jack Benny," she said.

"Who's Jack Benny?" Phillipa asked.

Devlin looked at her to see if she was serious this time. She was. Her little freckled face was all screwed up with curiosity. God, he *was* getting old. Just two birthdays away from the big one.

He shook his head. "Suddenly, I feel too old to go to work today. Maybe you could both help me back to bed."

"Uh-uh," Phillipa said. "I want to go to a rock concert . . . this afternoon."

*T*he cardinal's secretary gave him a broad smile.

His mother had once told Devlin to watch his step when a priest smiled at him. *They're either getting ready to ask you for money or to do work for no pay.* He had only been a child when she said it, but it endured as a truth from his mother's own lips.

"I appreciate your seeing me, Father," Devlin said.

Father James Arpie was close to Devlin's age. He was a slender man, barely average in height and balding prematurely. He also had busy hands, Devlin noticed. They seemed to move constantly, adjusting a paper here, picking up a pen there and putting it down again, brushing a bit of lint from the sleeve of his clerical coat, adjusting another piece of paper. Either the cardinal was a very hard man to work for or his secretary needed a prescription for Valium. Perhaps it was both.

"You said you needed the cardinal's help?" Arpie began. He was wasting little time.

"It's about the three priests who've been murdered," Devlin began.

"I know. You explained that on the phone. It's tragic," Arpie said coldly. "But still, I don't see how the cardinal can be of any help."

"I think there are going to be more. I believe the killer has a list of priests he intends to kill."

Arpie gave him a skeptical look. "That's a disturbing prediction."

Both men were still standing—Arpie behind his desk, Devlin in front of it—the secretary not having offered Devlin a chair or taken one himself. It was as though he expected the meeting to be a short one and wanted to let Devlin know that was his intention.

They were in a small office off a well-appointed reception area. The cardinal's office was marked by a set of double doors off that same reception room. Devlin had been there once, years ago. It had also involved police business—that time about a priest who had forgotten the commandment Thou shalt not kill. It had been a different cardinal then, and it had not been a pleasant experience. He had hoped this time would be different.

"The three priests who've been murdered were all suffering from AIDS." He let the statement sit. He wanted to force some response.

"The archdiocese is aware of that," Arpie finally conceded.

"Our investigation indicates that none of these men contracted the disease from tainted blood transfusions or intravenous drug use. The information we've gathered has convinced us that all three were gay." Devlin decided not to add the final conclusion that the disease had been contracted through sexual contact. He didn't want to antagonize Arpie unnecessarily.

The line of Arpie's mouth stiffened, and he lowered himself into his chair. He extended a hand toward another for Devlin. "I would have thought the existence of a few gay priests was an old story," Arpie said. "The fact that an even smaller number contract a disease associated with gay men also should not come as a surprise." He tried a smile that died quickly. "The vow of celibacy is a difficult one, and priests are all too capable of human failings, Inspector—be they heterosexual or otherwise inclined."

Devlin took the offered seat. Arpie, he decided, was obviously a student of Aquinas. His circular reasoning was almost classic.

"I'm not here to debate morals or sexuality or anything else, Father. We have several unpleasant facts staring us in the face. First, all the murdered priests were gay and all suffered from AIDS. Second, it appears they are being killed in alphabetical order. That leads us to believe that someone has found a way to use that illness to identify gay priests and has decided to eliminate them from the church."

Arpie leaned forward, resting his forearms on the desk. "I'm still at a loss about what the archdiocese can do to help you."

Like pulling teeth, Devlin thought. "We're also aware that these illnesses were reported to the archdiocese."

Arpie stiffened again. "And you think we compiled a list and that someone got that list from *us*?"

"I'm not saying that."

"Nor should you," Arpie snapped. "First of all, there is no such list. And I assure you no one here would ever compose such a list, even privately. It is not something we would choose to have on paper, if for no other reason than the very fact that it might fall into the wrong hands."

Meaning anyone's hands, Devlin thought. "But since you're aware of illnesses among your priests, you could create such a list, if asked."

"And what purpose would that serve?" Arpie's voice remained snappish, and his short, slender body seemed to have assumed a surprisingly combative posture. His hands were moving again like little pistons.

"It would allow us to figure out who might be next on this killer's list. And that would give us a chance to stop him."

Arpie waved his hand in the air, as though dismissing Devlin's suggestion as foolishness. "There are a great many assumptions here. First, that your theory is correct, and not merely a series of coincidences. Second, that every parish in the archdiocese follows our instructions and reports serious illnesses." He raised his eyes to the ceiling. "If only they all were that conscientious."

Devlin's jaw tightened. The small scar on his cheek became lighter, more pronounced. Arpie was looking for an excuse to turn him down. Any excuse, any reason to avoid acknowledging the problem. "It's not a perfect solution, Father. I accept that. It may not even work. I accept that as well. But it gives us a shot. *Before* another priest is murdered." He paused, hoping the final words would have some effect. They didn't. "I assure you, the list would be kept in confidence," he added.

Arpie's poor attempt at a smile came again. "Among how many detectives?" The words dripped sarcasm.

"The question is, How many more priests have to die before you agree?" Devlin snapped back.

Arpie glared at him, his face red, hands moving along his desk like two spiders. "You think I'm not concerned about that?"

"I think you care more about appearances."

"It's my job to protect the archdiocese, the reputation of the church."

"And it's my job to stop someone who's killing your priests. Prioritize, Father. That's all I'm asking. Or at least pass my request on to the cardinal."

Arpie leaned back in his chair, still glaring. "I'll pass on the request," he added at length. "But my recommendation, should I be asked for it, will not be affirmative."

Devlin offered up a smile as miserable as the ones he'd been given. "I didn't expect it would, Father. But I had to ask. It will help ease my conscience when I put the next priest in a body bag." He dropped his card on the desk as he stood. "All my phone numbers are there. Please call me when you have an answer from the cardinal."

*E*milio had taken up a position at the corner of Amsterdam Avenue and West 78th Street at seven that morning. It gave him a clear view of the address the man had given him. It was a four-story brownstone, and the doorbells next to the front door told him it had been divided into six apartments. Not bad, he had decided. How many tall redheads could there be in six apartments?

Sharon had come out at eight, and Emilio had stepped back around the corner and into the doorway of an antiques shop as soon as she turned in his direction. He was pleased he had guessed right, that she might work on Sundays. It pleased him even more when she walked past without glancing in his direction.

He had watched her walk toward the subway and had fallen in well behind her. She was a good-looking woman, he had decided. Beautiful legs and an even more beautiful ass. It would be a shame to put her away. He had consoled himself with the fact that she shared her beauty only with other women. She was already lost to the men of this world, he reasoned, so what did it matter?

He had followed her onto the subway, still only 90 percent sure he had the right woman. There could be two tall redheads in the building—unlikely but possible. He wanted to be certain. There was no point in wasting the risk on the wrong woman. To do so would be unprofessional.

Emilio's doubts evaporated when Sharon changed trains at Times Square and took the shuttle to Grand Central Station. From there she walked to Second Avenue and entered a coffee shop across from Opus Christi headquarters. Emilio walked farther up the avenue and hid himself in the doorway of a closed clothing shop.

It was a long wait. Occasionally, when women left the headquarters building, the detective would leave the coffee shop, catch up to them, and engage them in conversation. Then she would wait for others to leave and speak to them as well. When traffic slowed at the building she would return to the coffee shop and wait again, then start all over each time more women left the building.

The pattern was broken in the middle of the afternoon, when a young slender man left the building and headed south on Second Avenue. This time the detective caught up with him and continued down the street. Emilio followed, keeping well back.

"Hey, I'm already goin' crazy in there," Boom Boom said. "You tell the boss not to worry I'll come on to any women. They don't even let you *see* a woman, except when they go zippin' out the front door."

Sharon rolled her eyes. "Spare me your social problems, Boom Boom. Try and stick to business. *Police* business."

"Hey, I'm inside. I'm into their computer system. All I need now is a little space when nobody's watching me. Then it'll be magic time."

"The inspector thinks we should wire you up. For your own safety."

Boom Boom shook his head. "I dunno. It wouldn't surprise me if these guys sweep for bugs. They got security comin' out the wazoo in there. I start givin' off little beeps, and my ass is out the front door. Besides, I haven't seen any kind of physical threat in there. These guys threaten you with hell, not the boneyard."

"I still think it's a good idea. I can call Red on his cell phone and have him wire you up this afternoon. Where are you headed now?"

"Home to my apartment to pick up some clothes. If I'm not back pretty fast they'll get suspicious."

Sharon glanced at her watch. It was nearing noon. She knew Boom Boom's apartment was on Riverside Drive. Red Cunningham should still be at the Columbus Avenue church where the last priest was killed. He could be at Boom Boom's apartment by the time they got there.

"I'm gonna go with the wire," she said. "I don't want your sweet little buns to get bruised."

Boom Boom grinned as she took out her cell phone. "Hey, Sharon, you like my sweet little buns, maybe we should go to my apartment alone."

Sharon threw him a look. "Not till you've had a sex change, sweetie."

Boom Boom screwed up his face. "Sharon, don't even talk like that. Think of all the women who'd be in mourning."

Sharon gave him a mirthless smile. "You still wearing that little garter I put on you?" she asked.

"Yeah, I'm wearin' it."

"Then you better remember what I said about your mouth, unless you want me to tell Ollie all about it."

Boom Boom raised his hands in surrender. "Anything you want, Sergeant."

Sharon's cold smile widened. "That's what I like. A good little Boom Boom."

"Hey, don't get too overjoyed. I could tell them you're lyin' about the garter, you know."

"The inspector will back me up. I put it in my DD-Five. Everything except you wanting me to move it higher up your puny little leg."

*Charles, you must come. The most delightful people will be there.* Those trite and tired words had actually been spoken to him almost three weeks ago by the woman whose home he was about to enter. Now, as he thought back to that rather graceless conversation, a small sneer came to Charles Meyerson's lips. The most delightful people were those who were one with the Lord, and he knew this opulent Park Avenue apartment he was about to enter would be devoid of any.

The hostess, Margaret Dunstreet, greeted Charles warmly as soon as he entered. She was a slender bottle blond somewhere in her forties or fifties. Like that of most of the women of her set, her age was difficult to determine. Her face, like those of her friends, was fixed in a rigid mask, the skin drawn so tight by repeated facial surgeries that it appeared ready to crack if stretched in any direction. Even the smile she wore gave off hints of strain, as if it too had been surgically imposed. Margaret was the wife of a partner in one of the nation's major brokerage houses and in many ways reminded Charles of his own mother. He utterly despised her.

"Charles, I'm so delighted you came," Margaret said, as she leaned in to kiss the air near his cheek. "And you will be too," she added in a whisper. "Everyone is discussing money, money, money. Your expertise is very much needed."

Charles smiled, asked after her husband, and was told he was "milling about" somewhere.

"Just look for one of those little cartoon balloons hanging in the air," Margaret said. "If it's filled with dollar signs, you've found him."

Charles located Edgar Dunstreet just as Margaret had suggested, surrounded by men whose lives were consumed by investment. The wives who stood beside them were equally consumed, but simply with the rewards of that game. Charles always likened them to vultures at the site of a fresh kill—heads bobbing, pleased and reassured to see the carcass laid out before them, yet eager for the larger carnivores to finish so they could take over the feast. He immediately decided he did not want to join this group. He intended simply to compliment his host and move on to more gentle conversation. Edgar, however, would have none of it.

"Charles. We were talking about Indonesia. I'm trying to convince Harry, here, that they've bounced back and are a good target for investment." He clapped his friend on the shoulder. "He just won't agree with me. You're the foreign expert, what do you think?"

Charles gave Edgar a regretful smile. "I'm afraid I agree with Harry. Personally, I plan to hold off on Indonesia, at least for the next year or two." He offered a helpless gesture. "It's also the recommendation I've given my bank."

Edgar seemed confused. "Good Lord, why? I was sure you'd be hopping on their wagon."

Charles shook his head. "Corruption there has been so systemic, especially among the government-controlled banks, I'm just not convinced it's been reversed. If it hasn't, they'll be back in the same morass they encountered a few years ago. I'd give them another year or two, just to be safe."

Edgar's eyes brightened. "But the time to jump in is a year or two *ahead* of the herd."

Charles smiled. "You're probably right, Edgar. But you know how we bankers are. We want to be sure about our money before we hand it out. We've been burned too many times."

Edgar's friend, Harry, grunted agreement. "Haven't we all." He gave Charles a nod of approval. "I'm pleased to hear you share my view. I'm still not convinced the Pacific rim— excluding Japan, of course—is a good place to have one's money."

Charles turned to him. "In large part, I agree. Now, South Korea is a different matter. Their economy is strong, and they have some well-run companies: KIA, Samsung." He ticked them off on his fingers. "Some others as well. And if negotiations succeed with the north, they'll be positioned to tap into a very cheap source of labor. That's a country into which I'm eager to put our money."

"How do you feel about Cuba?" Harry asked. "When the embargo is eventually lifted, of course?"

Charles offered a pained shrug. "The Canadian, German, and Spanish firms that have done business there up to now have done reasonably well—primarily the tourist industry, of course. When U.S. companies join them, they can expect similar or perhaps slightly better results. But nothing dramatic is going to happen until Castro or his successor eases up on their model of joint-venture capitalism. The Cuban government is slow and inefficient and still far too entrenched in dogma to allow its economy to take off. Until that ends, or at least until they allow corporations fully to own their investments, U.S. banks are going to remain cautious about financing Cuban-based projects. U.S. companies who import *from* Cuba will have the strongest investment potential—again, because of cheap labor and low prices. However, I'm still skeptical about industry operating on the island itself. They'll have cheap labor, but they won't have full control of their capital investment, and at the same time the Cuban government will want to milk them to help maintain the rather extensive social programs they presently offer their people." He shrugged, dismissing the idea. "Nice for the Cuban people, but not terribly good for business."

Harry's wife—yet another plastic surgeon's meal ticket—cocked an eyebrow. "My, how unegalitarian of you, Charles."

Charles gave her a cold smile. "Is there such a word?" he asked.

Charles excused himself a few minutes later and moved about the gathering, finally stopping at a small group of women engaged in idle chatter. That suited him better and he joined them, only half listening to their words, satisfied with his role as a passive participant.

He accepted a glass of champagne from a waiter and turned slightly toward a nearby window. His reflection came back at him, and what he saw pleased him. He was dressed in a lightweight linen blazer, a traditional navy blue but lacking the brass buttons he had always regarded as a bit tawdry. Beneath the jacket was a matching collarless shirt, and the combination, he thought, seemed almost clerical. It was a satisfying vision. Without appearing to leave the group, he eased a bit closer to the glass and looked down onto Park Avenue. What he saw there tainted that earlier image.

The building he was in had a large courtyard, separated from the street by a high iron fence. Beyond it the median divider that bisected the roadway was awash with flowers. It was a beautiful ribbon of color, intended as a synonym for this wealthiest of New York addresses. Yet beneath those flowers, he knew, lay the burrows of an extraordinary concentration of rats, which for years the city had unsuccessfully fought to control. It was like so much of the city, he believed—so much of life. Beauty hiding corruption, the vileness below fully entrenched and inescapable. A small shiver passed through his body, but he pushed the accompanying thoughts away.

"They call it a civil union, and these two women were married last week, right on the lawn of the house next to ours."

Charles's head snapped around. "I'm sorry, I missed that," he said to the woman who was speaking.

She gave him a broad smile, pleased that he was interested. Her name was Beatrice—Beebee to her friends. "Well, you know we have a summer house in Vermont. In Dorset, actually. And there's this recent law that's been passed up there that allows homosexuals to marry." She waved a hand and hurried on. "Well, it's not marriage, really. They call it a civil union. I'm told it's intended to give them the same protections as married people—inheritance, various tax advantages, insurance benefits, even divorce settlements, if you can imagine that." She let out a little titter before continuing. "They even get a license when they do it, and they hold these little ceremonies, complete with a justice of the peace, or any minister who's willing to take part. I understand a Catholic priest even officiated at one not long ago. Isn't that remarkable? It's all so delightfully silly."

Charles's entire body went rigid. "I think it's an abomination," he hissed. His face became an angry mask. "Are you sure a priest actually conducted one of these ceremonies?"

"Oh, yes," Beebee said. "I gather there was quite a fuss about it. There's even talk about him being defrocked, or whatever it is one does to a priest."

"He was probably one himself," Charles snapped. He seemed unable to speak for a moment. "But to put his blessing on such deviancy. . . ." Again, he seemed to run out of words and just stood there, red-faced.

Beebee's eyebrows shot up in surprise. "Why, Charles, you're being so . . . so homophobic. I think it's all just a silly lark, and I always thought—well, you being such a confirmed bachelor and all . . . I always assumed you'd be . . . more sympathetic to those people." She glanced at the other women and began to laugh.

Charles's eyes widened in disbelief. "You thought *what*?" He stared at her, his face scarlet.

"Oh, Charles, I didn't mean a thing by it. It's just . . . well . . ."

Charles didn't wait for any more. He turned without another word and stalked across the room, straight to the front door.

Beebee watched him, her mouth forming a small circle of surprise. "Oh, dear," she said. "I seem to have made a little faux pas, haven't I?" She pressed her fingers to her lips and began to laugh again.

*E*milio had lost the woman when she and the young man entered the subway, so he had returned to Opus Christi headquarters hoping she would reappear.

The young man she had left with returned two hours later carrying a suitcase, and Emilio was preparing to give up his watch when the woman pulled up in a car driven by another man, who appeared to take up half the front seat. They parked slightly south of the building's entrance and remained inside.

Emilio watched them for another hour. The glare of the afternoon sun made it difficult to see into the car, and neither his target nor this new man seemed to have any intention of getting out. There was little question this new man was a police officer, and that made any action here hopeless. Emilio's pistol was equipped with a suppressor. Had the woman been alone, he could have waited for a lull in pedestrian traffic, walked by, and fired into the car. But two cops raised the risk, and risk was always best kept to a minimum. There was also the possibility they would drive off and he would lose track of her completely. Better to return to her apartment, he decided. If he could get inside he could lie in wait. Then it would be easy—nice and clean and quiet, just the way he liked it to be.

Emilio stepped out of the doorway and hailed a passing taxi. As he entered the rear seat he glanced at the unmarked police car. Just stay where you are for another half hour, he thought. A grimacelike smile flickered across his lips. He liked the idea of the woman sitting there, talking her stupid cop talk, never suspecting that she was being hunted. Another half hour, he thought again. It would be all the time he needed.

## Chapter Ten

"*S*o what's he doing?" Sharon asked.

Red removed the earplug he was wearing so he could better hear her. "Boom Boom's getting a religious lecture. Some crazy shit. Somethin' called self-mortification."

"I'd like to mortify the little weasel." A smile played across Sharon's lips. "Before you got to his apartment I helped him pack his suitcase." She had to hold down a laugh. "The little pervert put in a deck of condoms. Can you believe it?" She raised her chin toward the building. "The whole place is full of virgin celibates, but Boom Boom thinks he's still got a shot."

"Hey, where's there's life—"

Sharon raised a hand, stopping him. "Yeah, yeah, I know. Where men are concerned, where there's a heartbeat, there's a hard-on."

Red replaced the earplug and began monitoring the wire again. "Whoa," he said. "This guy's telling Boom Boom about this cord with knots tied in it. He's telling our boy how he should use it to whip his own butt." He listened again. "At least once a week he's supposed to do it. While he's saying his prayers." He pressed a finger against the earplug. "Oh, man, this is too much. I got this snitch, this crazy hooker who's into all that dominatrix crap. She'd love this place."

Sharon thought about the two young women they had interviewed; thought about them scourging themselves as they said their prayers; about the metal belt they wore around their legs for two hours each day, a belt they tightened so the small sharp spikes on the inner surface would cut into their flesh. If you could get young men and women to do that, you could get them to do anything, she reasoned—even swallow condoms filled with heroin.

"Sounds like they're finished up for the day," Red said, as he removed the earplug. "Boom Boom's been told to go to his room and meditate on what he's been told. They said a bell would ring for evening prayers and dinner. You wanna hang around or bag it?"

"Let's give it another hour, then bag it," Sharon said. "We can meet back here at seven tomorrow morning. Boom Boom's supposed to go to his regular job. I told him we'd pick him up at Grand Central, but I want to make sure no one's tailing him."

"What's he gonna to do if he's got a tail?" Red asked.

"He goes to the city office he's supposed to work at," Sharon said. "Paul's got it set up for him. If we don't pick him up at Grand Central, he'll figure we spotted a tail and he'll go straight there. We'll meet up with him there later."

"You trust this guy, Peter—the one who got him into this loony bin?"

Sharon thought about that. "I don't think we can trust anybody in that place. But with Peter we don't have much choice. We'll just have to watch Boom Boom's back."

*D*evlin took Adrianna and Phillipa to Umberto's, a Little Italy eatery made famous a quarter century ago when Crazy Joe Gallo was gunned down over a plate of scungilli. Ever since she'd learned about "the mob rubout," as she termed it, Umberto's had become Phillipa's favorite Italian restaurant. She had even asked her father to find out what table the Brooklyn mobster was seated at when two hit men sent him to "that big cannoli factory in the sky." It had prompted Devlin to ban New York's two tabloids, the *Daily News* and the *Post,* from their home.

Devlin's cell phone went off halfway through their Shrimp Diavolo, and he went out into the street to take the call. He felt awkward doing so. He hated cell phones, hated being part of the endless band of idiots who walked the city streets with the obnoxious devices pressed to their ears. In the past, if you heard someone babbling on the street, you knew a lunatic was nearby and you could give him a wide berth. Now every other person babbled, and the lunatics hid among them.

This time the cell phone paid off. The call was from Father Arpie, the cardinal's secretary, and Devlin listened as the priest seemed to choke on his words. The cardinal had agreed to provide a list of all AIDS-infected priests, providing it was kept in strict confidence. That, Arpie said, would mean that only Devlin had access to the full list, and that members of his squad would only be given the name of the one priest they would put under surveillance.

Devlin suspected the conditions were Arpie's, not the cardinal's. But it didn't matter. He needed the list, and Arpie said he'd have it ready early in the morning.

Adrianna and Phillipa both gave him questioning looks when he returned. Like those of all detectives, Devlin's calls often signaled his abrupt departure, and Adrianna and Phillipa—like all cop families—had learned to dread each inopportune ring.

Devlin smiled and winked at his daughter. "Not this time," he said. "I'm yours for the evening."

Phillipa's face broke into a wide smile. "Great," she said. "Because I want you to take me to Ferrara's for dessert."

Devlin winced at the thought. Ferrara's Bakery had been a regular haunt of mob boss Giovanni Rossi. At least it was until Devlin left "John the Boss" locked in a Cuban jail. The result, not surprisingly, had been icy treatment the next time he visited that Little Italy landmark.

"I don't know, honey. I'm not very high up on their hit parade. I don't think they like me anymore."

"Yeah, but they like little kids," Phillipa said. She seemed to think about that a moment. "But maybe you better wait outside. I'd hate it if I ended up with a stale pastry."

*I*t was almost seven when Sharon finally made it back to her apartment building, a bag of Chinese takeout in her hand. It had been a seven-day week, with no sign of a letup, and all she wanted now was to scarf down her spicy orange chicken and immerse her weary body in a hot bath.

Sharon opened the two locks on her third-floor apartment, never noticing the small scratches left by Emilio's picks. She scanned the room as she entered, just to be sure everything was still there. It had nothing to do with being a cop. Just being a New Yorker provided the necessary paranoia. Satisfied, she went straight to the kitchen and headed for the black-enameled refrigerator for the special bottle of soy sauce she kept there.

Emilio stepped into the doorway behind her and raised his pistol in both hands. Sharon caught his reflection on the refrigerator door, spun to her right, and sent the bag of orange chicken hurling toward his face.

The bag hit him just above the eyes, and his hand jerked to the right, sending his first shot an inch away from Sharon's ear.

There was no time to go for her own weapon. She crouched and rushed forward. Still off balance, Emilio fired again, this time nicking her left shoulder. Sharon came up under his arm, hitting him with all the force she could muster. The blow sent them both hurtling back into the living room, and Emilio's pistol flew from his hand as they hit the floor.

Sharon reached for the automatic tucked into a holster at the small of her back, but Emilio's fist crashed into her jaw, knocking her to one side. Then he was up like a cat and out the front door before she could recover.

By the time she reached the hall outside her apartment she could hear the front door of the building slam shut. Then the pain in her shoulder hit, and she slumped against the wall.

"Sonofabitch," she muttered.

She inspected the jagged rip in her lightweight linen jacket and thought immediately that it was brand-new. It was the first time she had worn it.

"Sonofabitch," she muttered again and headed back inside her apartment. Briefly, she debated whether to put in a 10–13 call—officer in need of assistance—as required by department policy. She wanted every patrol car in the area looking for the man who had shot her, and she knew a 10–13 would bring them all rushing to her door. There wasn't much choice. If she ignored regulations she'd have Internal Affairs climbing all over her. Besides, she wasn't sure she could even give an accurate description of the shooter. It had all happened too fast. She muttered again, picked up the telephone, and punched in 911. Then she spotted Emilio's pistol off in a corner of her living room.

"Maybe I've got you after all, you little prick," she growled.

**D**evlin's cell phone rang as he stood on the sidewalk outside Ferrara's as instructed. It was Red Cunningham, and Devlin paled with the first news and then blew out a long breath when he learned that Sharon's wound was superficial.

Red had been headed home when the 10–13 call had come over his radio. He had recognized the address and immediately doubled back.

"Was it a burglar?" Devlin asked.

"Doesn't look that way, boss. We got the gun he used. Sharon managed to knock it out of his hand." He paused. "It was equipped with a silencer. Looks like a straight-out hit to me. With any luck we'll lift some prints off it."

"Make sure it's bagged and tagged," Devlin snapped. "I want a clear chain of evidence."

"Already done," Red came back.

"Good. I also want a twenty-four-hour watch on her apartment. The hospital too, if she stays there. What hospital is she at?"

Red told him.

"I'll be there in fifteen minutes."

Adrianna and Phillipa came out of Ferrara's with a box of pastries.

"We decided to have dessert at home," Phillipa said. "They gave me one stale one. They said it was for you." She was grinning up at him, then noticed the look on his face and the smile evaporated.

"Sorry, honey. I have to take a pass." He glanced at Adrianna. "Sharon's been hurt." He raised his hands. "She'll be okay, it's not serious, but I've got to get over to Bellevue."

Fear had crept into Adrianna's eyes, and he glanced down and saw the same look in Phillipa's. It was another unwanted part of a cop's life.

He bent down and kissed his daughter. "I'll be home soon," he said. He cupped her chin and raised her face to meet his own. He smiled. "Save me that stale pastry, kiddo." The fear refused to leave Phillipa's eyes.

"It's not really stale, Daddy," she said. "I was only kidding."

**S**haron was in a black mood when Devlin arrived at Bellevue, the hospital of choice for all wounded cops because of its reputation as the city's finest trauma center. Red rolled his eyes, warning him, as he entered a small treatment room off the ER. Sharon was seated on the edge of an examining table and looked as though she might bite anyone who came too close. The sleeve of her blouse had been cut away and her left shoulder was swathed in bandages. Her eyes became even more hostile when she saw Devlin.

"I don't need a twenty-four-hour baby-sitter," she snapped.

Red gave Devlin a sheepish look. "Sorry, boss. I told her about the watch on her apartment."

"And I don't need it," Sharon snapped again.

Devlin ignored her. "How's the shoulder?" he asked.

Sharon glanced at the bandages, almost as if she hadn't noticed them before. "The jacket's hurt worse than I am," she said. "A hundred and sixty bucks. First time I ever wore it. And this blouse. Another eighty. Sonofabitch. When I find the little bastard I'm gonna shoot him and then I'm going through his wallet."

"You give Red a description?" Devlin asked.

"Yeah."

"Give it to me."

Sharon shook her head. "It makes me feel like an idiot, but all I have are impressions rather than a clear picture. It happened so damned fast." Her jaw tightened. "A weasel comes to mind. He was skinny, pinch-faced, dark complexion, dark eyes. I remember the eyes, both of them open, looking over the barrel of that automatic. And when I slammed into him, there wasn't a lot to him. Maybe he went one hundred forty, one hundred fifty pounds. But wiry and strong. The little bastard hit me a good shot in the jaw."

"You keep saying *little*. Was he short?"

"Maybe average height at the most. Probably less. As a guess, I'd say five-seven or five-eight. No more than that."

"What about his hair?"

Again, Sharon shook her head. "Dammit, I'm not sure. My eyes were on the damn automatic, and on his hands—to try and see what he was doing with them after I knocked him down." She gave a faint smile. "What he was doing with them was smacking me in the mouth. Shit, I didn't even know he had dropped his weapon; didn't even get another look at him until he was going out the door." She gritted her teeth in anger. "I was just trying to get my weapon out before he took another shot at me."

"What's your impression?" Devlin asked.

Sharon thought a moment. "Thin. Brushed straight back. Maybe a widow's peak. I do remember he was wearing gloves—skintight leather—so we'll probably get zip for prints."

"Maybe not," Devlin said. "Unless he was a real careful guy and wore them when he was loading the clip. We'll check the clip and the bullets. We might get some partials."

Sharon was still annoyed with herself and struggled to come up with something more. "If I had to pick a nationality or ethnic mix or whatever, I'd say Italian or Hispanic. But that's based on his coloring. I never heard him say anything. He just made his play and did a rabbit when it went sour."

Devlin stepped closer and placed a hand on her good shoulder. "I'm glad it went sour, kid. I hate inspector's funerals. The damned bagpipes always get me." His words got no reaction, and he realized she was still suffering some level of shock, if not physical, at least mental. "What does the hospital say?"

"They say I'm fine. They loaded me up on painkillers and

gave me a prescription for more. I can leave whenever I want."

Devlin nodded. "Red and I will take you home. And there *will* be a guard on your apartment, so don't even think about giving me grief about it. And you're off the chart until that shoulder heals."

"Give me twenty-four hours and I'll be fine."

Devlin shook his head. "Let's take it a day at a time and see how you feel. Tomorrow morning I want you to start talking to Ollie about any old cases that might have produced this. I can't see how it could be the one we're working on now, but we'll take a look at that too. In the meantime, we come up with some decent prints, we'll run this bastard down before he knows what hit him."

## Chapter Eleven

**D**evlin arrived at the cardinal's office at eight the next morning. Father Arpie was waiting for him in the empty reception area, and it seemed obvious the early meeting was intended to avoid other members of the archdiocese staff. Arpie was not a happy man and insisted on revisiting the conditions the cardinal had supposedly laid down.

He handed Devlin a sheet of paper. It was plain unmarked stationery with four names listed alphabetically—first and last names only, with no "Father" or "Reverend" in front of them, no visible connection to either the Catholic priesthood or the Archdiocese of New York.

"This, as they say, is for your eyes only," Arpie said. "No exceptions. I have not included the names of the dead priests. It seemed unnecessary." His voice and eyes were like ice.

Devlin was reminded of a priest from his youth, one he and his peers had avoided at Saturday confessions. The man's voice had been severe enough to conjure up the eternal flames of hell.

Arpie's eyes bored into him. "If I am ever asked about this list, I will deny any knowledge of it."

Devlin was so surprised by the words he couldn't avoid smiling. "That would be a lie, wouldn't it, Father?"

Arpie continued to glare at him. "Count on it," he snapped.

**I**t was raining heavily when Devlin left the chancery office. Men selling cheap umbrellas already occupied every corner and Devlin wondered, as he often had, where these men came from. Even unexpected showers brought them out. They seemed to materialize as soon as a drop of rain hit the pavement, each one ready with boxes of umbrellas. An old partner had once suggested they lived in a rabbit warren of tunnels beneath the sidewalks, where they lay in wait for the first clap of thunder.

Devlin was due to meet Ollie Pitts at Sharon's apartment, but first he took a cab north to Columbus Circle for a pre-arranged meeting with Father William Martin.

Seated in his cluttered office in Fordham's faculty building, Martin threw back his head and laughed when told of Arpie's warning.

"Ah, the archdiocese," he said. "I'm afraid it's staffed with bureaucrats and bankers, and somehow they've lost all sense of their priesthood somewhere along the way. Perhaps they should all have gone to law school instead." He shrugged. "It's the price of power, I'm afraid. Thank God I've been spared that temptation, at least."

"But how the hell do I deal with them? One bark from Arpie and the mayor jumps out of his shorts. All he can think about is the two and a half million Catholics who show up at mass every Sunday. There are a lot of voters in that number."

Again, Martin shrugged. "I'm not sure how many of those Catholics show up, let alone pay the slightest attention to archdiocesan pronouncements. You want my best advice? Ignore them. At least, ignore Arpie. I doubt this directive came from the cardinal. I've met his eminence. He's a so-phisticated man, sophisticated enough to know that unpleas-ant things occasionally hit the fan." He grinned. "Besides, you can lie as easily as Arpie can. You can say he never told you not to show the list to anyone else." He held up a cau-tioning finger. "Of course, as a priest, I'm not telling you to lie." He laughed again, then ran his fingers through his gray hair. "God, Paul, it's all insanity, isn't it? Just save the poor devils on that infernal list and to hell with the bureaucratic madness."

Devlin smiled at the idea of matching Arpie lie for lie. He pushed it away. "There are four priests on Arpie's list. That makes a total of seven with reported cases of AIDS. It seems like a high number to me."

Martin shook his head. "Not when you think of the large number of priests working in the archdiocese," he said. "Well over seven hundred, I'd guess, and I'd also speculate that they are not men who normally carry condoms around in their pockets." He raised a hand, begging Devlin's patience while he continued. "Now let's assume that we in the church follow the general population, and that ten percent of our number is gay." He paused. "Frankly, I'm sure the percentage is much higher. Even something close to fifty percent would not shock me. So seven gay priests with AIDS is not a surprise. It also shouldn't surprise you to find that you don't have a complete list in your hands. Remember, only the illnesses of diocesan priests are reported to the archdiocese. Those in religious orders would be reported to their specific superiors in that order."

He smiled at the look on Devlin's face. "Yes, those of us in the various orders face the same situation. I, for one, think we should ignore it. Just face the fact that it's part of the human condition and not something that should be shunned, or lied about, or hidden away. But for the present, at least, it is regarded as a central problem for today's church—whether or not its clergy will soon be dominated by gay men." He raised his hands out at his sides and let them fall away. "Of course, what the leaders of the church do not see is that it all stems from the intransigence of our popes, past and present. Like his recent predecessors, our current pope will not even consider the need to make celibacy voluntary. Married priests remain a taboo as far as he's concerned. The same is true with the ordination of women, even though neither ban can be found anywhere in the teachings of Christ." He shook his head. "Most of the first priests of the church, the apostles, were married men. Peter, our first pope, was married. And Christ's own veneration of his mother displayed no prejudice against women." He laughed again. "Fat old men in Rome came up with those ideas."

"So why so many gay priests today?" Devlin asked.

"Two reasons, really. First, it is very, very hard today to

convince young heterosexual men to go into the priesthood. It's a hard life, made even harder when one has to forgo the joys and pleasures of married life. No children of one's own, no companionship, and, unless illicitly taken, no relief from the sexual inclinations the good Lord built into all of us. Second, gay men—especially gay Catholic men—have been taught all their lives that responding to the sexual natures with which they were born is a grievous, grievous sin that they must avoid. Not an easy task, to say the least. It's like telling a child with two strong legs that he must never run." Martin raised a lecturing finger. "But for those poor souls there is hope—at least there appears to be. *Voilà!* They can overcome their natural instincts. They can enter the priesthood, where they will live lives of celibacy. And there it is, a solution to their problem: a life where sex is not even an option. Except it is, of course, as every priest learns. It's all around them, just as it is for every lay man and woman. And priests, unfortunately, lack even the blessing of a wife to ease those temptations. Meanwhile, we're called upon to do the same things that lead lay people into that temptation. We work with people who from time to time we find attractive. We attend cocktail parties and social gatherings. We even find ourselves being flirted with on occasion. Plus we must also sit down each week and hear confession—and that almost always includes a certain number of young men and women who are sexually active." He smiled broadly. "And we're told not to think about those things as part of our own lives." He leaned forward. "Fat chance, my friend. Fat chance."

"So you think about it, yourself," Devlin said.

"Never," Martin snapped. He tilted his head to one side and smiled. "Only every time a young coed sashays down the hall in a pair of too-tight jeans."

"So what do you do?"

Martin grinned at him. "I pray a lot, rather than surrender to my baser nature." He sighed. "However, I'm told by my noncelibate friends that the results are not quite the same."

*T*he rain had stopped when Devlin reached Sharon's apartment at ten o'clock, and the sun streamed down on the wet sidewalks, driving all the umbrella salesmen back to their rabbit warrens.

A patrol car was parked in front of Sharon's building, and the two uniforms inside jumped out and stopped Devlin when he headed for the front door. It was a good protective response, although he doubted Sharon would share that view. When she opened the door to her apartment, she looked even angrier than he expected. Across the room Devlin could see Ollie Pitts grinning at him, and he wondered if Ollie's special charm had added fuel to the humiliating presence of the patrol car. It would be safer to ignore the entire subject.

"So what have we come up with?" he asked, as he took a seat next to Pitts.

"*Bubkes,*" Sharon snarled. "There's nothing there, dammit. Nothing in any of my past cases that would warrant a professional hit. Hell, I can't even think of anybody who could *afford* a professional hit." She paused to stare at Devlin. "And this was a pro, Paul. It went sour on him, but he was good. He got in here. He waited for me. He came up behind me without a sound. If it hadn't been for his reflection on the door of the refrigerator, he would've had me cold." She shook her head. "Christ, if I hadn't had a bag of Chinese food in my hands, he would have had me anyway."

"Then it has to be this case."

Sharon stared at him in disbelief. "You think someone from Opus Christi hired a hit man?"

Devlin made a helpless gesture with his hands. "It's like Sherlock said: When you eliminate everything else . . ."

"I think the boss is right," Ollie added. "Don't forget there's a drug dealer involved in this somewhere."

Sharon glared at him. "And I'm not even close to finding out who that is."

"You must be close to something," Devlin said. "Someone's scared enough to try to kill a cop."

Sharon shook her head. She was dressed in jeans and a baggy T-shirt. She walked to an overstuffed chair, dropped into it, and tucked her bare feet beneath her legs, yoga style. "I've gone over every interview in my mind. I've gone over every one of them again with Ollie." She looked across at the hulking detective. "Has anything I said suggested any threat to you . . . to anyone?"

Ollie turned to Devlin. "It's like she said. *Bubkes*."

"I've been stonewalled at every turn," Sharon added. "It's like this nun I've been trying to see. Nobody comes out and says I can't talk to her. They just smile and say they're sorry and keep insisting they're not sure where she is." She threw up her hands in exasperation. "Like nuns just wander off and disappear all the time," she added.

Sharon's telephone interrupted them. It was Stan Samuels calling for Devlin. She and Ollie listened to Devlin's end of the conversation as a hint of excitement seemed to creep into his voice. He had taken out his notebook and was jotting down information.

"Okay, Stan, great work. Now, I need you to contact the head of our intelligence unit. See if anybody knows this guy. If not, ask him if he can put us in touch with somebody at the Colombian embassy who might. Just lay it out for him. Tell him it involves an attempt on a cop's life. That should get everybody up off their asses. I'll be back in about an hour. See what you can set up for me by then."

When he replaced the receiver, there was a small smile playing at the corners of Devlin's mouth. "Stan got a hit on the prints we lifted from the automatic. Nothing here in the U.S., but Interpol had him as a drug-smuggling suspect five years ago in Spain. He walked, but not before they printed and photographed him."

He glanced at his notebook. "His name is Emilio Valdez. He's a Colombian national, thirty-four years old, five feet, eight inches, slender build, one hundred forty-five pounds, black hair, brown eyes." He grinned at Sharon. "Looks like your description was right on the money . . . for a cop who didn't see anything."

Sharon ignored the compliment. "We got pictures?"

"We've got one. Interpol faxed it to us. The only problem is the guy had a full beard five years ago. Stan says he looks like Fidel. But it's a starting point. We'll find out who he's connected to here in the States. Then we'll run his skinny butt into the ground."

"You want me to work it?" Ollie asked.

Sharon's eyes snapped to him. "It's mine."

"It's Stan's," Devlin countered. He held up a hand as Sharon wheeled on him. "You'll be there when we bust him, I promise. But as soon as you're up to it, I want you back on the Opus Christi case. You're doing something there that drew somebody out, so I don't want to let up now."

He turned to Ollie. "You and I are going to work on these murdered priests. The archdiocese finally coughed up the name of every one of their priests who's been diagnosed with AIDS. We're going to play out our hunch that somebody's after them and is working from an alphabetized list." Devlin took out the typewritten sheet Father Arpie had given him. "If we're right, our next target's name is James Janis. He's a curate at the Church of Our Savior at Park and Thirty-eighth."

"He know we're gonna be on him?" Ollie asked.

Devlin glanced at his watch. "He will in about half an hour. You and I are going to stop and see him on our way back to the office."

"What about me?" Sharon demanded.

"You get a day sitting on your butt." He raised a hand, stopping her objection. "We'll see how you feel tomorrow. We get anything on the shooter before then, I promise we'll get you there before we take him down."

*F*ather James Janis had the saddest eyes Devlin had ever seen on a young man.

"I want you to know that the information about your illness will be kept in strict confidence," Devlin said, as he finished explaining why they believed the priest, along with others, was in danger of being murdered.

They were seated in a large office in the church rectory. The room held all the opulence one would expect on Park Avenue: Oriental carpets scattered across a highly polished oak floor, hand-carved tables and chairs that were clearly antiques, heavy brocaded draperies pulled back to reveal floor-to-ceiling windows. It reminded Devlin of photographs he had seen depicting the homes of robber barons of the past century.

Father Janis didn't seem to fit his surroundings. He was a slender man in his early thirties, with unruly brown hair that grew in several directions at once. His hands were clasped tightly in his lap, cornflower-blue eyes staring at them as Devlin spoke. He looked like a farm boy who had just wandered in from Iowa, still uncertain of his surroundings.

"It doesn't really matter, does it?" he said, his voice barely audible. He looked up. "I mean, if you catch this man, it will all come out eventually." He gave Devlin a weak smile. "I mean, the reasons for his doing it."

"That's possible," Devlin said. "I won't lie to you. Once we make an arrest, it's out of our hands. But the archdiocese carries a lot of weight in this city. And they've made it very clear—to me, at least—that they want everything kept in strict confidence."

The priest gave out a small unhappy laugh. "Oh, yes. I'm sure they do. No fags in the priesthood. And certainly none who are sexually active." He let out a long sigh. "And they're right, of course. I vowed to put that all aside. I just couldn't live up to my good intentions." The weak smile returned. "In Rome they would call that an *infamia.*"

"I think they said the same thing in *The Godfather,*" Ollie interjected. "The hoods, I mean."

The priest smiled more sincerely. "There's a lesson there, I think. But I won't comment on it."

Devlin leaned forward in his chair. "Have you had any counseling, either individually or in a group?"

Father Janis shook his head. "I was diagnosed six months ago. I had all the symptoms for a long time—almost two years—but I chose to ignore them. I think, at first, I just didn't want to acknowledge it. Then, subconsciously at least—when I really knew in my own mind—I looked at it as a punishment for my sins." He looked at his hands again, as if unable to meet anyone's eyes. "You see, I never should have become a priest. I was sexually active in the seminary, and I knew—oh, yes, deep down I knew—I would continue. But I lied to myself. I kept telling myself that I would stop once I was ordained—that I was only having a last fling before I gave it all up." He shook his head. "But it doesn't work that way, does it?"

Devlin was hearing more confession than he wanted. He needed to get the priest back on point. "Father, what we have to do here is keep you under close surveillance. And we need to do it as unobtrusively as possible."

The priest looked up. He seemed clearly shocked by what he was hearing. Devlin had decided to treat it as a fait accompli, giving the priest no room to refuse their offer. He nodded toward Ollie. "Detective Pitts will be running the operation. He'll be with you, or as close as possible, from the time you get up in the morning until you go to bed at night. There will also be a surveillance team on the rectory at night. Hopefully we'll have one man inside and two watching the exterior of the building. So far, at least in the deaths of the other three priests, we haven't had any attacks during the night. But we don't want to take any chances. The most important thing is that you tell Detective Pitts every move you're going to make before you make it. If you're going to visit someone, you tell him. If you're going to say mass, you tell him. Anything at all. That will allow him to position himself so he can watch you without being seen. He'll have backup men close by that he can call in if he needs them. They also won't be easy to spot, but they'll be there."

Father Janis glanced at Ollie. The detective was dressed in his usually baggy suit, sturdy black brogans, and wrinkled shirt and tie. He looked like a slob, a very large, imposing one. "I think Detective Pitts may stand out. Certainly here in the rectory and the church proper."

Devlin nodded. "I was going to ask if you had any . . . priestly attire . . . he could wear. A large cassock, or something like that."

Ollie threw Devlin a look. "What?"

Devlin raised a hand, shutting him off, as he awaited the priest's reply.

"A cassock, yes. I think we could do that. Then he'd look like another priest moving about."

"Wait a minute, boss. I dunno."

"You have a better idea, Ollie?" There was a sharp warning in Devlin's words.

"How about a janitor? Somethin' like that," Ollie offered. "I mean, a cassock is like a dress, right? I mean how am I gonna get to my piece if I need it?"

"Actually our janitor is a rather large man. And he keeps extra clothes in the basement," Father Janis said.

"All right," Devlin said. "But use a cassock too, if you need to. I don't want you easily spotted."

Devlin began to rise from his chair. The priest's words stopped him.

"Inspector, can you tell me . . . these other priests, the ones who were murdered . . . were they also infected?"

Devlin paused, thinking about Father Arpie. He dismissed the man and his warnings. "Yes, Father, they were. It seems to be the common thread."

Father Janis nodded. "Retribution for our sins." His voice had become almost a whisper again. "It's odd, isn't it?"

"What is, Father?" Devlin asked.

"That they should want to punish us by ending our lives a little earlier." His weak, sad smile had returned. "If they knew anything about the final stages of this illness, they'd realize they weren't punishing us at all. They'd realize they were actually being merciful."

Xavier de la Mayo was listed as a military attaché to the Colombian Mission to the United Nations. He was actually a colonel in his country's newly formed antidrug force and had been assigned to the UN to plan and coordinate joint operations with the U.S. Drug Enforcement Agency and the Federal Bureau of Investigation.

The NYPD Intelligence Unit recommended the colonel as a top authority on Colombian drug traffic, and to Devlin's surprise de la Mayo offered to come to the squad's office for their first meeting.

The colonel was dressed in a business suit when he arrived, and like most career military men he seemed slightly uncomfortable in civilian clothes. He was a short square man with dark hair, graying at the temples, and dark brown eyes that seemed to look right through you. *Severe* was the only word you could use to describe the man. Devlin felt immediately that life as a private under the colonel's command would be one long road to hell.

"What do you know about Colombia?" the colonel asked, when Devlin had outlined the problem. He seemed to snap the words out as a challenge.

"Not a great deal," Devlin conceded. "What I do know comes from the job, and that's pretty much been limited to the major drug cartels."

De la Mayo gave Devlin a knowing smile. "Few people in the north know very much about my country," he said. "First, the major cartels no longer exist. Get that straight in your mind from the outset. The Medellín and Cali cartels have been destroyed. It is to the credit of our new president, Andrés Pastrana, who, before he became president, was himself kidnapped by these madmen."

He gave Devlin a broad shrug, as if what he had said meant nothing. "What we have now is worse. Now there are dozens of smaller cartels, each one run by men who are even more violent than their predecessors." He leaned forward in his chair. "What you are dealing with here, my friend, is the most vicious group of criminals the world has ever seen." He waved a hand in front of his broad body. "Nothing is beyond them. No atrocity is too great. Providing it gives them what they want."

Devlin sat back in his chair and studied the man. De la Mayo's words seemed flamboyant, perhaps even overly dramatic. Devlin chalked it up to Spanish machismo and a need to have his own work appreciated. Still, he had to get back to their subject.

"I understand the problems you face, and I don't envy you those difficulties," he said. "It's a formidable task." De la Mayo nodded his approval and Devlin pushed ahead. "But regrettably my focus is a bit narrower. I believe this man, Emilio Valdez, attempted to murder one of my detectives. Right now all I have is a name and an old photograph, so anything you can tell me about him will help. Especially any connections he might have to people here in the States."

De la Mayo shrugged away the question, as if the answer were obvious. "Valdez is a killer. It is what he does. It is all that he does." He nodded his head for emphasis. "In the past he has worked for several of the smaller cartels. Presently, we believe, he is part of a group that operates out of Bucaramanga, which is a city northeast of Medellín. This particular group is run by Ernesto Chavarría, a man who would order the death of his own mother if it would put more pesos in his pockets." De la Mayo brought a hand up and shook his finger for emphasis. "These are not sophisticated men. These are men whose thoughts are governed by only two questions: What can I get? and What do I have to do to get it? If money is involved, they will do anything. For them, life is not a complicated matter." The colonel paused, as if deciding how much more he should say. "I believe this would be the first time Valdez has been in your country, although he speaks your language fluently." He raised a lecturing finger again. "But be assured of one thing, my friend. If this man you are searching for is indeed Valdez, he is here for only one purpose. He is here to kill."

"Is Chavarría here?"

The colonel shook his head. "To my knowledge he has never come north. He is unsophisticated but not stupid. He knows he cannot buy his way out of the legal system here or intimidate its judges and prosecutors with death threats. Your country is too large and complex, so regrettably he remains where he is safe." He tapped his chest. "In my country."

"How about his connections here? Someone who might be giving Valdez his orders?"

"Yes, Chavarría has these connections. Together with the FBI, we are presently investigating a particular bank that we believe is laundering money for him."

"Can you tell me which bank?"

De la Mayo shook his head. "It is not for me to do so. Perhaps you can learn this from your Federal Bureau of Investigation."

Fat chance, Devlin thought. But he would try anyway. "What about contacts outside that bank? Is there anyone else Valdez might go to for instructions?"

De la Mayo flashed a smile that seemed to soften his otherwise severe demeanor. "That I can tell you. There is a man named Ricardo Estaves, who was once suspected of having ties to the Cali group. He is supposedly a coffee importer who maintains an office here. We have never been able to prove his connection to narcotics, but on several occasions in the past he was seen with members of the old Cali cartel. On his last visit to Colombia he also was observed entering Chavarría's home in Bucaramanga. Since there is no longer any coffee grown in that region, we can only assume he was there on drug business and is now connected with that group."

"What specifically does he do for them here in the States?" Devlin asked.

"We suspect he is a contact for distributors and also plays a role in the cartel's need to launder money."

"Is he under surveillance—a wiretap—anything?"

De la Mayo gave him a pained look. "We have tried. Both legally and illegally. But he knows the game. His office and his apartment here are swept for listening devices at least twice each week, and when he wants to meet with someone he simply goes to a large hotel, rents a room, and has his meeting. He is in and out before we can mount an adequate surveillance."

"So this Estaves might be our boy's contact."

"It would be my best guess," De la Mayo said. "But I doubt he would ever meet with him in person. Estaves is regularly seen using pay phones. Never the same one, of course. But we suspect his arrangements for meetings and all other contacts are made in this way."

Devlin shook his head. "It doesn't sound promising." He paused to think it through. "What else can you tell me about Estaves? Any particular habits, places he goes to regularly, anything at all?"

De la Mayo began drumming his fingers together. "He actually leads a rather quiet life." His face broke into another smile. "He is, I'm told, a very devout Catholic. In fact, I myself have followed him to mass on several Sundays. It is odd—no?—that a man could be involved in this filthy trade and still consider himself a religious man."

"No odder than a nun carrying heroin in her body," Devlin said. He paused again. "What do you know about this Opus Christi group?"

"I know they are very powerful in my country. I know that many influential men are members, both within the government and in the business community. I also know that this group is very secretive and very devious. And for these reasons I do not trust them."

"You think they could be involved in drug trafficking?"

Again, De la Mayo smiled. "Señor, I have dealt with drug traffickers for most of my life. Now, as my career nears its end, I find I am very much like the famous fictional detective Hercule Poirot. Now, my little gray cells tell me to suspect everyone."

# Chapter Twelve

*R*icardo Estaves sat in a battered desk chair in the cramped, cluttered office normally used by the building superintendent of the First Avenue co-op in which he lived. Unknown to those who would keep him under surveillance, Estaves paid the superintendent a generous monthly fee to make the office available and to provide access to the "workmen" who occasionally visited by way of the building's service entrance.

Emilio sat before him now, dressed in blue work pants and a matching shirt that had the name *Joe* stitched above its breast pocket. He had come to the short, fat, balding coffee importer to complain about Charles.

"*Patrón,* this man is going to get us killed," he said in Spanish. "Or even worse, sent to some stinking Yankee prison."

Estaves leaned back in his chair and gave Emilio a benign look. Normally he would not meet with the man. He would keep their contacts limited to the telephone. But there had been a hint of panic in Emilio's voice when they had spoken earlier, and he had decided to see the man's eyes so he could tell if he was still capable of carrying out their contract.

"I'm told that Yankee prisons are actually quite satisfactory," he said. "Compared to our own, at least." He waved a plump hand, dismissing his own words. "But I agree. It was unwise to order the death of this woman police officer. It throws too great a light on us, and that is something that should be avoided." Emilio started to speak, but Estaves's raised hand stopped him. "Now that this woman detective has seen you, perhaps that has changed things."

Emilio studied his shoes to keep Estaves from seeing the anger in his eyes. The fat little man had surprising power within their organization. Ernesto Chavarría trusted him, and that made him a man to be feared.

"If it is your wish that she be killed, it will be done, *patrón*."

Estaves toyed with his brightly patterned silk necktie. It was an affectation that gave him comfort. As a child raised in the slums of Bogotá, he had been poor; and now that he had found prosperity, the feel of silk was reassuring. For years he had worn nothing else. His shirts, his ties—the very suit that now adorned his plump body—were all handmade in that soothing fabric.

The superintendent's office lacked air-conditioning, and he ran a handkerchief over his sweaty jowls. "What is your opinion, Emilio? You are the expert in these matters."

Emilio's eyes came up slowly. They were cold and hard and unflinching. "If it was my decision, *patrón*, I would finish these priests we have agreed to put away. Then I would leave the country."

"And this woman detective?" Estaves asked.

"Only if she came close to me would I kill her." He raised his hands, palms up, in front of him. "Her death will only complicate the work you have given me, *patrón*. It will make it harder for me to kill these other priests."

Estaves considered Emilio's words. "Yes, I see that. But Charles fears this woman is getting too close to our other enterprise—our *important* enterprise—the narcotics we are bringing into this country. He fears what this detective might discover if she reaches this second nun who was with the unfortunate Sister Manuela." He paused, his eyes narrowing on Emilio. "The death of that young nun was a serious mistake, my friend."

Emilio's back stiffened. "I assure you, *patrón,* I had nothing to do with that."

The lie flowed smoothly off Emilio's lips, and Estaves found himself admiring the man's ability to make it so. And he understood the need. The cartel had long overlooked the side deals their employees occasionally made—as long as they remained small and did not interfere with the cartel's profits. It was a small perquisite, a bonus for other work well done. And Emilio's side effort—forcing the nun to smuggle a small amount of heroin—had been brilliant. After all, who would suspect that a nun had swallowed condoms filled with narcotics? By itself, even her death had been acceptable. Allowing her to reach a hospital where the police could question her would have put their larger operation in jeopardy. But the combination of factors—the cause and effect—was something that required punishment. And despite his facile lying, Estaves knew that permanent punishment awaited Emilio upon his return to Colombia.

Estaves allowed his hands to rest on his protruding stomach. "Do you have another solution, my friend?" He kept his eyes on Emilio's face, noting a small tic that had come to one eye.

"All the city's police would be after us if we killed this detective," he said. "But only a few would be after us if we killed someone else."

"And who would you kill instead?" Estaves asked.

Emilio gave a small shrug. "I would kill the other nun," he said. "Then this woman detective could discover nothing from her."

An appreciative smile formed on Estaves's lips. "That is very good. Very good indeed. I will speak with Charles and find out where you can find this other nun." He raised a finger. "In the meantime, you will continue with the priests. I want this matter concluded quickly."

Emilio stood, preparing to leave. "As you wish, *patrón*." He paused a moment. "And the woman detective?" he asked.

Estaves gave him a noncommittal shrug. "For now, you can forget her." He leaned closer to Emilio. "That, of course, means you will lose the ten thousand dollars you were to collect for her life." He watched Emilio flush with embarrassment. "Yes, my friend. We always know what our people are doing."

Emilio lowered his eyes momentarily. "I am sorry, *patrón*."

Estaves waved a hand, dismissing him. It would be a shame to lose Emilio, he thought. He was a clever man and good at his work. But then, there were many clever men, and for most of them killing was not a difficult matter.

*I*t was late afternoon when Boom Boom returned from his "day job." He had come back loaded down with miniature technology. Now, in addition to the small automatic in its garter holster, a Palm 7 wireless Palm Pilot and an enhanced cell phone were taped to his leg. He would be able to use the cell phone to send e-mail back to the squad without risking messages on the closely monitored Opus Christi system. He would also be able to sit in the safety of his room and use the Palm 7 to hack into that very system.

Peter was waiting when Boom Boom entered the lobby. He seemed nervous and kept glancing around to see if anyone was watching. "I have to talk to you," he whispered. "Please come into the dayroom with me."

"Okay," Boom Boom whispered back. "But play it cool, my man. If I saw you acting this way on the street, I'd figure somethin' was goin' down."

Boom Boom followed the young numerarier to a large first-floor room at the rear of the building. Sofas and chairs were scattered about. One wall was lined with bookshelves, containing works with religious themes. There was a large television set, equipped with a VCR. There was also a young man stationed nearby to monitor its use. Boom Boom had already learned that very little television fare was deemed "spiritually appropriate."

Peter and Boom Boom took chairs as far away from the young man as possible. To anyone watching from a distance it would, they hoped, look like an impromptu session of spiritual guidance.

"Whassup?' Boom Boom asked.

Peter glanced nervously across the room.

"Stop that," Boom Boom warned. "You look like some kid who just swiped a candy bar. You keep it up, you're gonna make somebody wonder what you're up to."

Peter twisted in his chair. "I can't help it," he whispered.

"Thomas has been after me all day. He keeps asking questions about you. I'm sure he suspects something."

Boom Boom smiled at him. He needed the man to chill out. "Hey, Peter, don't worry about it. Just stick to the story we laid out for you. It's covered. Thomas can check all he wants. The story's gonna hold up." He gave him a wink. "I'm just worried about *you* holdin' up. You gotta stay cool and trust that we know what we're doin' here."

Peter began wringing his fingers. First one hand, then the other. "It's just that Thomas is so intimidating."

"But he's not your boss or anything, right?"

Peter shook his head. "We're actually equals, as far as rank is concerned."

"So tell him to piss off." Boom Boom grinned at him. "Or however you say it so it's not a sin."

Peter shook his head. "I can't. He's older, and I think those higher in the order will listen to him if he raises any doubts about you. Or about me."

Boom Boom leaned in closer. He needed to calm the man before he started jumping out of his chair. "What's his problem?"

Peter glanced toward the young man monitoring the television. The television was off. There was no one else in the room, and the young man was deeply engrossed in a thick book.

"He doesn't like you working on the computer system. He doesn't feel you can be trusted . . . yet."

"Hey, man, that's easy. I won't work on it."

Peter looked confused. "But I thought you had to—"

"Not anymore." He patted one leg. "I brought back some stuff that will let me work from my room. All I need now are the passwords."

Peter seemed relieved; then his brow furrowed again. "He also said he saw you looking at some of the women when they were leaving the building. He said the look was lustful."

Boom Boom grinned at him. "Hey, man, I'm Spanish. Lust is my thing." He raised a hand. "But I'll watch it, man. I promise. If Thomas is around and some lady walks by, I'll make a little sign of the cross, like I'm warding off sinful thoughts." He grinned again. "Thomas won't know what I'm *really* praying for, you dig?"

"Please don't talk like that." Peter's face had flushed.

He thinks about it too, Boom Boom thought. Thank God, he added to himself. He had begun to think the young man was dead from the waist down. "Hey, it's just between you and me," Boom Boom said. "I'm just tryin' to lighten things up here."

Peter absently rubbed his leg, and Boom Boom thought he saw a thin band under the compressed fabric.

"You wearin' that thing again?" he asked. "That mortification belt or whatever you call it?"

Peter nodded. "A repentance belt. I wear it for two hours every day." His eyes held Boom Boom's. "You're supposed to do that too."

"No way, José." Boom Boom leaned in closer. "And I haven't been floggin' my butt, either." He raised his chin, indicating the belt on Peter's leg. "You should stop doin' that, man. That can't be doin' you any good, havin' those little steel spikes cuttin' into your skin like that."

Peter lowered his eyes. "It's good for my immortal soul," he said softly. "Lately, I've been wearing it for four hours each day." He hesitated, then continued. "To atone for what we're doing."

Boom Boom shook his head. He wished the guy would stop thinking like that. If he didn't, sooner or later it would all come crashing down on him, and he'd end up turning them both in. "Hey, my man, we're not doin' nothin' that doesn't have to be done. You get yourself straight on that. You hear me?"

Peter nodded, but Boom Boom could tell his words had just flown past the man. Nothing but guilt was registering, guilt and fear. Boom Boom hoped that fear would keep his mouth shut.

Peter glanced at his watch. "You're supposed to be in the computer room in a few minutes. I scheduled you for five. I thought you still needed time on the machines."

"That's cool. We'll go through the motions."

"I think Thomas will be there to watch you."

Boom Boom shrugged. "That's cool, too, Peter." He ran his fingers over an imaginary keyboard. "He can watch all he wants. He's not gonna see nothin' I don't want him to see." He gave Peter a smile he hoped would calm him. "We're safe here, my man. I promise you. Just trust me on this. There is *nothing* to worry about."

Charles sat in the living room of his Central Park West apartment. He was staring at his statue of the Virgin Mary. He had taken it from his bedroom and placed it on the glass cocktail table, a small votive candle flickering before it. His mind raced with prayers, each coming so fast that the phrases of one began to mix with those of another, until his mind was filled with an incoherent jumble of devotional thought. He forced himself to stop, his eyes still fixed on the statue of the Virgin, his mind trying to absorb the calm, soothing warmth that seemed to emanate from the painted plaster. His hands were balled into fists.

He had created the makeshift shrine as soon as he got home. He had left his office earlier than planned. The telephone call he had received from Ricardo Estaves had been too disturbing. It had forced him away from his office . . . forced him to seek out some sanctuary . . . some solace . . . some peace of mind.

The Virgin had always done that for him. She had always provided the food for meditation that soothed his soul. But not today. When Estaves had telephoned to ask where Sister Margaret could be found, Charles had known his intentions and had refused to tell him. But the matter would not die there. Eventually, if pressed, he would be forced to do as they wished. There would be no other choice. Estaves and that bastard Chavarría could destroy him anytime they chose.

And that policewoman—that filthy homosexual creature. Estaves had said nothing more would be done to her. She would simply escape punishment. His jaw tightened. No, she would not. Not even if he had to punish her himself.

Charles didn't hear the doorbell when it first rang. Only when it was followed by a loud knock did he rise and cross the room. His movements were slow and uncertain, like those of a somnambulist.

Suddenly Ginger stood before him, although he could not remember opening the door. She was smiling, one hand against the doorframe, her large shoulder bag against one hip, which was provocatively cocked.

"Hi, sailor," she said.

Charles didn't respond but merely stepped back to allow her to enter. Ginger walked slowly into the living room, hips swaying, her tight skirt revealing every subtle movement of her slender body.

She stopped next to the coffee table and stared down at the statue of the Virgin and the flickering votive candle. Then she turned and smiled again.

"Charles, this is just too kinky," she said.

Charles moved across the room and picked up the statue and the candle. "I'll put them away," he said.

"Honey, don't do it on my account." There was laughter in Ginger's voice. "If it makes you happy to have them here, it makes me happy."

Charles's eyes hardened. "I said I'll put them away."

Ginger took an involuntary step back. She had seen this mood before, and she didn't like it. But she knew she could control him. And five hundred bucks was five hundred bucks. Whatever you want, creep, she told herself.

She smiled again. "Well, why don't you do that. Just make sure you hurry back. I have some very special ideas about making you happy, and they're getting me really, really hot." She patted her large bag to let him know what he wanted was inside, then placed it on the table and began unbuttoning her blouse. "Don't keep me waiting *tooo* long, honey. You don't want me to cool off now, do you?"

*D*evlin sat in a back pew, his eyes lowered in what he hoped an observer would interpret as prayer or meditation. Actually he was watching Father James Janis as the priest instructed a group of would-be altar boys. They were practicing the Mass for the Dead, something Devlin hoped would not prove prophetic. The bier that would normally hold the coffin had been placed at the foot of the altar. Father Janis was demonstrating how a priest would circle the coffin, first sprinkling it with holy water and then anointing it with incense. Two altar boys would have to follow close behind, assisting with the various implements, without bumping into each other or the priest—or, God forbid, the coffin itself. Janis told the boys a story about a mass in another church in some unnamed city, where a coffin had actually been knocked over by two altar boys. The resulting crash, he explained, had sprung the locks on the casket and sent the body rolling to the floor. Devlin smiled at the story. He doubted its veracity. Priests and nuns, he knew from childhood, were very good at fabricating horrific tales to achieve desired behavior.

Movement on the other side of the church caught Devlin's eye. When he looked he saw Ollie Pitts pushing a broom down a side aisle. Pitts was dressed in a brown work shirt and trousers, his weapon secured in an ankle holster. Ollie's appearance in the church was Devlin's signal to leave. He would go out the front door, then go directly to the rectory, where he would reenter the church through the sacristy behind the altar. When Ollie left the church proper, a third detective would enter the front door and assume Devlin's previous position. The plan was designed to rotate personnel: to keep one person in visual contact with Father Janis at all times and not tip off the fact that surveillance was under way.

Fifteen minutes later, Father Janis finished his rehearsal and entered the sacristy.

"What's on your schedule now?" Devlin asked.

The priest glanced at his watch. "I'll be having my dinner. Then I have a novena at seven-thirty."

"Then you're in for the night?"

"Yes."

Devlin nodded. "We'll have one man inside the rectory and two outside. How's your pastor taking all this? I know it's a bit intrusive."

The priest gave him a weak smile. "He's not pleased. But it's not really you and your men who are displeasing him."

"You, huh?"

Father Janis nodded. "Me, my lifestyle—which of course he was not aware of before—everything that produced the need for all this. He has some very strong ideas about how a priest should behave. And rightly so, I'm afraid."

"Would you like me to talk to him?"

Janis shook his head. "I don't think it would do any good. After all, as I said, he's right. My actions brought this on everyone."

Devlin took the priest's arm and began walking him to the door that led to the rectory. "Not for a minute, Father," he said. "One thing you learn, being a cop, is that people make choices that get them into trouble. Sometimes it's as simple as walking down the wrong street at the wrong time. But they don't *cause* the trouble. The person waiting on that street causes it. Right now we've got someone who's playing God because he disapproves of the way you live your life. He's the one who's causing this, not you."

Janis stopped walking and offered up his weak smile again. "But he's right. I chose my sins."

Devlin shrugged the statement away. "You're in a better position to judge that than I am, Father, but I suspect we all choose our sins. I do know our perpetrator doesn't have the right to play God—or, from my standpoint, to anoint himself judge and jury and executioner. I also know you can't be blamed for our killer's madness any more than I can."

The priest nodded, the smile becoming a bit stronger. "Thank you," he said. "I do appreciate everything you and your men are doing."

"It's what we're supposed to do, Father," Devlin said. "We're supposed to keep the bastards from winning."

# Chapter Thirteen

*T*he church was dark except for the light that came from the altar, and it cast only a faint glow out into the pews where the parishioners knelt. There weren't many, and again it was mostly older women. Emilio liked that. It gave him a sense of security.

He watched the priest move about the altar, preparing to offer his final benediction. The thought brought a faint smile to his lips. It was amusing, this final benediction. It would be final in more ways than the priest understood.

Emilio was seated near the front of the church, close to a side door that led into a small garden that sat between the rectory and the church proper. When the service ended, and the priest and altar boys went into the sacristy to disrobe, he would enter the garden and wait. He had watched once before, and he knew it was the route the priest would take when he left the church. It was a good place, a quiet place.

Emilio sat back in the pew and immediately took comfort from the pressure at the small of his back. A 32-caliber Beretta was tucked into the rear of his waistband, replacing the one he had left behind in the woman detective's apartment. He touched his side pocket, assuring himself that the three-inch-long suppressor was there. Once it was fitted to the Beretta, the sound of each shot would be no louder than a small book falling against a table. This would be his weapon of choice from now on. There would be no more special instructions from Charles, no more variations that made the job harder. There were only a few priests left, and he intended to put them away as quickly and quietly and safely as he could. Then he would leave the country.

He had not yet decided if he would return to Colombia or, if he did, if he would continue to work for the Chavarría cartel. He had not liked the look in Estaves's eyes. The man had stared at him as though he were already in his grave. But he could stop that from happening. There were others he could work for whose own power would forestall any punishment Chavarría might have planned. His failings had not been so great that Chavarría would risk warfare with a rival group.

A stirring in the congregation brought him back from his reverie, and when he looked toward the altar he saw the priest and the altar boys moving toward the door that led to the sacristy. He slipped from his pew and quietly walked to the side door, glancing back once, then again, to be sure no one was watching him.

Outside, the air was sultry, trapped as it was between the church and the three-story rectory. There was also a smell of roses. He followed the scent to a large bush, momentarily thought about using it for concealment, and then noticed a small stone bench slightly to its left. It was situated in a dark corner, perfect for his purposes. He could sit and wait. It would all be so easy.

He had barely seated himself, the thought of how simple it would be still in his mind, when the door of the rectory opened and another priest started down the path to the church. This one was older than the one he had targeted. He had a full head of gray hair and a slight stoop to his walk.

Emilio muttered an oath under his breath as various scenarios rushed through his mind. He could kill this old priest, pull his body off the path, and wait for the other. Or he could let the priest pass, hope he did not notice someone resting in his garden, and then hope again that he would not return with the priest he was waiting to kill.

Emilio rejected the first two ideas. He had no interest in killing anyone he had not been paid to kill. It was a waste of effort, and it also brought additional danger. Every killing, he knew too well, offered the possibility that clues to his identity would be left behind. The fewer the killings, the fewer chances that would happen.

But allowing the priest to enter the church also presented dangers. The church would be his route of escape when he left the garden, and having this priest inside raised the possibility of a confrontation. If that happened, and if any old women were left inside, it would be even more dangerous. Then, if the old priest confronted him about his presence in the garden, he would have to kill everyone present.

As the priest tottered toward him, Emilio made up his mind. He eased back into the darkness of the rosebush and allowed the priest to move past. Then he came up quickly behind him. A solitary blow from the butt of his pistol dropped the old priest like a stone.

Just as quickly Emilio returned to the shadow of the rosebush. Now the old priest was not only out of the way but provided a service as well. Now he was a decoy. With any luck he would distract the targeted priest and make Emilio's job that much easier.

Five minutes later the priest he was waiting for left the church through the side door and started across the garden. Halfway down the path he came to an abrupt halt, uttered a quick, "Oh, my God,"and rushed to the fallen body.

Emilio stepped from behind the bush and moved forward, the noise of his steps hidden by the sound of the priest's voice as he tried to rouse his fallen comrade.

Emilio stopped behind him and raised the pistol until the end of the suppressor was only inches from the priest's head. Then something happened that he had not anticipated. Somehow the priest sensed his movement and spun around, one hand striking the side of the pistol. The silenced shot made hardly a sound, but the bullet went harmlessly past the priest's shoulder and plowed into the garden.

The priest was on him immediately, his eyes filled with rage.

"What did you do to him?" he hissed. "What did you do?"

The priest's hand had clamped onto Emilio's wrist, and twisted the automatic away. It was a fierce grip, stronger than Emilio ever would have expected. Desperately, he brought his knee up into the priest's groin, but the man only grunted and held fast to his wrist.

Emilio drove the crown of his head forward, striking the man squarely in the face: once, twice, then a third time. Finally the grip loosened, but almost instinctively the priest's hand shot out, his fist connecting with the side of Emilio's jaw.

The next thing Emilio knew, he was on his back, staring up at the man. The pistol was still in his hand, and he raised it and fired two quick shots. Each struck the priest in the chest, and he staggered back and finally dropped to his knees.

Emilio was up immediately. He raised the pistol until it was again only inches from the priest's forehead.

Blood and bone and tissue flew from the back of the priest's head. His entire body jerked and then he slumped forward like a rag doll, all muscle control gone as every nerve in his shattered brain shut down.

Emilio didn't wait. He bent and fired an insurance round into the back of the priest's neck. A chill went through his body, and his arms and legs began to tremble. He was unable to move for several moments. Finally, he turned and walked haltingly back toward the church. The man had almost had him—*this* man, this *maricón*. The realization frightened and then disgusted him, and it sent another involuntary shiver through his body. He glanced back, almost fearfully, almost as though he expected the dead priest to rise and come at him again. The man was still lying there, put away for good. Normally Emilio would take pleasure in that—pleasure in another job done well. This time he was just grateful to have escaped. This time he had no reason to admire his work, no reason at all.

# Chapter Fourteen

**D**evlin did not admire the assassin's work. The other hits had been clean and neat with no witnesses left behind. This one had been sloppy from start to finish. The crime scene showed the dead priest had fought, which raised the possibility that forensic evidence had been left behind. All of which was good. It was what every detective wanted from a murder scene. But it wasn't enough to improve Devlin's black mood. There was one damned problem. The victim had been the wrong priest.

Father Arpie's words came back to him. *You're assuming that every parish in the archdiocese follows our instructions and reports serious illnesses.* Devlin stood in the small garden looking down at the body. His theory about alphabetized murders still fit. Father William Halloran's name was correctly situated in the alphabet. It just didn't appear on the list Arpie had given him. Devlin shook his head in frustration. Father Halloran's decision not to report his illness to the archdiocese, or his delay in doing so, had been as good as signing his own death warrant.

And that was the problem, the immediate question he now had to answer. How many more names between the letter *H,* for Halloran, and the letter *J,* for Janis, were on the killer's list and not on Arpie's? That, and where the hell were the names coming from? His interview with the older priest—the one the killer had knocked unconscious (and the pastor of the church, as it turned out)—confirmed that Halloran had indeed contracted the AIDS virus. It also confirmed that like the other murdered priests he had not been involved in any therapy or counseling. He had been diagnosed by his personal physician three months earlier and began treatment under his care. Nothing more, no other contacts. It was another dead end.

Devlin had already determined that there had been no common doctor for the four slain priests and no common insurance carrier. Nor had their prescriptions been filled by the same pharmacy. Even the laboratories that had done the individual blood work were different. Efforts to find out if the information was coming through a central insurance information center were meeting resistance and would probably require a subpoena. So far the only common factor had been the archdiocese, and Father William Halloran's murder had just blown that all to hell.

This last murder had taken place in the Flushing section of Queens, as he and Ollie Pitts had meticulously guarded Father James Janis in Manhattan. Devlin didn't even want to think about how foolish he looked. While he and Ollie played cat and mouse, Queens precinct detectives had caught the latest case and had initiated the preliminary investigation. As he had with the other murders, Devlin had arrived at the scene and immediately reassigned those detectives to work with his unit until the murders were solved. Soon their precinct commander would complain to his superiors at One Police Plaza, who would promptly pass his objections on to the mayor's office. Complaints were fast becoming a chorus. Devlin had now treaded on the turf of four precinct commanders in three of the city's boroughs, and—with a little urging from the brass at the Puzzle Palace—they all had bitched about their diminished personnel. It was something Devlin lived with on each case. The "mayor's squad," as the unit was derisively known, was not a favorite with the NYPD brass. Devlin's ability to supersede senior commanders under a mayoral directive—including those who outranked him—challenged the department's closely guarded power structure. Lower-ranking commanders, especially those who wished to curry favor with the top brass, were quick to add their voices to a long list of complaints.

Soon, if the investigation didn't take a dramatic turn, the press would join in, eagerly fed by the senior commanders Devlin had bypassed.

The press had already gathered when Devlin left the church. There were at least thirty reporters and photographers milling behind a police barricade, print and radio jockeying for position with four TV crews in what had commonly become known as "the swarm." He debated passing them by with his usual *No comment* but decided it might not be wise. Not this time.

When he turned toward them, cameras immediately zeroed in and the questions began to fly. He always marveled at the way the press responded to any offer of information. It was an immediate feeding frenzy, each of them fearful that some morsel might escape their eager jaws. He held up a hand and waited. It was a way to force a temporary silence—make them fear they might get nothing at all.

Devlin started with the basics, the dead priest's name and age; the fact that he was a curate at this church for the past six years, where the body had been found, and the apparent cause of death—numerous bullet wounds from shots fired at close range.

Again the questions flew at him, and he waited patiently for the one he wanted.

"Is there any connection between the murder of Father Halloran and the other priests' deaths?"

Devlin turned to the questioner, ready to offer the bit of information that might keep them at bay for at least a day or two.

"We're looking into that, of course," he began. "But our preliminary investigation has come up with a number of discrepancies that make that possibility questionable."

Again the hungry voices sang out their demands for more.

Devlin raised a hand. "First, this murder involved the use of a pistol. In the other deaths, weapons were used that allowed the killer or killers to commit the crime more quietly and to escape without creating any unwanted attention. Second, Father Halloran was killed when he stumbled onto another crime in progress. The killer had just attacked another priest, the pastor of this church, Father Vincent Clabby. The killer had knocked Father Clabby unconscious in an apparent robbery attempt."

"Did Father Clabby see the killer?" a voice shouted.

Devlin held up his hand again, stopping another barrage.

"Father Clabby was struck from behind. Father Halloran apparently came on the scene and rushed to his defense. We know he struggled with the killer and was shot and killed. The killer then apparently panicked and fled. Except for a very bad lump on his head, Father Clabby is unhurt."

"Did the killer take anything—money, whatever?"

Devlin shook his head. "Nothing that we can determine at this time. We believe the killer fled immediately. Father Halloran had given him all the trouble he could handle." He waved off another barrage. "There's just one more thing I can tell you. The evidence clearly shows that Father Halloran saved his pastor from more serious harm. He may have even saved his life. He was a hero. He gave his own life in defense of another priest."

There it was. The easy headline, the tear-jerking story they would all chase—at least for a day, maybe two if he was lucky.

More questions erupted from the swarm—gluttons not yet sated and still wanting.

"That's really all I can give you now. Until the forensic and medical work is finished, we won't have anything else. Thank you."

With that Devlin turned and fled, followed by more uselessly shouted questions. It was the best he could do: buy some time and hope for a break before the vultures gathered again.

*H*owie Silver looked like one of those vultures when Devlin entered the office the mayor kept at Gracie Mansion, his official residence in Carl Schurz Park on Manhattan's Upper East Side. Dressed in a silk bathrobe and leather slippers, he paced back and forth behind an antique desk. He needed to shave and run a comb through his hair. His eyes were shadowed and sunken from lack of sleep. In short, he looked very tired and very unhappy.

"I heard a radio report, quoting you," he snapped. "It said this killing may not be connected to the others."

Devlin, seated in an oversized club chair, shook his head. "Don't believe everything you hear."

The mayor stopped pacing and stared down at him. "It's bullshit?" he demanded.

Devlin shrugged. "It could be exactly what I said it was. But I'd bet the pension it's the same killer." He paused to give the mayor time to absorb that. "The dead priest was infected with the virus, like all the others. He just wasn't on the list we got from the archdiocese."

"Why the hell not?" Silver was staring at him as though he had personally done something to keep Halloran's name off the list.

Devlin kept his voice calm. "The list the archdiocese gave us was based on information reported from the various parishes. They're supposed to report serious illnesses so the archdiocese can plan for possible replacements, or whatever other needs an illness creates." He waved a hand, taking in other things that went unspoken. "Father Halloran's illness wasn't reported, so he never made the archdiocese's list. We believe the murders are being committed in alphabetical order. We thought the killer was using the same list the archdiocese gave us. Obviously, that's not the case. We were watching the priest who was next on the archdiocese's list. And while we were doing that, Father Halloran got iced."

The mayor ground his teeth. "But this Halloran fit the pattern? Alphabetically, I mean?"

Devlin nodded. The mayor already knew the names of the dead priests. He just needed reassurance. "Donovan, Falco, and Hall were the first three names on the archdiocese list. They were also the first three hits. Father James Janis was next on that list, and he's the one we had under protective surveillance. Unfortunately, the killer has his own list, and it seems to be more complete than the one we were given." He watched the mayor place his hands over his eyes and shake his head. "There's more bad news, Howie, and you might as well hear it. Right now, we don't know if there's somebody else who fits in before Father Janis."

"Jesus Christ." Again the mayor shook his head. "So now you just sit and wait, and you hope this Father What's-his-name is really the next one on the killer's list. Is that it?"

Devlin inclined his head to one side. "Unless the archdiocese does something I asked them to do about an hour ago."

"And what's that?"

"I asked Father Arpie—that's the cardinal's secretary—to contact every parish, explain the situation, and ask if they have any priests who've been diagnosed with AIDS."

"What did he say?"

"He said he'd ask the cardinal."

"Shit."

"My feelings exactly," Devlin said. "If you could urge the cardinal to agree, it would help."

The mayor looked stricken by the thought. He immediately changed the subject. "What about this dead nun and the guy who shot one of your detectives?"

Devlin leaned forward in his chair and rested his forearms on his knees. "We've identified the shooter in Sergeant Levy's apartment. His name is Emilio Valdez. He's a Colombian hit man who works for one of the smaller drug cartels. We're reasonably sure he's the same person who forced Sister Manuela to carry drugs into the country and then killed her. But we need to reach the other nun—the one Sister Manuela was traveling with—to get a more positive ID. So far Opus Christi has refused to tell us how to reach her." Devlin paused. "I could really use a court order to force the issue."

The mayor shook his head emphatically. "We're not hauling any church group before a judge. Period. You must be working on it in some other way."

"I am," Devlin said, "but it's slow going."

"Do I want to know what you're doing?" the mayor asked.

"No, you don't," Devlin said. "And even if you do, I won't tell you. I've got a cop hanging out on a limb on this."

The mayor raised both hands. "That's fine. I don't want to know. Just get it done. Christ, solve *something!* Those bastards at One Police Plaza are beating the war drums. They want me to cut you off at the knees. It's only a matter of time before they start spreading that idea to the press so they can put me in a box on this."

Devlin leaned back in his chair. "And what happens when they do?' he asked.

"You don't want to know, and I won't tell you even if you do,"  the mayor said, mimicking him, "*I'm* hanging out on a limb on this one."

Charles looked out of place in the basement office. He was dressed in a pale-gray summer-weight suit, a crisply starched shirt, and a regimental tie. Estaves sat across from him, behind the building superintendent's desk. He was wearing a flamboyant silk shirt opened halfway down his fleshy chest.

"I dislike meeting here," Charles said. "I've told you that before." His face twisted in displeasure, very much the business executive forced to go somewhere not befitting his station.

Estaves gave him a patient smile. He didn't care what Charles liked or disliked. He didn't care anything about the man, other than his value as an asset. And that was a temporary circumstance. Only for the present, he told himself.

"The police watch me closely," Estaves said with a shrug. "It's the price of doing business."

"What is it you want?" The impatience in Charles's voice was palpable.

"We have a problem we must resolve. I told you this when we spoke before, but you refused to help me." He waited and then, when Charles failed to respond, continued. "This nun who has disappeared—the one who was traveling with the unfortunate Sister Manuela—we need to know where she is."

"Sister Margaret? Why?"

Estaves offered up another shrug. "As I explained before, she has become a problem to us."

Charles's face flushed with anger. "She's done nothing. She's a problem to no one."

Estaves shook his head sadly. "Charles, you identified the problem yourself. If the police find her, there may be things she could tell them."

Charles's back straightened, every muscle suddenly rigid. "The police officer, that vile woman, is the problem," he snapped. "And your man was supposed to resolve it."

Estaves smiled coldly. "You are mistaken, my friend. Oh, it's true; the police are a problem. But eliminating this particular woman will solve nothing. There are many detectives. If this one is eliminated, another will take her place. Emilio was foolish to agree to your proposal." He smiled. "I think greed for the money you offered got in the way of his good judgment." He shook his head again. "No, Charles. The solution is not eliminating one police officer. The solution is eliminating the information the police seek." He placed his elbows on the battered desk and clasped his hands. "There are two ways to do this. First is the nun. Tell me where she is, and we will begin to solve this problem. The second way I will describe in a few minutes. *After* you tell me what I want to know."

Charles's face was stricken. "I won't. I won't do it."

Estaves smiled at him as he might smile at a small child who had said something foolish. The man had so much power in his work, so much respect, and yet he was a fool. "Yes, you will, Charles. You will do as we ask." He took in a deep breath. "Please don't make me tell you why you will do this. It would only offend your manly pride, and that is something I do not wish to do."

Charles stared at him. His jaw began to tremble. "You bastard," he said. "I never should have done business with you."

Estaves began to laugh. "Oh, Charles, why do you say such things? If you had not done business with us you would not have had your share of the profits, and you would not have been able to use those profits to save your church." The laughter ended in a broad smile. "It would be unfortunate if the public learned how that money was used, would it not?

It would also be unfortunate if we were forced to end our agreement and withdraw our help in your other cause." He shook his head. "If we were forced to do that, all these priests you hate so much, they would still be at the altar every Sunday, would they not?" He forced away more laughter. "But let us not talk of these things. We want to continue offering our help in these matters. After all, this is all for the greater good. It is God's work. Is that not what you told me?"

"I didn't expect you to blackmail me," Charles snapped.

Estaves leaned back in his chair. "Let's not use ugly words with each other," he said. "It is simply a question of leverage. As a banker you understand that, am I not right?"

Charles glared at him. "We had a straightforward business deal. I provided you with a service. You agreed to a certain share in the profits and to provide an extra service in return. But that wasn't enough for you, was it? You spied on me. You discovered what I was using the money for, and now you are using it against me."

Estaves leaned forward, his features no longer benign. "You listen to me, you foolish man. You will have everything you want. *Everything!*" He shouted the final word, his eyes glaring anger. "*If* you live up to your end of our bargain. I assure you we will live up to our end. We will kill your priests for you. And you will continue to provide a means to bring our product into this country and be free to use your share of the profits in any way you choose." He leaned forward, still glaring. "But we also will do whatever is necessary to protect our interests. And if you interfere with that . . ." He left the warning unspoken. "Do we understand each other?"

Charles's hands began trembling, and he clenched his fists to hide it. "I understand," he said. "I understand all too well."

Estaves smiled at him. "Good, Charles. Very good. Now you will tell me where this nun is." He waited as Charles told him. "Very good, Charles. Very good. Now we will eliminate our problem with this nun. And we will also do the second thing I spoke of. We will convince these police to"—

he waved his hand in the air, then continued—"to *soften* their investigation."

Charles stared at him, his eyes filled with suspicion. "How will you do that?" he demanded.

Estaves smiled. "As I told you, Charles, eliminating this one police officer accomplishes nothing. Another would only take her place. But all police officers have commanders who direct their efforts. I have looked into this situation. The commander in this matter is a man named Devlin. He has a daughter he loves deeply." A smile returned to Estaves's lips. "So . . . we will send him a message about his daughter . . . along with a very simple suggestion. It is something that has worked very well in my own country. And I assure you it will work here as well."

## Chapter Fifteen

*T*homas glanced at the others who were gathered around him and let his eyes come to rest on Boom Boom Rivera. He disliked this man Ramon. He distrusted him, and he was frustrated that the others could not see the reason for his concern.

Thomas had gathered a small group in the dayroom to discuss their spiritual well-being. The two young men who were among those under his charge had come willingly. He also had insisted that Peter attend with this new probationer, Ramon Rivera. It was not common for probationary members to take part in these sessions, and Peter had resisted at first. But Thomas had exerted his will, and the younger numerarier had finally given in, as Thomas knew he would. Peter was no match for him and never would be.

He kept his eyes fixed on Boom Boom as he began. "I want you to listen to our discussion, Ramon. Feel free to ask any questions at the appropriate time. Also be prepared to answer questions that we may ask you." He paused, keeping his eyes hard. "Do you understand?"

Boom Boom gave him a friendly smile. It was all facade. What he really wanted was a chance to grab the sonofabitch by the throat and choke the bastard until he turned just a little bit blue. He hoped this job ended with some arrests. He also hoped Thomas was one of those arrested. He very much wanted to slap the cuffs on him and see his hard little self-important eyes turn to jelly.

"I'm looking forward to it," Boom Boom said. "I need all the spiritual guidance I can get." He fought his facial expression, kept the smile from becoming a smirk.

Thomas didn't seem to notice. He nodded and turned back to the others. Then his eyes snapped back to Boom Boom, as though preparing to catch him out.

"How do you feel today, Ramon?" The words came out more a demand than a question.

Boom Boom placed a hand on his chest. "Me? I feel great. Hey, I feel really at one with the Lord." I also feel horny as a motherfucker, Boom Boom thought. And if I don't get out of this nuthouse soon I'm gonna go outa my gourd.

Thomas's eyes filled with challenge, eager, ready to pounce.

"I envy Ramon."

The thin, reedy voice snapped Thomas's attention away. The words had come from a plump young man with an acne-stained face. They had been spoken almost as a plea, and his eyes seemed to hold that same begging quality.

"What do you mean, Joseph?" Thomas seemed annoyed by the interruption, and the angry tone in his voice made the plump young man cringe.

Joseph lowered his eyes, and for a moment Boom Boom thought he might burst into tears. "I'm sorry. I didn't mean to interrupt. I just . . . I just . . ."

"It's all right, Joseph. Finish what you started to say." Thomas's voice had softened, but just barely.

Joseph glanced at him nervously, then fell to his knees as if about to confess some sin. "It's just that I try so hard to be one with the Lord." He hesitated. His eyes seemed to be searching Thomas's face for some sign that he would understand. "I just . . . I just always seem to fail. I become distracted . . . and tempted."

Thomas leaned forward, the cat with the mouse again. "What tempts you, Joseph?"

His voice was demanding, even a bit threatening, Boom Boom thought. He stared at the kneeling figure, somewhat shocked by his sudden supplication. He could see fear creep into

Joseph's eyes and felt an instinctive urge to say something that would sweep that fear away. He looked at the other young man whom Thomas had brought into the room and decided to hold back. His name was Howard and he was no more than twenty or twenty-one, and his eyes flitted from Thomas to Joseph, clearly pleased that it was not he who was being challenged. Boom Boom decided to back off. Joseph was on his own.

"I asked you a question," Thomas said. "I'm waiting for your answer."

Joseph's lips moved silently. Then he forced the words out. "I just . . . I just get tempted to do things I shouldn't."

Thomas leaned forward, eyes glaring. "You haven't been masturbating, have you, Joseph?" His body seemed coiled, all the muscles tight and ready.

"Oh, no. God, no!" Joseph seemed horrified by the thought.

"But you've been tempted, haven't you?" Thomas demanded.

Joseph shook his head rapidly. He was about the same age as the other young man, perhaps nineteen or twenty, but the fear in his eyes made him seem much younger. "I've been having thoughts I know I shouldn't," he said. "I try to force them away, but . . ."

"Thoughts about women? Thoughts about performing impure acts with them?" Thomas's eyes were glittering now. He watched Joseph nod, and a small, satisfied smile came to his lips. "You know what that leads to, don't you, Joseph?"

Again Joseph nodded but said nothing.

Boom Boom cringed inwardly but also kept silent. He glanced at Peter and found him staring at the floor.

Thomas turned to the other young man. "Howard, what do you do when you're faced with temptation?" he asked.

Howard's face beamed. He was painfully thin, with lank brown hair plastered to one side, and the white dress shirt he wore ballooned around his skinny arms and chest. Now he seemed to swell within it like a grammar-school kid who knows the answer to the teacher's question.

"I increase my self-mortification," he said. "I wear the repentance belt for three hours instead of two. I use the scourge with more intensity."

Thomas nodded. "And this drives away your impure thoughts, doesn't it, Howard?"

"Oh, yes."

"And you're not tempted to masturbate, are you, Howard?"

Howard confirmed that he was not so tempted, but Thomas wasn't listening. His eyes had snapped back to Joseph, who was now staring at the floor, lips trembling. Thomas's entire body seemed filled with accusation.

Boom Boom couldn't stand it any longer. "That's really bad, huh?" he asked. "I mean impure thoughts and masturbation." He waved away his words. "Like I know it's supposed to be a sin, okay? I mean, it's something you gotta confess and all. But you make it sound like it's even worse than I thought it was."

Thomas turned to him, incredulous. "*Supposed* to be a sin?" He repeated Boom Boom's words as though they had been spoken in some incomprehensible language. "Masturbation damns you to hell for eternity. There is no redemption, no forgiveness. And impurities of the mind lead you to that sin." He turned sharply on Peter, who was still staring at the floor, his face flushed. "Have you taught Ramon none of this, Peter?" he demanded.

Peter looked up slowly. "Our instruction hasn't gotten that far," he said.

"It hasn't?" Thomas seemed overwhelmed. "When were you planning to discuss this with him?"

Peter looked away. "Soon," he said, his voice barely above a whisper.

Again, Boom Boom felt he had to jump in—this time to save Peter further humiliation. "Hey, it's my fault, here. I was always taught all sins could be forgiven." He shrugged as if now concerned that he might have misunderstood. "I mean, I thought a priest could forgive anything in confession, or you could even get it done yourself by saying a perfect Act of Contrition."

Thomas glared at him with undisguised contempt, and Boom Boom wondered if throwing the teachings of the Catholic Church back at him was yet another unforgivable act.

"Well, you are wrong," Thomas snapped. "And the people who taught you that were wrong. The Father has taught us that masturbation is beyond forgiveness. It condemns one to hell without hope of redemption."

The man's voice was so harsh, so filled with finality, that Boom Boom raised his hands defensively. "Okay, man, I didn't know." He paused a beat and then pushed ahead, unable to resist offering Thomas another challenge. "You mean, like, if a fourteen-year-old kid . . . you know, like, does it . . . he's doomed for eternity?"

The absurdity of the statement almost made Boom Boom break into a grin. Then he saw a look of horror crease the faces of Joseph and Howard.

"Of course that's not what I mean," Thomas said. "But once one is shown the way, once one hears the true teachings of the Father, one must follow those teachings or be damned for eternity."

Boom Boom leaned forward, trying to appear earnest. "And the Father teaches that masturbation is, like, unforgivable?"

"He does," Thomas snapped.

"Are there, like, any more unforgivable sins?" Boom Boom asked.

Again, Thomas glared at him. "Only one, Ramon. Only one more." He let the sentence die as if Boom Boom were unworthy of that particular bit of information.

"And what's that?" Boom Boom finally asked.

Thomas stared at him for several long seconds. Then he leaned forward, matching Boom Boom's earnestness. "Lying to your spiritual guide," he said. "That is the other unforgivable sin."

"So who's this Father guy who teaches all this unforgivable crap?" Boom Boom asked. "I mean, Thomas isn't talking about God, right?"

Boom Boom and Peter had returned to the computer room after their disastrous session with Thomas. Peter lowered his eyes and shook his head. "No," he said. "The Father, as we use the term here, refers to Father José Chavarría de

Mata. He was the founder of our order. He wrote *The Way* under divine inspiration. It's the book of teachings that we follow to make our lives one with Christ. Thomas was trying to explain that to you—that once you know the teachings of *The Way,* you must follow them or be condemned."

Boom Boom gave him a long look. "And you believe that, right?"

Peter lowered his eyes. "Yes," he said softly. "I believe the Father's teachings are the truth. I believe they were divinely inspired, a message from God about how we must live our lives."

Boom Boom kept staring at him. "You don't think, like, maybe these people are telling you these things so they can control you?"

Peter's eyes shot up, now tinged with anger. "No, I do not. I believe in the Father's teachings."

Boom Boom waved a hand around in a small circle, as if trying to get a hold on what he wanted to say next. "Then why are you helping us, man? I don't understand."

Peter's hands tightened into fists. "Because someone is doing something here that is corrupting the order. And it has to be stopped." He drew a long breath, fighting to control his emotions. "It has to be stopped," he said again, his voice sounding very tired now, "even if it means I'm no longer welcome here."

*B*oom Boom's room reminded him of an oversized jail cell. It was eight by ten feet, furnished with a narrow metal-framed bed, a small metal writing desk, and a straight-back chair. There was a washbasin in one corner and a metal armoire in another. Between them a solitary window looked out onto an airshaft. A plain wooden crucifix provided the only decorative touch.

Boom Boom had checked the room for listening devices and found none. But there was little need. There was no telephone or computer terminal that would give a resident access to the outside world. Once inside the building, every part of a resident's life was controlled and directed by the order. The isolation was intended, and it was completely inescapable unless you planned ahead.

With a slight smirk he removed his trousers and retrieved the Palm Pilot and cellular phone that were taped to his leg. He took them to the small desk and went to work.

Devlin wanted a complete list of all members of the order and their present locations. He also wanted any information about work assignments, family history, and any personal background the order had collected on its members. Obtaining that information from the main system had proven impossible. His activities were too closely monitored. But the work he had done on that system had given him access to various codes and passwords, which he could now use to hack into the system by using the Palm Pilot and his cellular network.

By ten o'clock that evening he had what he wanted. He converted it into a file and e-mailed it to the squad's office. Then he called Devlin at home.

# Chapter Sixteen

"**S**ister Margaret has been stashed at some kind of cloistered convent in Westchester County. You feel up to chasing her down?"

"Try to stop me," Sharon said.

Devlin handed her the list Boom Boom had e-mailed. It carried the name of every Opus Christi member in greater New York and included his or her place of residence and current work assignment—except for the supernumerarier, whose identities were concealed even from the members. Boom Boom had already made the list, along with his cover job as a computer technician for the City of New York. His name, along with half a dozen others, was marked with an asterisk to indicate his probationary status.

Sharon smiled as she flipped through the names. "Nice that they have all this. I wonder how they'll explain not giving it to us a week ago when all they had to do was click the mouse on their damned computer? It's obvious—with Boom Boom on the list—that they keep it pretty current."

"You never heard of a computer going down?" Devlin said sarcastically. He took the list back, laid it on his desk, and gave it a gentle pat. "I think we'll find out they update this little baby every day." He grinned across the desk. "Ironic, isn't it? How their need to know where everyone is every minute of the day put this in our hands."

"Could piss them off when they realize it," Sharon said.

Devlin nodded. "A sense of humor, it's a terrible thing to waste. Who knows? Maybe this will help them catch on to an idea like that." He turned serious and gave Sharon a long look. "You sure you're really up to this? The effects of a bullet wound can stay with you quite a while. I know from personal experience."

They were seated across from each other in Devlin's office, and throughout their conversation Sharon had struggled to conceal the dull, throbbing pain in her shoulder. "I'm fine," she said. "Your bullet wound was a lot worse than the little nick I got." She gave him an all-knowing smile. "And if I'm not mistaken, *sir*, you climbed out of a hospital bed and went after the person who set you up."

Devlin nodded. "Yeah, I seem to remember that. I also seem to remember how useless I was, and how a certain lady sergeant had to come along and save my sorry ass."

Sharon gave him a small shrug. "That's what lady sergeants are for."

Devlin leveled a finger at her. "You're *sure* you're up to this?"

"I'm sure."

"You may hit the same stone wall again. This is a cloistered convent, and it's run by the same people."

Sharon's eyes hardened. "I'll get in," she said, "and I'll see that nun."

A small smile played at the corners of Devlin's mouth. He had no doubt she would. "I'm sending someone with you," he said.

Sharon's eyes narrowed. "Not Ollie, for chrissake."

Devlin laughed, then shook his head. "He's busy playing watchdog for Father Janis. I'll send Red. He looks like an overweight Boy Scout. Maybe it'll help get you inside the convent."

*O*ur Lady of Perpetual Light convent sat on fifty acres of meticulously groomed woodland and lawn located just north of Bedford in Westchester County. Originally owned by another Catholic order, the convent had occupied the site since 1925 and had provided a steady stream of teaching nuns for Catholic schools along much of the East Coast. Then modernity had struck, bringing with it the rise of feminism and a steady decline in the number of young women seeking the veil. The convent struggled on for three decades but ultimately became obsolete; as the end of the century approached, the property was reluctantly put up for sale.

It was prime real estate, enough to make any developer drool, and offers poured in proposing everything from an office complex to a shopping mall to an upscale residential community. None of those offers, however, matched the one made by Opus Christi, which was rumored to have been twice the appraised value.

Now, five years later, the convent shared the property with a conference center and religious retreat, all situated behind a high stone wall that kept the site hidden from intruding eyes. Sharon and Red drove up to an imposing iron gate that closed off the main entrance. A call box was fixed to the stone wall, and Sharon got out and pressed the button.

A high, faint, timid voice answered, asking if she could help.

"Sergeant Levy and Detective Cunningham," Sharon snapped. "We were sent up by New York Headquarters. Please open the gate."

There was a short pause, and then the timid voice returned. "Please drive up to the main house."

With that the gate slowly began to open.

The main house turned out to be a large three-story stone building with the air of a once-great home. Long small-paned windows looked out over a wide lawn that was dotted with stone benches set under arbors and surrounded by massive old trees. To the right, some distance from the house, stood a shrine to Our Lady of Fatima, depicting three small children kneeling before a beneficent and serene Virgin.

Sharon and Red parked their car in the circular drive and climbed wide stone steps to a massive oak door. Sharon rang the bell, and the door was opened immediately by a young nun who had obviously been awaiting their arrival.

The young woman smiled warmly, her slightly chubby face framed by the veil of her black-and-white habit. She was no more than eighteen or nineteen, and her unlined face radiated an inner peace that seemed almost unnatural.

"Are you the two police officers who called from the gate?" she asked. There was eagerness in her voice, as though their arrival was something exciting.

"Yes," Sharon said. "We were sent up to see Sister Margaret. We were told we'd find her here."

The young woman blinked several times, as if confused by the information. "I wonder why they didn't call us," she said. "They always call us when someone's coming. They even call us when someone's coming who's a member of the order."

Sharon was about to make an impromptu excuse but the young nun prattled on.

"There must be someone new working in the main office. They sent up another custodian this morning, and they didn't call about him either. It's very confusing when they do that." She smiled at them warmly. "I mean, they have such very strict rules and then they don't follow them."

"It's the same everywhere," Sharon said. She wanted to end the young woman's senseless prattle and get to Sister Margaret before someone a little brighter came along. "Is Sister Margaret here?"

"Oh, yes," the young nun said. She laughed. "I mean she's not *here* here. But she's on the grounds. She's over at the conference center. She's taking part in a pro-life clinic. Just about everyone is there." A small pout formed on her lips. "Except me. I had to stay behind to answer the phones and the door." She brightened again, suddenly, unexpectedly. "But work—whatever we're given—is an expression of our love of God, a path of knowledge toward Him." She smiled, all happiness now. "They teach us here that all work is worthy and lifts us up toward a higher love of God."

Sharon winced inwardly. "I'm sure that's true," she said. "How do we get to the conference center? We really need to see Sister Margaret."

"Oh, it's simple," the young nun said. She stepped across the threshold and pointed toward a path laid with paving stones. "Follow the path, the one that goes past Our Lady of Fatima, and go on through the trees. The center's just on the other side. Oh, and if you see a man wandering around like he's lost, it's probably the new custodian. Please tell him to follow you. He was going to the center too, but I don't think he understood my directions. He didn't seem to understand English too well." She blinked. "That surprised me, because he spoke it well enough."

"If we see him, we'll tell him," Sharon said.

They went along the path and passed the shrine. Up close the plaster figures of the Virgin and the three children were much larger than they had seemed from a distance. They were life-sized, Sharon realized, the children kneeling, eyes raised to the Virgin, who rose above them. The statue had been placed so it appeared to be standing on a live flowering bush that Sharon could not identify. The main figure's eyes gazed down at the children, its face filled with maternal warmth. Beneath the grouping were numerous offerings of cut flowers, intermingled with pieces of paper held down with small stones, each seeming to hold a written prayer or entreaty. Sharon wondered if one of those written pleas had come from the young nun they had just left, some search for support in joyfully accepting the mundane tasks she was given.

"Jesus," she said, more to herself than to Red.

"What?" Red asked.

"That young kid back there," Sharon said. "Babbling away by rote all that stuff they've been feeding her."

"Spooky," Red agreed.

"Worse than spooky," Sharon said. "I bet they could tell that kid to do anything, and she'd do it."

"You thinking about the nun who smuggled the heroin?" Red asked.

"You bet your ass I am," Sharon said.

They followed the path through a dense patch of trees and came out onto another sprawling lawn. Ahead, a long single-story building stood at the end of the path. It was on a raised circular pedestal, the upper portion built in a misshapen U with unsupported wings extending out and tilted at sweeping angles so the entire building looked like a bird in flight. Here again, the exterior grounds held numerous stone benches, each one situated so it faced a central point: a large wooden cross, bearing a plaster representation of the crucified body of Christ. Places to sit and meditate, Sharon guessed. And to have your thoughts directed only where intended.

They entered the main door and found another young nun seated at a long table that was filled with pro-life literature. A poster hung on the wall behind her, depicting the mutilated remains of an aborted fetus. Beneath the photo were the words THE WORST KIND OF CHILD ABUSE. Sharon ground her teeth. She wished she could drag the person who had dreamed up that poster to some of the crime scenes she'd been forced to visit. Make that sucker look at the real bodies of some unwanted and unloved children, she told herself. Then send him back to the drawing board.

The young nun at the table fixed them with a broad smile, not unlike the one they'd been favored with at the convent.

"Are you here for the training session?" she asked. Then, not waiting for an answer added, "You're late, you know. The session started at eight."

"We're here to see Sister Margaret," Sharon said.

"Oh!" the young nun said, obviously surprised. "Well, she's in the training session, and I can't disturb her."

"If you could just point her out," Sharon said. "Then we'll just wait until she's finished."

"Oh, yes, I can do that," the young nun said.

They followed her to a set of double doors. She opened one barely a foot, and pointed to a long table set before an audience of about two hundred.

"There, at the end of the table on the left," she said. "That's Sister Margaret."

"Thanks," Sharon said. "We'll just sit inside and wait until she's finished."

They took seats at the rear. The audience was made up of young men and women, all early to mid-twenties, each sex seated separately, divided by the aisle.

Red leaned in close and whispered. "You think we're sinning by sitting next to each other?"

"Only in our hearts, sweetie," Sharon whispered back, "so don't get any false hopes up."

A middle-aged man stood before the group in a sharply

pressed summer-weight suit. He was tall and slender, with neatly barbered hair, and he spoke with the easy intensity of the professional instructor.

"Now," he intoned, pausing for effect, "the important thing to remember is that we are doing God's work. We are saving the lives of the unborn. We are there to help these young women—to help them decide against the murder of their unborn infants. God's children. Children our Lord has placed in their wombs because he has decided to give them life." The instructor raised a solitary finger as if pointing toward the heavens. "And that, my friends, is an act *no one* has the right to alter. Under no circumstances, at any time. To do so is to go against the will of the Almighty."

The instructor smiled easily as he took a few steps, nodding to himself about the truth of what he had just said. Then he stopped and wheeled abruptly, to point at various individuals as he continued.

"And you, each and every one of you, will be doing the work of our Lord when you force these young women to abandon the heinous plan they have been coerced into. One day, when their children are grown, they will thank you for your actions. They will see what you did as the work of God, as the *will* of God, and they will bless you every day of their lives."

He paused, walked again, and then stopped, his hands out at his sides. "So how shall we do the work of the Lord?" Again, he raised a solitary finger. "We shall do it by any means at our disposal." He offered them a face filled with regret. "Unfortunately, one of the most effective means is through intimidation. Now this may sound cruel. We know that many of these young women are under enormous pressure. Some of them are unwed. Some are living in disadvantageous economic circumstances. A few may even have been the victims of unwanted sexual advances. But we are talking about murder here. We are talking about a greater crime—the taking of life that God has willed into the world.

"Some of you will be given cameras. We have found this a very effective means of driving these women away from these abhorrent clinics. As they approach, you step in front of them in teams of two or three people. One of you will take their photograph." He raised a cautionary finger. "And always use the flash, even if it's bright and sunny. The flash enhances the intimidation factor.

"You take their photograph, and you tell them it will be published in advertisements we plan to run. Tell them it will be published in our monthly newsletter and sent to thousands of people.

"Tell them they don't want to be publicly identified as a killer of the unborn. Tell them there are other choices— charities that will help them raise their child, adoption agencies that will place that child in a loving home. Show them photographs of the mutilated bodies of the unborn and ask them if that is what they want for the life they carry inside their bodies. Ask them if that is their idea of motherhood."

The instructor stopped and shook his head. "It may sound hard-hearted. But I tell you that every woman you drive away from these places of death will further brighten the crown you will one day wear in heaven, and when you stand before our Lord on judgment day, He will look upon you and say, "You have done well, my child. In you I am well pleased."

The instructor stopped, arms outstretched, and called for questions. A hand went up. Sharon could not see who it was, but the would-be questioner was on the women's side of the audience.

At that same moment Sharon noticed a bearded man in a custodian's uniform standing at a partially opened door behind the speaker. Something struck her as odd, but she couldn't quite place what it was. Her attention was drawn away by a question directed at the instructor.

"What about women whose health makes it dangerous to have children, or the ones who have been the victims of rape or incest? Should we make exceptions for them?"

The instructor looked at the questioner with what seemed to be great sadness. He shook his head. "This is the type of propaganda hurled at us by the abortionists." He raised his voice to a near shout. "But don't be fooled by it. Don't be fooled by talk about children raised in abject poverty. Don't be fooled by talk about children forced to live their lives with hideous physical and mental defects. Don't be fooled by concern for a mother's health. *God* makes the choice of who will live and who will die, only God. Never man." He lowered his voice again. It was almost a whisper now, sadness creeping into his words. "And do not be fooled by talk of rape or incest. God has chosen how these children—*his* children—will come into this world. God has chosen the moment and the means of their conception. All of it is God's will. There are no victims here except the unborn who are about to have life stolen from them."

Sharon was still seething when the instructor called a twenty-minute break. She fantasized about grabbing him by his pencil neck and strangling him until he realized that *some* women did have control over their bodies and their ability to use them. Instead, she and Red moved out into the hall and waited for Sister Margaret. She just wanted to finish the interview and get out of there. The next item on the printed agenda dealt with birth control and the steps that could be taken to keep women from accepting contraceptive devices offered by parenthood clinics. If she were forced to listen to that she would strangle every simpering sonofabitch in the room.

The crowd pushed out of the auditorium en masse, creating a barrier that cut Sharon and Red off from Sister Margaret. They followed her outside and caught up with her just before she reached a stone bench near a small copse of trees.

Sharon introduced herself and Red and explained why they were there.

Sister Margaret seemed surprised at first; then a look of relief came to her face. She was about twenty-five, small-boned and slender, with a long nose and doelike brown eyes. Her voice was soft, almost like that of a supplicant.

"I was warned that someone might come, and I was told not to speak to anyone unless one of the numerarier was with me," she said. She looked around, as if searching to see if one was nearby. "I told my superiors that I wanted to talk to the police, but they said that might not be wise. They said to wait until everyone was certain the time was right."

"When will that be?" Sharon asked. She struggled to keep sarcasm out of her voice.

Sister Margaret shook her head. "I don't know. But I still want to talk to you. I just . . . I just . . ."

"Let's sit down," Sharon suggested. "We can talk off the record if you want. Then later, if a formal statement is needed, we can do it when one of your numerarier can be there."

That seemed to satisfy the nun, and she smiled with obvious relief. They sat on the stone bench; Sister Margaret perched delicately on its edge, Sharon and Red on either side. To their right, the custodian Sharon had noticed inside was now kneeling beside a garden about twenty yards from the bench.

"Tell us about the last time you saw Sister Manuela," Sharon began, still watching the bearded custodian as he worked in the garden. Again, something that she couldn't quite identify seemed wrong about the man.

Tears suddenly filled the nun's eyes and she sniffed them back, the sound of her distress drawing Sharon's attention. "It was at the airport," she said. "We had just returned from Colombia. Sister had become ill on the plane, and she seemed to get worse after we passed through customs. We sat down to rest. Then a man came up to her and spoke to her in Spanish." She shook her head. "I don't understand the language very well, only a word or two, but he seemed to be asking what was wrong. I wasn't concerned, because I had seen him before we left, at the airport in Bogotá. Sister had introduced him as a relative who was also traveling to the United States. So it made sense that he would come up to us, especially if he thought Sister wasn't well."

"And Sister Manuela left with him?" Red asked.

The nun nodded. "That was strange, and it did concern me. Sister said he was going to take her to a doctor, and that I should take our things back to our headquarters in Manhattan, and she would meet me there later." She shook her head. "But that isn't how things are supposed to be with us. We're not supposed to go places alone. We're always supposed to go in pairs. I tried to tell Sister that, but the man just took her and started off, and I had all our bags there, so I couldn't just leave them and follow." Tears filled her eyes again. "I didn't know what to do."

"What did this man look like?" Sharon asked.

Sister Margaret began to describe the man.

"Hey, that sounds like the guy at your apartment," Red said.

Sharon's head snapped back to the garden. That was it. That was what was wrong. The beard on the custodian was fake; without it—

Sharon rose quickly, her hand going to the automatic at her hip. "Get the nun under cover," she snapped at Red, as she pulled the pistol from her holster.

Emilio had already taken his own automatic from inside his shirt, and Sharon could see the bulbous suppressor attached to the barrel.

Behind her Red had seen it too, and he pushed Sister Margaret roughly off the bench and dropped in front of her, shielding her body with his own.

Emilio fired first, three rapid rounds. Sharon assumed a shooter's two-handed stance and returned fire. She was short of her target, the bullets kicking up turf and dirt a foot in front of the Colombian.

The surrounding lawn was crowded with people from the pro-life training session, and the sound of gunfire set them screaming and racing for cover.

Emilio fired again and Sharon felt a gust of air by her cheek as the bullet passed within inches of her head. Then the Colombian was up and running. He headed directly into the scattering crowd of people, forcing Sharon to withhold fire.

"I'm going after him." She glanced back over her shoulder and saw Red clutching his thigh. Blood seeped through his fingers.

"You're hit," she said, finding the words unbelievable even as she spoke them.

"I'm okay," he snapped. "So's the sister. Get the sonofabitch. I'll call for help on my cell phone."

Sharon took off at a fast trot, ready to dive for cover if the shooter turned to fire again. He was thirty or more yards ahead now, but his progress was slowed by his decision to weave in and out of the scattering crowd to use people for cover. Sharon chose a straight course and began to close on him quickly as he cut away from the others and plunged into a wooded grove.

They left the trees with Sharon only fifteen yards behind. Emilio turned suddenly and fired three wild shots in her direction and then spun around and was off again.

Sharon dropped to one knee and raised her Berretta, steadied it in both hands, and emptied the remainder of the sixteen-shot clip. Emilio screamed in pain and crumpled to the ground.

Sharon replaced the empty clip and got to her feet, her weapon still leveled at her target. Emilio's automatic had fallen to his side, and he reached out for it. Sharon fired two shots into the ground in front of him and continued to advance as his hand froze.

"Reach for it again, you slimy little prick, and I'll blow your fucking head off."

Emilio stared up at her as she approached. The false beard hung loosely to one side, and his lips curled with unadulterated hatred. *"Puta,"* he muttered.

Sharon stepped forward and kicked him in the groin and then stepped back and watched him hunch into a ball of pain. "I prefer to be called a ballbreaker, not a whore," she said. "And by the way, you owe me for a new fucking suit."

## *Chapter Seventeen*

**D**evlin met Sharon at Westchester County Hospital, where both Emilio and Red had been taken. Red's wound was superficial, and he was already hobbling around with the aid of a cane. Emilio's was more serious. Sharon's bullet had broken his left femur and chewed up much of the muscle in his thigh. Westchester police had been called in to guard his room until Devlin could arrange transport back to a city hospital. They had also provided units to seal off the convent and guard Sister Margaret from further attack. Devlin had tried to place the nun in protective custody but had been told he could not enter the convent without a court order. Howie Silver had called and ordered him to back off. He was out of his jurisdiction, Silver had warned, and Westchester police had refused to act after Opus Christi had claimed religious sanctuary for the nun. Nothing was to be done, Silver had said, until something could be negotiated with Opus Christi and the archdiocese.

"At least we got to interview her before they brought down the fucking curtain," Sharon said, as they sat in a small office the hospital had provided.

"Tell me what else you got from her," Devlin said.

Sharon was pacing the floor, the adrenaline from the gunfight still pumping through her system. "The nun identified the little prick as the man who took Sister Manuela from the airport, the same man she saw her with earlier in Bogotá, whom Sister Manuela had identified as a relative."

"And he's the same shooter you found in your apartment, right? You're sure of it?"

"No question. It's the same fucking weasel. I didn't make him at first because of the phony beard, but as soon as Sister Margaret started describing the man she saw at the airport it all clicked. I tried to question him, but he's not talking. The guy's obviously a pro. He knows better than to open his yap."

"That's okay. We know who he is. You were able to ID him when the Colombians gave us his mug shot. The prints we just took will confirm that ID. We've got enough to indict him for Sister Manuela, the attempt on your life last week, and attempted murder on Red today." Devlin paused a moment. "And you think he was going to kill the nun, too."

Sharon nodded vigorously. "Had to be. He had no way of knowing I was coming here. Shit, *I* didn't know until yesterday, and nobody else in the squad knew except you, Red, and me. I think he would have offed her if we hadn't shown up. And I think he tried to nail me earlier because I was dogging her, and somebody thought I was getting too close. You know where that points."

Devlin steepled his fingers. "Yeah, the only people who knew you were chasing her down were those hard-asses at Opus Christi." He shook his head. The prospect of what lay ahead promised to be a political quagmire. "What else did she tell you?"

Sharon took out her notebook. "I didn't have a lot of time with her after the shit went down. As soon as everything got sorted out, they took her away from me as quickly as they could. I did have time to get her to tell me everything she knew about Sister Manuela." She paused, flipping the pages of her notebook. "According to Sister Margaret, Sister Manuela joined up two and half years ago and started training as a nun about a year and a half later. Until that time she worked at a bank in Manhattan in its foreign investment department. Sister Margaret said Manuela told her she worked for one of the big honchos there, a VP named Meyerson. Sister Margaret said she got the impression that he had some connection to Opus Christi and may have been the person who recruited her into the order, but she wasn't sure. It's not surprising she doesn't know for sure," Sharon added, "since they run that outfit like the fucking CIA."

Devlin took out his own notebook and jotted down Meyerson's name. "You know the name of the bank?" he asked, and wrote it down when Sharon gave it to him.

"It's a place to start," Devlin said, as he put the notebook away. "Somebody was behind this Valdez guy. Maybe Meyerson can give us a lead on who that might be. I'll get to him as soon as I finish up with the mayor. I've got a meeting with him later today. Seems like the honchos at Opus Christi are unhappy with us. Claim we used subterfuge to get into their training center and then turned it into a real-life Hogan's Alley."

Sharon smiled at the image. Hogan's Alley was a term used for a police combat pistol range, where you fired at pop-up targets, some armed, some not. It tested a cop's skill in deciding whether to shoot or withhold fire. "Nice comparison," she said. "Except this target fired back with real bullets. You want me there to help straighten it out?"

Devlin shook his head. "It's what they pay me the big bucks for," he said. "It's called being a human commode." He smiled at her. "The mayor will live with it. We've got a Colombian hit man in custody who shot two of our cops, and we've got a nun he'd targeted who's still breathing. If he takes us to task about our methods he looks like a fool. And Howie Silver never lets himself look like a fool." He gave Sharon an approving nod. "You did good, lady sergeant. Wounded cop chasing down an armed killer. The mayor just might end up giving you a commendation. It'll be a damned medal if I've got anything to say about it."

"I'm just happy I finally got to kick the little weasel in the balls," Sharon said.

"Don't tell me about any police brutality," Devlin said. His smile widened. "You know, you're getting more like Ollie every day."

"Oh, shit," Sharon said.

*G*ood news arrived by way of Stan Samuels a half hour before Devlin's meeting in the mayor's office.

"Did the prints come up positive?" Devlin asked.

"It's better than that," Samuels said. "First, our guy is definitely Emilio Valdez. No question about it. We got a positive on the prints we took up in Westchester with the prints the Colombians gave us. But just on a chance I also asked them to run them against the partials we got at the crime scene of the last priest who was iced. And guess what? That came up positive too. Not enough for a lock in court, maybe, but enough for us to be certain he's our guy for that killing. All we gotta do now is dig out the rest, a little legwork to place him at the scene."

Devlin sat back, taking it all in. "You get on that," he told Samuels. "Use the precinct detectives in Flushing who caught the case. And pull anybody else you need. I want you to identify everyone who was at the service in that church the night Father Halloran was murdered. Talk to the pastor. They usually have regulars at those services, old ladies who go to all of them, and who know everybody else who shows up and everybody who misses a night. Take the new mug shot we have on Valdez and show it around. Also show it in every store and gin mill in the surrounding area. Then do the same thing at every crime scene where a priest was murdered. If this guy Valdez did one, he probably did them all. I want to be able to prove it, and I need to do it fast. We're running out of time on this thing."

Samuels nodded but didn't move.

"What is it, Stan?" Devlin asked.

"You know what this is starting to look like? I mean with the nun and at least one of these priests tied to the same killer?"

Devlin placed both hands on his face and ran them down toward his chin. "Yeah," he said. "It's all falling into place. And I sure as hell don't like what I'm seeing." He leaned back in his chair and gave Samuels a weary smile. "Now I just have to go to the mayor's office and let the archdiocese and Opus Christi chew on my ass without letting them find out just how much we do know."

"Not even the mayor?" Samuels asked.

"Not even him," Devlin said. "Not yet. I want to see this Meyerson guy first. And I can't do that until I hold the mayor's hand for an hour or two."

*D*evlin entered Charles Meyerson's office at five that afternoon. It was impressive: a great deal of open space dotted with starkly modern furniture, each piece artfully placed to take advantage of a wall of windows that overlooked Park Avenue. Devlin also found Meyerson impressive. He was tall and fit, somewhere in his mid-forties, with prematurely gray hair and piercing blue eyes, a no-nonsense banking executive who seemed fully secure in his element. Devlin couldn't help wondering what else he was.

"You told my secretary that you wanted to speak to me about Maria Escavera," Meyerson began, when Devlin was seated in a visitor's chair across from his desk. Meyerson's own chair had a high back of black leather. There was not a scrap of paper in front of him, although numerous documents filled a console behind him, along with a computer and two multiline telephones. "I had my secretary pull Maria's employment records in case you wanted to look at them. We can, of course, provide you with copies if you wish. Since she's deceased, our usual employee confidentiality appears to be moot."

With that he spun his chair around, retrieved a large blue folder, and placed it before him on his desk.

"I've taken the liberty to review it myself," Meyerson continued. "Just to refresh my memory. But I actually remember Maria quite well and quite fondly. She was an excellent employee, and one I was sorry to lose."

"What type of work did she do?" Devlin asked. He was studying Meyerson's eyes, as every good cop does, always looking for some telltale hint of deception.

Meyerson leaned back in his chair. "Our office handles international investments for the bank. Our brief is worldwide, but our primary effort has been in South America, and to some extent Central America. There are many emerging companies there who offer good opportunities for investment. We also consider loans to several Latin American nations as well. Brazil, Colombia, and Argentina are of particular interest, and Maria spoke both Spanish and Portuguese, which made her quite valuable. She also had a very good business sense for such a young woman. We hired her right out of high school, based on her language and secretarial skills, and were quite impressed with how rapidly she

adapted herself to our needs." He gave Devlin a small, regretful shrug. "As I said, we were sorry to see her leave. She
was difficult to replace. Skill in more than one language is
not easy to find these days."

"So she remained in your employ until she decided to
enter the convent."

"Yes. It was a year and a half ago."

"And she still worked here when she became a member
of Opus Christi?"

"Yes, I believe that's correct."

There was a hint of something in Meyerson's eyes now,
and Devlin leaned forward, trying to narrow the distance between them. It was a mild attempt at intimidation, one he
had found effective when people were trying to conceal
something.

"Are you familiar with Opus Christi?" Devlin asked.

Meyerson hesitated, then offered Devlin a smile. "I'm a
Catholic myself," he said, "so I'm acquainted with The Holy
Order."

The use of the term set off an alarm in Devlin's head, and
he glanced down at his shoes to try and hide anything his
eyes might give away. When he looked up, his face was
blank. "Do any other members of the order work here?" he
asked.

Meyerson's jaw clenched slightly. He seemed to ponder
the question. "I really don't know," he said at length. "We try
not to pry into our employees' religious affiliations. Maria
raised it with me because she knew I was a Catholic. I got
the impression she was very devout in her beliefs, especially
those she had adopted since joining Opus Christi."

"Did you ever see her after she became Sister Manuela?"

Again, Meyerson hesitated. "Yes," he said. "When the
new cardinal was installed I was invited to the ceremony. I
ran into her when I was leaving. I believe she was with some
other nuns who were part of the crowd outside Saint
Patrick's Cathedral."

Devlin leaned in even closer. "I'm impressed," he said.
"At your getting an invitation to the cardinal's installation
ceremony. That was quite a hot ticket. I know that several of

our chiefs tried like hell to wangle an invitation. They weren't successful."

Meyerson gave Devlin another shrug, one intended to convey humility. "The bank does some rather extensive work with the archdiocese. I believe I was considered a suitable representative. I'm afraid it wasn't much more than that."

There was another flicker in Meyerson's eyes, and now Devlin was certain he was being lied to. He decided it was time to rattle the man a bit.

"Did Sister Manuela—I'm sorry, I mean Ms. Escavera—ever travel to Colombia for the bank?"

Meyerson's arms went momentarily rigid, but he forced himself to relax almost at once. If Devlin hadn't been looking for the telltale he probably would not have noticed.

"She traveled with me to Colombia on two occasions, I believe," Meyerson said. "I can check our records and confirm the number if you wish."

"That would be helpful," Devlin said. "Also the dates."

Meyerson made a note on the cover of Maria's folder. "She was part of a small group that went," he added, unnecessarily. "We traveled there on several occasions, and the personnel varied each time. That's why I can't recall exactly how many times she accompanied us. I do remember she was very useful as a translator. She had also lived in Bogotá as a child and had family there, so she was eager to go."

"Did Maria or any member of her family ever have any involvement with narcotics?" Devlin threw the question out like a heavy punch. This time the rigidity did not leave Meyerson so easily.

His face flushed and his eyes filled with anger. "Of course not," he snapped, then seemed to get a grip on himself. "I have no way of knowing about her family, of course. But as far as Maria was concerned, I'm certain she wasn't involved in anything so unsavory. She was a very devout young woman."

Devlin nodded as though thinking that over. Slowly, he raised his eyes back to Meyerson. "The autopsy showed that she had a lethal amount of heroin in her system when she died. It also showed that it got there when one of several condoms she had swallowed burst in her stomach. It didn't kill her, however. She died when the drug trafficker she was working for gutted her to retrieve the drugs." Devlin paused a beat, letting it all sink in, before continuing. "Yesterday we arrested the man who killed her. His name is Emilio Valdez, and Colombian authorities have identified him as a professional killer for one of the Colombian drug cartels." Again, Devlin paused, noting the pallor that had crept into Meyerson's face. "He was arrested while he was attempting to murder a second nun—the one who was traveling with Sister Manuela. Oddly enough, the two nuns were returning from Bogotá. According to this other nun they were also bringing in some religious artifacts for Opus Christi. I wondered if you knew about any history with drugs that might help us."

Meyerson stared at him for several seconds. "None whatsoever," he said.

"Well, it doesn't matter," Devlin said. "We're bringing this Valdez back from Westchester County tonight. We intend to lean on him until he tells us what we need to know. He will." He gave Meyerson a bright smile. "It's the only chance he has to save his ass."

*D*evlin took up a surveillance post outside Meyerson's office building. He had telephoned Ollie and pulled him off the unit guarding Father Janis. He wanted to tail Meyerson when he left work, and then he wanted Ollie to stay on him throughout the night. Something smelled about the man, and he wanted to know what it was.

Meyerson left his office at six-thirty, grabbed a cab, and headed across town. Ollie and Devlin followed in Ollie's unmarked car. When the cab stopped in front of Opus Christi headquarters, Devlin got on his cell phone and contacted Boom Boom, who was already en route to Opus Christi headquarters from his cover job with the city.

"Get here as quick as you can," Devlin said. "I want you to eyeball somebody."

*"T*hat's Father Charles," Boom Boom said, as he watched Meyerson leave Opus Christi headquarters. He continued to

study the man as he went to the curb to flag down another taxi. "Yeah, that's him. I'm sure of it. Our boy Peter pointed him out to me a few days back. Said he was one of the supernumerarier, a real bigwig. I guess I should have checked him out."

"You didn't have any reason to," Devlin said. "But you do now. I want you to get into the order's computer system and pull anything that even touches on him. I also want you to find out if there are any links to Meyerson's personal computer or the one he uses at the bank." Devlin gave him a long look. "I especially want you to look for any connection to Colombian religious artifacts, Maria Escavera, this hit man, Valdez, or any of the priests who've been killed. Got it?"

"You got it, Inspector."

A cab pulled up and Meyerson climbed into the rear seat. "Ollie, drop us off at the first corner you can without losing him," Devlin said. "Then you stay with Meyerson for the rest of the night. I want to know everything he does. Call me at home if you see anything that looks even a little suspicious."

As Ollie started after the taxi, Devlin turned to Boom Boom again. "I want *you* to call me too, if you hit on anything. This guy stinks. He lied through his teeth when I interviewed him. So get me something on him. And get it fast."

# Chapter Eighteen

Charles Meyerson was sweating. He sat in the rear of the cab dabbing his face with a folded handkerchief, surprised that he was suddenly awash. It had not been an unusually hot day. On the contrary, he thought, a heavy rain the previous evening had cooled things considerably. He rolled down the window, and a gust of noxious fumes poured in. He reached out again to close it and noticed his hand was trembling. Damn.

He stared out at the sidewalks, still filled with people who had worked later than most, all of them unaware of him as he drove past—a man whose life was crumbling. He clenched his fists in his lap, struggling to drive the tremors away. Father George had just confirmed his worst fears. Everything he had planned, everything he had tried to do for the church, was falling apart. And the man had just sat there, fuming about the police incursion on the order's property. It had been all he could think about. Of course he didn't know the rest. It had been held very closely, as any good business arrangement should be. And now, if that fool Emilio talked, it would all come back on him. And on Estaves.

He straightened in his seat. Yes, that was it, Estaves! Estaves had assured him he could make the police back off.

He leaned forward and told the driver to change his destination. It was his only hope now, and he would have to risk it.

Devlin entered the loft and found Phillipa on a chair in a far corner, her face in an angry pout. Adrianna was at the opposite end of the loft, cleaning the brushes she had used that day. She did not look happy either.

"Hi, guys. Why does everybody look so glum?"

Adrianna's eyes met his in a hard, even line. "I think you should ask your daughter," she said.

He turned to Phillipa, who was staring at him as well. "I think you should ask your girlfriend," she snapped.

Devlin blew out a breath, removed his jacket and sidearm, and placed each in the coat closet by the door, the pistol going into the lockbox he kept on the top shelf. He turned back to the two women in his life. "So, tell me about your fun day," he said.

"I really don't care to speak about it," Adrianna said.

"Neither do I," Phillipa chimed in.

Devlin let out another breath. Then he walked to the kitchen counter, where he kept their modest supply of liquor. "I think I'll have a comforting after-work drink," he said.

"Make me one too," Adrianna said.

He glanced at his daughter. "Martini?"

She gave him an evil look, the kind young girls master before they learn to walk, and turned back to the Harry Potter novel that lay in her lap.

It took another half hour before the complaints of the day unfolded. A friend of Phillipa's—an older woman, age twelve—had two tickets to a rock concert at Madison Square Garden. The group was one Devlin had never heard of, but that was far from a surprise. The point of contention was Phillipa's attendance, unchaperoned, solely in the company of her twelve-year-old friend Joslyn.

Adrianna had suggested it was unwise and not something she could agree to.

Phillipa had argued that *all* her friends were allowed to go to rock concerts alone.

Adrianna had questioned that assertion and offered to telephone Joslyn's mother to see if a proper chaperone could be arranged.

Phillipa had insisted that would be embarrassing and make her feel like a child.

Adrianna had pointed out that she was ten years old, which qualified as being a child.

Phillipa had snapped back, "You're not my mother!"

The discussion ended there until Devlin came home.

"You can't go unless there's a parent with you," he said.

"Daaad. Joslyn only got two tickets, and one of them's *mine*," Phillipa whined. "And there are a hundred thousand cops at Madison Square Garden. It's the safest place you can be."

He looked into her beautiful young face, at the spray of freckles now tinged red with adolescent anger. "There aren't a hundred thousand cops on the entire force," he said.

"You know what I mean. It's safe. It's protected. . . ."

"It's filled with lunatics and people using dope," he countered.

"No, it's not. It's safe. It really is. Joslyn's been to concerts there before."

"Alone?"

Phillipa didn't answer. Instead she again offered her assurances that the concert would be safe.

"I'm a cop, and you're telling me what's safe in New York?" he asked.

Phillipa glared at him. "You're just like *her*," she snapped.

"Does that mean I'm not your parent either?" Devlin asked.

That seemed to stop her, and she stared angrily at her lap.

The telephone postponed further comment. It was Ollie.

"Guess where our boy has been for the last half hour?" he began.

"Tell me."

"A certain co-op on First Avenue."

"Estaves?" Devlin said.

"The same. I double-checked with the doorman. Our boy asked for Estaves and went on up."

"Make sure the doorman knows he should keep his trap shut," Devlin said.

"I already told him," Ollie said. "It's not a problem. He's an old hairbag, used to be on the job."

"Stay with Meyerson, Ollie. See where he goes next. And keep me posted."

Devlin returned to the large sitting area where Phillipa and Adrianna remained, equally silent.

He took a chair next to his daughter. "I want to talk to you about Adrianna *not* being your parent," he began softly. "I want to talk to you about how she feels about that. Especially when she helps you get all the stuff you need—like your clothing for school, your meals—all the time she spends with you talking about your problems, the sports programs and dance classes, all the stuff she's helped you do all these years. You think when she does all that stuff she sits around saying: 'Well this isn't really my kid'? "

Phillipa continued to stare into her lap. In a tiny voice she whispered the word "No."

"I don't think so either," Devlin said. "I think she does all that stuff because, to her, you *are* her kid, and she loves you. We both love you. And that's the reason you can't go to this concert without an adult along. We don't think it's a safe thing to do. And you don't let people you love do things that aren't safe. Even if it makes them mad at you."

He knelt in front of her and covered her hand with his. "If Joslyn's parents think it's safe for her, that's their decision. But we don't feel that way, and we love you enough to let you be mad at us about that."

Phillipa licked her lips and looked up at her father. "Joslyn hasn't told her parents about the tickets yet," she said. "She was going to tell them tonight."

Devlin fought to keep a smile from his lips. "I see," he said. "Well, I wouldn't be surprised if she's hearing the same thing you are, right about now."

Phillipa nodded, rose slowly from her chair, walked to the sofa where Adrianna was sitting, and gave her a hug.

"**Y**our fears are unwarranted. Emilio will say nothing about our arrangement. Not to the police, not to anyone." Estaves held out his hands and let them fall away, as though the gesture itself gave validity to his words.

They were seated in a garishly decorated living room, couch and chairs upholstered in faux leopard, every side table etched with gold leaf. A sweeping window offered the room its only saving grace, a long southward view down the East River.

"How can you be certain?" Charles asked. "They will offer him things. Promise him his freedom if he tells them what they want to know."

"Still, he will not tell them," Estaves said. "Just as I would not tell them. He knows the kind of death that will be his if he talks. No man would want to die that way. It would not be quick, and that is what Emilio will want."

"You intend to kill him?" Charles seemed genuinely shocked by the thought. He had hoped Estaves would provide a lawyer who would thwart the police.

Estaves laughed, almost contemptuously, Charles thought.

"Of course," Estaves said. He spoke the words as though discussing some mundane matter that was of little concern. "We would never take the chance that we are wrong. Emilio understands that. He also understands that it will be done quickly and mercifully. And he knows how it would be done if he talked to the police. He will die because of his failure and his clumsiness. It is the way we do business, and he knows this."

"Then he has nothing to lose by talking to them," Charles insisted.

Estaves's lips formed into an all-knowing smile. "Oh, yes, my friend. Yes, he does."

"How will you do it?" Charles asked. "When they bring him back he'll be heavily guarded, won't he?"

Estaves shook his head and let out a long breath. "You have no need to know how it will be done." His eyes hardened, then softened again almost immediately. "But I will tell you enough to put your mind at rest." He shifted in his leopard-spotted chair, the movement lending him an air of self-assurance. "We already know he is to be housed in the hospital ward of the Brooklyn House of Detention. The policeman in charge of this matter has insisted on it. It is a very secure facility, the same place, I believe, where they first kept your famous serial killer, the Son of Sam." He let out a low baritone laugh. "You have such strange names for killers in this country."

Charles ignored the digression. "And you can get to him there, despite the security?"

"My friend, you can get to anyone, anywhere—providing you are willing to pay the price asked."

"And our arrangement?" Charles asked. "The other priests?"

Again, Estaves raised his hands and let them fall back. "It will take a few days, but Emilio will be replaced and the work we have agreed upon will continue."

Charles shook his head, still uncertain. "You said you could get to the police too," he said. "But today I had this Devlin in my office asking questions."

Estaves smiled. "I have already gotten to him," he said. "He simply does not know it yet." The smile broadened, as he explained.

"But . . . but what good is it if he doesn't know?" Charles demanded.

Estaves raised a finger. "But now he will. Would you like to take a small walk to a secure telephone booth and listen while I tell him?"

*D*evlin had just finished dinner when the call came. Phillipa answered the phone and told him it was for him.

"Your daughter sounds most lovely," a man's voice said. The words were spoken in a heavy Hispanic accent.

Devlin hesitated, not liking the tone he detected. "Thank you," he said, his words filled with caution. "Can I help you?"

"Oh, yes, indeed," the voice said.

"And how's that?"

A small laugh. "Your detectives are currently investigating a matter that is causing concern to some friends of mine. It would be most helpful if you softened their efforts just a bit."

Devlin gave him his own laugh now, but with a harder edge to it. "Now, why would I do that?" he asked.

"Why, if for no other reason than you realize we are serious people." He hurried on before Devlin could answer. "You also realize, of course, that I am calling you at home on a number that is not available to the public."

"Yes, I noticed that. So you're telling me you know where I live. I'm impressed. But not all that impressed."

"Perhaps your daughter would be more impressed," the voice said.

"*What?* Now you listen to me, you sonofabitch, and you listen good—"

"I have no time to listen, my friend," the voice said. "But, please, do me one small favor. Tell your daughter I hope she enjoys her concert at Madison Square Garden."

The dial tone assaulted Devlin's ears and became a dull bleating repetition he barely heard. He replaced the receiver and turned to his daughter, struggling to keep his voice calm. "Where did your friend get those concert tickets?" he asked.

Phillipa's face paled. "Um . . ."

"I need to know," he said. "It's important."

Phillipa studied her shoes. "Someone gave them to us," she said.

"Did you know the person?" Devlin asked.

Phillipa shook her head.

"Where were you when he gave them to you?" he asked.

Phillipa refused to raise her eyes. "We were standing in front of school," she said. Now she looked up quickly. "But he wasn't a stranger, Dad. He said he was there to pick up his daughter but had just missed her. He was somebody's *father.*"

"Did he tell you who his kid was?"

Phillipa lowered her eyes again and shook her head. "We kinda forgot to ask. He just said he had these tickets to the concert that he couldn't use, and we could have them if we wanted. Joslyn just grabbed them and showed them to me. So you see it was really Joslyn who got them, not me. And then we were so excited all we could do was stare at the tickets, and when we remembered we should thank him . . . well . . . he was just gone."

Devlin fought for control. "What did he look like?" he asked.

"Well, he was old . . . I mean, at least forty . . . and he was kinda fat."

"Do you remember the color of his hair, his eyes, anything like that?"

Phillipa shrugged. "They were both dark, I think. I guess

I was so excited about the tickets I really didn't look. Then . . . then it's like what I said. He was just gone."

"Did he have an accent?"

Phillipa seemed to think about it. "Yeah . . . maybe. I think maybe he did."

"What kind?"

Phillipa shrugged. "I dunno . . . Spanish, maybe. At least it sounded like maybe it was Spanish."

"God, Paul, what's this all about?" It was Adrianna. She had come up behind Phillipa and had her hands protectively on her shoulders.

Devlin debated what he should say in his daughter's presence and opted for the truth. The more she knew, he decided, the safer she'd be. "The person who gave Phillipa those tickets just called me. He told me he'd like my detectives to ease up on our investigation. He made it very clear that he knew where I lived. Then he told me he hoped Phillipa enjoyed the concert."

"He *threatened* her?"

"Not in so many words. But, yes, it was a threat." He looked back at his daughter. "You and Joslyn did something very stupid," he said. "You've known about taking things from strangers—or even talking to them—since you were three years old." Phillipa started to speak, but Devlin held up a hand, cutting off any reply. "Now, I'm not sure if there's any real danger, or not. This . . . *person* . . . would have to be crazy to try anything with a police inspector's kid. But there are crazy people out there. So here's what's going to happen. Within the next hour there's going to be a patrol car parked in front of our building twenty-four hours a day, and it's going to stay there until this case I'm working on is over. There are also going to be two plainclothes detectives here in the morning. They are going to be with you everywhere you go. If you see this man again, you will tell them. Understood?"

He waited until Phillipa had nodded her head. "You will go *nowhere* without them. Do you understand?" Another nod. "Good. Now you can get yourself to bed and try and figure out some way to be a little smarter by morning."

As Phillipa headed for her bedroom, Adrianna came to him. "Paul . . . ?"

He placed his hands on her arms. "It'll be all right," he said. He glanced toward Phillipa's retreating back. "Maybe you better go with her," he said. "I came down pretty hard. She's probably a little shaky."

"Maybe we both should," Adrianna said. She said the words gently, knowing Phillipa was not the only one who was shaken.

Devlin lowered his eyes. He knew he hadn't handled the situation as he would have liked. "I'll be there in a few minutes. I have to make some phone calls to set things up."

*B*oom Boom called on his cell phone just before ten. Devlin answered, afraid it was yet another call from the Hispanic man.

"Bingo," Boom Boom said, when Devlin answered.

"I take it that means you found something," Devlin said. His heartbeat and respiration had slowed when he heard Boom Boom's voice, then increased again as he realized the possible meaning of the young detective's single word. It was not unlike a hunter who felt his quarry was about to walk into a clearing.

"It was just like you thought," Boom Boom said. "There was a very big and very secure file on Meyerson." He let out a little chuckle. "At least these humps thought it was very secure. Anyway, it gives all kinds of background about his affiliation with Opus Christi and the ties they have to the bank he works for. The bank, by the way, financed the deal when they bought that land up in Westchester. It was done the same way they financed their headquarters building here on Second Avenue; the bank made loans to companies that the order controlled. But the money eventually came home to Momma. All of it's made Meyerson a big cheese around here, no doubt about it."

"What else?" Devlin snapped.

"Oh, you want the good stuff too," Boom Boom teased.

"Don't play with me," Devlin warned. "Not tonight. Not unless you like the idea of dusting off your blue bag and working Staten Island for a long, long time." He quickly told Boom Boom about the phone call he had received.

"Jeez, I'm sorry, boss. But we got this bastard, I promise. Hey, you're gonna give me a medal, Inspector. Believe me, you will."

"Tell me, dammit."

"Okay, okay. Well, you were right about a tie-in to Meyerson's computer at the bank. It looks like he set it up about a year ago so he could access stuff from here without anybody at the bank knowing he was doing it. It was a bitch to crack into, but he forgot one little security step—"

"Get to the damned point," Devlin snapped.

"Okay, sorry, boss. There's a list of names in Meyerson's computer. And every priest who's been killed is on it. Plus the names of the other priests that you got from the archdiocese. Plus a couple of others we don't have on that list."

Devlin's heart was racing now. "Are there any priests on that list whose names come alphabetically before Father Janis, the one we're guarding now?"

"No," Boom Boom said. "He's the next guy on the list. Right before him is Father Halloran, the one we missed."

"I want all the names, fast. I want to set up a watch on all of them, just in case."

"No problem," Boom Boom said. "I'll download it on the office computer as soon as I hang up." He paused a few seconds, as if savoring his next words. "You wanna know how Meyerson found out about these priests?" he finally asked.

"That was going to be my next question."

Again, Boom Boom let out a soft chuckle. "Seems like Sharon was right about this central medical database that insurance companies use. It's sort of hush-hush. At least they don't talk about it a lot, like maybe they think the public wouldn't like it. But anyway, all the doctors and clinics who work for HMOs are required to feed in medical information about their patients. Then all the insurance companies can use it to help them decide if they wanna take a risk on covering somebody. Even when you get insurance for your car, you get checked to see if you've ever had any treatment for drugs or alcohol, or any kind of psychological problem that might increase the risk. Thing is, they sell that information to anybody who wants it: banks, credit card companies, whatever—anybody who wants to know just how healthy or reliable somebody is before they decide to lend them money, or cover his mortgage, or offer him a job, or whatever. It's fucking Big Brother with a stethoscope. And guess whose bank is a subscriber to this service?"

"Meyerson's."

"Big-time," Boom Boom said.

"And Meyerson used this outfit himself?" Devlin asked.

"You bet he did. He fed in the names of every priest in the archdiocese about six months ago. Got medical reports on each and every one of them. Must've cost him a nice piece of change. But he got what he wanted. Enough medical information to put together one very complete list of every priest who was ever treated for AIDS."

"You cross-checked the names?"

"From one list to the other," Boom Boom said. "Meyerson's our boy, boss. Maybe we can't prove he ordered the hits yet. But we sure as hell can prove he had the list."

"Download that, too," Devlin said.

"You got it." He paused a beat. "There's one other thing, too—another list that I can't make heads or tails out of."

"Tell me about it."

"Well, maybe it's real bank stuff, I dunno. It's a list of names and addresses, and next to each one is a date— pretty far back, like ten or even twenty years. And next to that is a dollar amount. Each amount is pretty heavy—the lowest is about twenty Gs, the highest over a hundred. It's like a list of people who owe money or are maybe getting it. There's nothing to say exactly what. But there's also nothing to indicate it's strictly bank business either, and I don't think it is."

"Why?" Devlin asked.

"It's just that it was hidden like the other list was— you know, like, to be sure nobody could stumble across it without the right password or codes. It just smells bad to me."

"You better send that too. We'll have Stan check it out." Devlin hesitated. "You still wearing that wire?" he asked.

"Yeah, I am."

"Then Stan already knows. He's monitoring you tonight."

There was no immediate response. Then Boom Boom pushed ahead. "Hey, Inspector, speaking of that, can I get outa this place now? These people are driving me nuts." He paused. "I mean, I really gotta get laid."

Devlin fought down a smile. "Give it another day. Just in case. I'll try my best to have you out of there by tomorrow night."

"Jesus."

"Just think about how restful it's going to be."

"Hey, boss, my pecker don't need the rest. This is an Olympian I got here."

"I'll try for tomorrow," Devlin said. "I promise."

**D**evlin was in bed when Ollie called an hour later. He sat up as soon as he heard Ollie's voice.

"Our boy's home," Ollie said, "but he just got himself a visitor."

"Who?" Devlin asked.

Ollie started to laugh. Devlin marveled at how much his men seemed to enjoy their work.

"Stop laughing and tell me," he snapped.

"A certain high-class hooker by the name of Ginger. I know her from another case I worked a few years back."

"You sure she went to visit Meyerson?"

"Oh, yeah," Ollie said. "Doorman told me she's a regular. Comes by at least once or twice a week." He chuckled again, seemed to realize it, and stopped. "I think our boy is trying to ease the tension by getting his goose drained. You want me to pick her up?"

"As soon as she walks out the door," Devlin said. "Then call me and I'll meet you at the office. I want to have a little talk with Ginger."

"Who's Ginger?" Adrianna asked, as Devlin slipped back between the covers.

He picked up the book he'd been reading when Ollie called. It was Stuart Kaminsky's *Blood and Rubles*. The older he got, the more Devlin identified with Porfiry Petrovich Rostnikov, Kaminsky's aging and always beleaguered Russian detective.

He had been reading it tonight to distract himself, to try to push away the threat that had been made against Phillipa.

"She's a high-class call girl who happens to be spending some time with our prime suspect," he said.

"So you're leaving soon to meet Ollie Pitts and a high-priced call girl?"

"Afraid so."

Adrianna turned to him, propped on one elbow. "You're lucky you have an understanding girlfriend," she said.

"I know I am." He also knew she was using it—playing this little game—to further ease the pressure she knew he was feeling.

Adrianna poked him in the ribs. "Just leave your wallet and credit cards at home," she said. "I'm not *that* understanding."

"I doubt if she takes credit cards," Devlin said, playing the game out, grateful for it. "Hooking is usually a cash-and-carry business."

She poked him again. "Leave them anyway."

"Yes, ma'am."

Adrianna nestled into the crook of his shoulder and ran her fingers through the hair on his chest. "You were great with Phillipa tonight," she said.

Devlin nodded, still doubting it was true. "I hope *she* thinks so," he said. "Maybe not tonight but someday. I just want to keep her safe, and I want her to grow up knowing how much I love her."

Adrianna put her arm across his chest and hugged him. "She will, and she does. More often than you let yourself think," she said.

*B*oom Boom was just getting ready for bed when the door of his room flew open and Thomas rushed in, followed by two large young men.

"Hey, what's goin' on here?" Boom Boom demanded.

Thomas smiled as his eyes flashed around the sparsely furnished room. "A little inspection, Ramon. I hope you don't mind." He spotted the Palm Pilot and cellular phone and went directly to them. "And what are these?" he asked, picking up the small hand-held computer.

"Hey, man, you know what that stuff is. You're not exactly a novice when it comes to technology." He offered Thomas a smile with the compliment, then put on the most innocent look he could muster, and added, "What is this?"

"Why do you have them?" Thomas demanded.

"It's for my job with the city. No big deal," Boom Boom said.

"But you're not supposed to have them *here*. No form of outside communication. You know that, don't you, Ramon?" Thomas was smiling coldly now, enjoying the power of the moment.

"Hey, I had to go out on a call to a city office in Brooklyn. I finished late and didn't go back to the main office, so I brought my stuff back with me. What's the problem?"

"The problem," Thomas said, pausing for effect, "is that I don't believe you. I don't believe you're who you say you are. I don't believe you've joined us out of a true spiritual conviction. I don't believe anything you say."

"Yeah? Well maybe I don't belong here then. So maybe I'll just pack up my stuff and blow this place."

The two large young men stepped in front of him as soon as he had spoken the words. Thomas's smile widened. "I don't think so," Thomas said. "At least not until we search your room and search you."

Boom Boom took a step back. "In a pig's ass you're gonna search me," he snarled. "Stan, get up here. Room Four-oh-five. Use the elevator on the left."

The words seemed to startle Thomas. "Who are you talking to?" he demanded.

"The fucking Holy Spirit," Boom Boom snapped. "Better watch out for bolts of fucking lightning, you piece of shit."

"Stop him," Thomas hissed.

The two young men moved in. The first one was on his knees almost immediately, as Boom Boom kicked him in the groin. The second threw his arms around the much smaller detective but went staggering back from a head butt to his nose. Boom Boom moved past them, heading for Thomas, and watched with satisfaction as he backed away.

"Time for *you* to turn the other cheek, tough guy."

But the man he had kicked proved less injured than he thought. He grabbed Boom Boom from behind, pinning his arms to his sides. Thomas stepped forward now, and Boom Boom lashed out with his foot, catching him squarely in the knee. Thomas howled in pain. Next Boom Boom brought his foot down sharply on the instep of the man holding him, and felt his grip loosen. He swung his arm back and pulled up his hand, grabbing the man's testicles. The man let out his own howl of pain as Boom Boom held on and kept pulling up. One final pull and the larger man collapsed to the floor.

Boom Boom moved back so he could keep all three in sight, then dug one hand into the waist of his baggy trousers and with the other pulled the small automatic from Sharon's garter holster.

"Freeze, you pricks," he hissed. From his back pocket he removed his shield and held it up. Slowly, taking pleasure in the stunned look on Thomas's face, he began to recite the Miranda warning.

"You're . . . you're . . . a cop?" Thomas's eyes were wide and horrified; his mouth hung open.

Boom Boom grinned at him. "This ain't a Boy Scout badge, hump."

The door flew open again and Stan Samuels filled the frame, his pistol held out in front of him in a shooter's stance.

"Hey, here's the Holy Ghost," Boom Boom said.

Samuels took in the room: Thomas still on the seat of his pants, holding one of his knees; a second man on the floor, his testicles cupped in both hands; a third, with blood dripping down his face. "I thought you needed help," he said, glancing at Boom Boom.

"I didn't know they'd turn out to be a bunch of pussies," Boom Boom said, grinning again.

"So whaddaya wanna do now?" Samuels asked.

"I wanna lock their sorry asses up for assaulting a police officer," Boom Boom said.

Samuels stepped over to him and leaned into his ear, still keeping an eye on the men in the room. "Let's check with the boss first," he whispered.

Boom Boom thought about that and grimaced. "Yeah, you're right," he whispered back. "He ain't gonna be happy. Lemme get my stuff and we'll get out of here. We can call him from the car, then come back for these humps if that's the way he wants to go. But first I gotta find Peter and tell him to get his ass out of here. These humps will go after him next."

"Do it," Samuels said. He turned back to the three injured men. "Don't even think about moving," he said.

"Hey, it's unethical for me to talk about my clients."

They were in Devlin's office, Ginger seated in a chair with Ollie, Sharon, and Devlin facing her.

Ollie let out a snort and leaned forward, bringing his big square head within inches of Ginger's. "What do you think you are, a fucking shrink?"

Devlin put out a hand, touching Ollie's shoulder. Sharon Levy sat to Ollie's right. Devlin had called her in, hoping her presence might help the interrogation.

"You've got two choices," Devlin said. "You talk to us or you spend the night in the tank."

Ginger stared at him, unmoved. She gave him a warm, inviting smile. "Maybe I should talk to my lawyer," she said.

Now it was Sharon's turn. "Hey, whatever makes you happy. The phone's on the desk. Call him." She paused a beat. "But when he comes, you won't be here, sweetie. And I think he might have a little bit of trouble finding you. We've lost a lot of people lately. Seems they get taken to one precinct for booking, then everybody finds out it's just too crowded so they get moved to another precinct, and somehow their paperwork gets misplaced, and their lawyers just go around in circles looking for them. By the time the paperwork gets found, they've spent an ugly, ugly night with some people you wouldn't want to meet in your worst dreams."

"You wouldn't do that," Ginger said.

Sharon placed a hand over her heart. "Me? Of course not. I would never do that to another woman. Unfortunately, I'm not the one who's gonna book you." She inclined her head toward Ollie. "He is. He's the one who brought you in. And Detective Pitts? Well, I'm afraid Detective Pitts is not a nice man."

Ginger glanced at Ollie, who gave her a toothy grin. She turned to Devlin. "You gonna let them do this?"

"I'm going home to bed," Devlin said. "I came down here to talk to you, but cooperation doesn't seem to be your thing. So I'm ordering you held as a material witness. Where you go is up to Ollie, here. He knows departmental regulations. I'm sure he'll follow them to the letter."

Ginger looked at Ollie again and got another grin. She looked up at the ceiling and rolled her eyes. "If Charles finds out about this, you guys are costing me an easy five hundred a week."

Ollie leaned in again. "You can kiss those five C-notes goodbye anyway, lover. Your boy Charles ain't gonna be around to pick up the tab."

"Tell us about Meyerson," Devlin said.

Ginger looked at him, then shook her head again. "He's weird. What else do you wanna know?"

"Tell us how weird he is," Sharon said.

Ginger let out an unladylike snort. "Tell you! Shit, I'll show you." She reached down and picked up her carryall, placed it on her lap, and opened it.

*T*he call from Samuels and Boom Boom came in just as they were sending Ginger on her way. Devlin listened quietly as Samuels put the best possible spin on it.

"Was Boom Boom hurt?" Devlin asked, when Samuels had finished. He listened again. "Okay, then, no charges. We'll hold the possibility of future charges over their heads, but to be honest I don't think the DA would touch it unless they threaten to sue the city." He listened again, his eyebrows rising, as Samuels explained about the condition of the three Opus Christi men. "Three guys, and Boom Boom cleaned house?" he said. "Sonofabitch." He shook his head and fought back a laugh. "Okay, both of you pack it in for tonight. But I need you here first thing in the morning to start on that new list Boom Boom found on Meyerson's computer. Make it early," he ordered. "And tell Boom Boom not to worry. Getting caught was always in the cards. One more thing. Did that kid Peter get out okay?" He listened to the affirmative response. "Okay, that's good. Both of you get some rest. I need you both sharp tomorrow."

When Devlin explained what Samuels had told him, Sharon stared at him in disbelief. "Boom Boom?" she said. "That skinny little shit kicked ass in a rumble with three guys?"

"Hey, he's a macho little guy," Devlin said, fighting off laughter.

"You know what this means, though, don't you?" Ollie chimed in.

"Yeah," Sharon snapped. "Now we'll have to listen to his bullshit about being a fucking superhero."

"No," Ollie said. "I mean with the mayor."

Devlin looked at him. He had already thought the same thing. "Yeah, I know what it means," he said. "Big-time."

# Chapter Nineteen

*F*ather Arpie and Father George sat together on a sofa in Howie Silver's office, looking, Devlin thought, like a pair of grand inquisitors. The mayor and Devlin sat opposite in two chairs, both very much hot seats at the moment.

"What you did, what your people did, was unconscionable," Father George said, his heavy jowls shaking with anger. "First you used deception to get inside our facility in Westchester County—which was out of your legitimate jurisdiction, I might add—and then you turned it into a shooting gallery that placed the lives of our people in serious jeopardy. Now we find out you also infiltrated our headquarters in New York and placed one of your men in a position to spy on our most sensitive computer files. But even that was not enough. When our people discovered your spy they were viciously attacked and held at gunpoint." He shook his head angrily. "I must tell you, Mr. Mayor, that I am astonished by these unwarranted Gestapo-like tactics, which I regard as a complete violation of our rights of religious freedom."

"I fully agree," Father Arpie chimed in. His face was red and angry—and just a bit pleased, Devlin thought.

The mayor turned to Devlin, his eyes pleading for something that would ease the situation.

"I don't agree," Devlin said.

Both clerics seemed surprised by the terse, unrepentant response.

"You *don't*?" Arpie said. His voice dripped with sarcasm. "Would you care to explain *why*?"

"I'd be happy to, Father," Devlin said. He leaned forward and raised one finger. "First, the man your people discovered in your headquarters was, as you say, a detective who worked for me. It is also true that he went there on my orders. But it is not true that he attacked your people. They in fact attacked him and he defended himself. We can prove it. He was wearing a wire—a recording device—for his own protection at the time, and we have both a tape recording of their attack and the testimony of the officer who was monitoring the wire to back that up." Devlin paused and looked at each man in turn. "That's a crime, by the way—assaulting a police officer—but it's something we don't intend to pursue . . . at present."

Both men had stunned expressions on their faces, and Devlin hurried on before they could regain their composure, raising a second finger. "Next, on the question of your Westchester facility. We repeatedly asked officials at Opus Christi headquarters to tell us where we could contact Sister Margaret. She traveled from Bogotá with Sister Manuela and was one of the last people to see her alive. It was imperative that we interview her. However, we were repeatedly told that Sister Margaret was not available, her whereabouts not known. All the while that information, we later learned, was right there in the order's computer files."

A third finger joined the first two. "Next, when we finally learned where Sister Margaret was—"

"And how did you learn that?" Father George demanded.

Devlin blew out a long breath, letting the priest know he did not appreciate the interruption. "The officer we placed in your organization found that information in your computer records."

"Private records, I might add," Father George snapped.

Devlin ignored the comment and went on. "That officer was brought into your organization *voluntarily* by one of your people, and there was no pressure, no threat of any kind, made against the person who brought him in. That officer was then assigned to your computer room by *you*. He never requested the assignment. His sole job from our standpoint was to see if he could learn where Sister Margaret was by talking with other members of your order. Any information he got from your computer system was purely accidental." He hurried on before Father George pressed the matter further.

"When we did learn where Sister Margaret was, Sergeant Levy and Detective Cunningham were sent to conduct this crucial interview. When they arrived at your Westchester facility, Sergeant Levy identified them as police officers, and a young nun let them in and told them where they could find Sister Margaret."

"Your sergeant told the nun she had been sent from our headquarters," Father George snapped. "A deliberate fabrication that violated our religious sanctuary."

"Not so," Devlin said, shutting him off. "Sergeant Levy—and this has been confirmed by Detective Cunningham—told your nun they were *from headquarters*, that's true. But she meant *our* headquarters." The lie flowed easily from Devlin's lips, so easily it almost surprised him. "Technically," he added, "we are a headquarters unit, even though we work directly for the mayor, so she was simply explaining where they were coming from." Again he hurried on before Father George could press the issue.

"And it was fortunate that we found out where Sister Margaret was and got there as quickly as we did. We've since learned that Sister Margaret was the only person who had seen Sister Manuela's killer—both in Bogotá and again when they returned to the United States. She was also the only person who knew that Sister Manuela left the airport with her killer. She could both identify him and testify to those facts."

Father George started to speak, but Devlin raised a hand, cutting him off. "This man, Emilio Valdez, was sent there to kill Sister Margaret. He had already attempted to kill Sergeant Levy because he feared she would reach Sister Margaret before he did. And if Sergeant Levy hadn't been there—and hadn't recognized him—there is no question in my mind that Sister Margaret would have been murdered."

Again, Devlin raised a hand, even though no objection had been made. "I would like to point out, gentlemen, that Detective Cunningham was wounded by this killer when he used his body to shield Sister Margaret. Frankly, I think you should be thanking both these brave officers, rather than condemning them for their actions."

"But . . . but . . ." Father George stuttered.

"No *buts* about it," Devlin said. He kept his eyes hard on the man. "This man, Valdez, works for a Colombian drug cartel. His sole job for them is killing people. We have this directly from Colombian authorities. Somehow, he got Sister Manuela to smuggle drugs into this country inside her body, and when that went wrong he killed her to recover those drugs."

"That's only supposition," Father George snapped.

"No, it is not, sir," Devlin countered. "It is a fact of forensic evidence—evidence, by the way, that up to now we have withheld from the media to protect the good name of your order and of the Catholic Church." Devlin paused, allowing the implied threat to linger in their minds.

"It is also a fact," he continued, "that had we known what we do now—that Sister Margaret could positively identify Sister Manuela's killer—we would have insisted that she be placed in protective custody, and this whole incident at your Westchester facility could have been avoided." Devlin hardened his stare. "Your organization kept that information from us and, in doing so, jeopardized that nun's life and put my detectives at risk."

"I . . . I . . ." Father George stuttered again.

Devlin jumped on him immediately. "What I want now," he said, "is the ability to protect Sister Margaret from another attempt on her life. Because these people won't stop. She's a threat to them, and in their minds that means only one thing: She has to be eliminated."

Father Arpie had been silent, avoiding Devlin's onslaught. Now a small sneer came to his lips. "You haven't done much of a job protecting the priests who are being murdered," he snapped. "Or have you placed a spy in the archdiocese as well to accomplish that end?" He turned to the mayor. "The inspector has a very facile tongue, but his tactics are still inexcusable. I think you know what we want, Howie."

Devlin turned to the cardinal's secretary before the mayor could answer. He kept his voice almost unnaturally soft. "The answer to your second question is no, Father. None of my men have been placed in the archdiocese. The answer to the first is that I expect to have those murders solved within days. Providing *you* continue to cooperate."

Arpie stared at him; he too was now flustered. "What are you asking?" he said at length.

"I'll contact you about that in the next forty-eight hours," Devlin said. "If you agree to do as I ask, we'll have the person behind those killings as well."

*W*hen the priests left, Howie Silver let out a long ragged breath. "You're a good tap dancer, Paul. I'm just hoping it's not all flash and no substance. If it is I can't back you." He gave Devlin a regretful look. "They want you off this case— the archdiocese and Opus Christi both. That's what they expected to get when they came here."

Devlin held his eyes. "I'm not walking away from the case, Howie, and I'll fight any attempt to force me out."

The mayor stared at him. "Don't threaten me, Paul. If I decide you're out, you're out. I can't excuse what you've done. It was a stupid move, and now it's coming back on me."

"It was the only option I had, Howie. You closed off everything else." He continued to hold Silver's eyes. "This case has become personal to me. I won't leave it without a fight."

The anger seemed to flow off Silver in waves. "Personal how?" he snapped.

Devlin told him.

"They threatened your daughter?" he said, when Devlin had finished.

"That's right, Howie." Devlin paused briefly, giving the mayor time to digest the information. "And I'm going to nail the sonofabitch who called me. It's the only way I can be sure my kid is safe. I intend to get them all, every last sonofabitch who's involved." He paused again, wanting his final words to weigh heavily on the mayor. "I'm going to do it, Howie, even if I have to fight *you*."

Devlin could see the political wheels turning in the mayor's head. It wasn't that Silver lacked concern for Phillipa. Devlin knew him better than that. It was just the way his mind worked. Like any politician, he was a survivor first and foremost, and this case was a time bomb. The mayor knew it, and Devlin knew it. If that bomb exploded it would tarnish everyone—especially a mayor who was publicly fighting with the cop he had put in charge of the investigation.

Silver sat back and let out a long breath. "All right, Paul. You've got forty-eight hours to make good on the promise you made to Arpie. Don't push it beyond that." He gave Devlin another hard, cold stare. "And don't ever threaten me again."

Devlin remained silent. He took no pleasure in the small victory. He also knew there still might be a price to pay down the road. He decided to give the mayor something to smooth his ruffled feathers and to keep his courage up. "There's something you should know," he said, "but what I'm going to tell you can't leave this room."

The mayor raised his eyebrows. "This better be good news, Paul. I'm not a very happy man right now."

Devlin held his eyes. "Valdez also killed the priests."

The mayor's jaw dropped. "You're sure?"

"We have his prints at the scene of the last murder, the one in Flushing. And I'm ninety-nine percent sure, when we start showing his photograph around, we're going to be able to place him at some of the others, too."

"Then it's wrapped up," the mayor said. A large smile creased his face. "We can tell the press we've got it locked up and get the archdiocese off our backs. How soon can we do that?"

Devlin raised a cautioning hand. "We can't. Not yet, at least. You've got to give me at least forty-eight hours before we say anything."

"Why?" Silver demanded. Like all politicians he wanted the heat off and the good news spread fast. And he couldn't wait to take his bows before the public.

"Because whoever sent Valdez to kill these priests is still out there. And we've got to nail him before he sends anyone else." Devlin had a plan for that, but it was something the mayor didn't need to know.

The mayor pondered what he'd been told. "So the killings are all connected," he said at length. "What exactly does that mean?"

Devlin had hoped he would not be asked that question. "It means a lot of bad news, at least as far as Opus Christi and the archdiocese are concerned."

The mayor's eyebrows furrowed. "Is there a way out of that?" he asked.

"I don't know," Devlin said. "We'll have to see how it shakes out. Here's what I think has happened."

He drew a long breath. "Somebody—I'm not sure who yet, but I'm getting close—made a deal with a Colombian drug cartel. The *deal* involved smuggling junk into the country in religious artifacts. The *payment* for that service was bumping off gay priests." Devlin shrugged. "Maybe this somebody was getting part of the profits from the drug shipments as well, but I don't know. It's something we're still looking into. It could have been a strictly service-for-service deal."

"But why, for chrissake?" the mayor demanded.

Devlin shook his head. "Opus Christi is supremely homophobic, from what I gather. They're fanatical about it. I think—at least for some person or group within their organization—that fanaticism simply went over the top."

The mayor closed his eyes, as if severe pain were suddenly coursing through his brain. "So how do you get to this person?" he finally asked.

Devlin told him.

"Jesus Christ," Silver said. "That's pretty goddamned Byzantine."

"It's complicated," Devlin conceded, "but if everything goes right, I think it will work."

"No deal," Devlin said. "I can't believe this guy. He shoots two of my people, and now he's looking for a deal."

Devlin was seated in a small office at the Brooklyn House of Detention with the assistant district attorney in charge of Sister Manuela's murder. William Gray was a sparrow-thin thirty-something man, and everything about him matched his name, right down to his perception of proper legal ethics.

Gray toyed with his thinning gray hair. He was dressed in a light-gray summer suit that seemed to have wilted on his way to work. His necktie was a mix of gray and white stripes. "Slow down, Paul," he said. "Let's not close this door too fast. Look, I'm not going to try to ride roughshod over you on this. It's too politically hot. But why not listen and see if what he has to say is worth anything?" Gray suggested. "At least then we know. If we don't get something we want, we tell him what he has to offer is shit. Thanks but no thanks."

"Uh-uh," Devlin said. "I want to talk to him, sure, but I don't want to offer him a thing. This guy killed a nun, period. And I'm ninety-nine percent sure he killed four priests. And when we nailed him he was trying to kill another nun. He also shot two of my cops. What kind of reduced charge could we talk about with this guy, being naughty? The press and the public would have us both for lunch, and they'd be right." He shook his head. "Besides, I like to be able to sleep at night."

Gray raised his hands. "All right. Have it your way. But I'm telling you right now, somewhere down the road we are going to plea-bargain this case." Gray jabbed a finger against the office desk. "I do *not* want to go to trial and present evidence about a nun swallowing fucking condoms filled with heroin. And I do *not* want to go to trial and present testimony about a priest who picked up AIDS in a Greenwich Village bathhouse." Gray tapped the side of his long nose. "And I'll tell you a little secret, Paul. The DAs in Brooklyn and Queens are not going to want to present that kind of evidence about the priests who got bumped off in *their* jurisdictions. We'd all like to have some kind of future, thank you very much."

Devlin grinned at him. "What, were you scared by some nun when you were a kid?"

"Ha-ha. Very funny," Gray said. "Like the boys up at the archdiocese don't scare a big bad police inspector like Paul

Devlin. Like Paul Devlin thinks they only call those boys the Powerhouse because they're trying to be clever. I tell you, my friend, those people eat their young. Fuck with them at your peril."

Devlin raised his hands. "I've already had a run-in with them. I also had a run-in with them a few years back. I'm not a novice at having my ass handed to me by fat old men in dresses. That's part of the reason I've been tiptoeing around them ever since this mess got dumped in my lap. I *knew* how they play the game. And I knew if I didn't watch my step I'd be out, and the case would get handed to one of the hear-no-evil see-no-evil clowns at the Puzzle Palace, because Howie Silver has been shitting bricks ever since he heard the word *archdiocese*."

"Howie Silver's a smart man," Gray said. "I hope you are too."

Devlin nodded. "Let's go talk to this little prick and see how smart I am."

*E*milio Valdez lay in a bed in the hospital wing. His lawyer, a public defender named Walter Shultz, sat in a chair at his bedside. This surprised Devlin. He had expected a high-priced narco attorney who would shut the door in the DA's face and then pull out his bag of expensive and time-consuming tricks. What Valdez had instead was a tired middle-aged guy in a rumpled suit, who looked like he hadn't slept in a year. He also looked like a lawyer who was very used to losing in court. On the surface, at least, it appeared as though the Colombians had kissed Emilio Valdez goodbye.

"So what have you got for us?" Gray began.

The public defender gave Gray a weary look, as though he knew he was wasting time he didn't have. "Mr. Valdez is fearful for his life," Shultz began. "He would like an opportunity to enter the witness protection program in exchange for information about Colombian drug dealers."

Gray smiled at the idea. "That's a nice thought. But your client is forgetting something, isn't he? We're here to talk about the murder of a nun, the attempted murder of two police officers, the attempted murder of a second nun"—he paused for effect—"and, according to what I've just learned from Inspector Devlin, the murder of four Catholic priests. All of which we believe Mr. Valdez was involved in. We're not even talking drugs here, except how they might relate to the murder of Sister Manuela."

Shultz turned to the bed and had a whispered conversation with his client. When he turned back the weary look had not improved. "Mr. Valdez says he's willing to talk about those things, but only after he's guaranteed immunity and has a written guarantee that he'll be placed in witness protection. He insists he has a lot to offer."

Devlin folded his hands across his chest. "Like what?" he asked. His eyes remained fixed on Valdez. "Are you going to tell us about Charles Meyerson?" He watched a twitch come to Valdez's eye. "Or maybe you're going to tell us about his little deal with your friend Estaves?" A second twitch. Devlin smiled at him. "But we already know those things. So what have you got to offer?"

Valdez stared at him. Devlin noticed his hands were now balled into fists. "I can testify," Valdez finally said.

Shultz turned to him, ready to warn his client not to speak—to let the attorneys do all the talking. Valdez held up a hand and waved him off.

"You'll testify against Meyerson?" Devlin asked. "That he set up the drug deal that got Sister Manuela killed?"

Valdez nodded.

"You'll testify that, as part of the deal, he wanted certain priests dead because they were homosexuals?" Devlin saw William Gray wince at the suggestion.

Another nod from Valdez. "I'll also testify that he got some of the profits and it wasn't no chump change."

Devlin nodded, storing away that unexpected bit of information. "You'll testify that you killed the priests—all of them—on his orders?"

Valdez shook his head. "I'm not gonna admit I killed nobody unless you promise I'm gonna walk," he said. "And until I walk I wanna be protected." He waved his hand, taking in the hospital cell. "Not like this shit here."

Devlin looked around the hospital cell. "This is the best we've got," he said. "You were supposed to go to the prison ward at Bellevue, but I vetoed that. The place is like a sieve. Here you're inside a secure prison." He inclined his head toward the door behind him. "You've got a solid steel door between you and the corridor, and two barred doors locking down both ends of that."

"It's shit," Valdez snapped. "Hey, I give you what you want, you give me what I want. It's simple."

Devlin smiled at him. "There *is* one thing I want. Maybe you can buy yourself something if you give me that. It involves my daughter." He waited, offering Valdez nothing more.

Valdez's face broke into a broad grin. "She got the tickets, huh?" he said.

Devlin stared at him, his eyes ice. "Tell me all of it."

Valdez shrugged, still grinning. "Hey, man, I don't know no more. I was supposed to do it—like, give the tickets to her, you know? But you busted me before I could."

"Who told you to give her the tickets?" Devlin asked.

"Hey, a little bird." He was smirking now.

Devlin turned to the door. "Let's get out of here," he said to Gray.

"Okay, okay," Valdez called, stopping him. "It was Estaves. He's the one who told me to give them to her. All right?"

Devlin looked back over his shoulder. "You gave me what I want, Emilio. We'll be back when I check it out."

Shultz joined Devlin and Gray out in the corridor. He was a soft, slovenly man who gave off the aroma of someone who knew he had chosen the wrong career. "I'm sorry," he said. "I told him it wouldn't fly, but he wouldn't listen. I do think he's desperate enough to give you whatever you want. He's convinced if he stays in prison, he's dead. What's this about your daughter?" he asked.

"Nothing you need to know," Devlin said. "It doesn't relate to any of the charges."

Gray put his arm around Shultz's shoulders and shook his head. "Look, I'm not going to kid you. The guy tells what he knows, he's a good witness. Maybe a perfect witness." He glanced at Devlin. "I'm just not sure we're going to need him." He shrugged. "But don't close the door. Maybe we'll be back."

Shultz seemed to sense a glimmer of weakness, something he was obviously not used to in his practice. He puffed himself up slightly. "I can't guarantee his offer will hold past today," he said.

Gray stepped away. "Listen to me, counselor. Your client is a first-class scumbag. I wouldn't count on his testimony until he gave it in court and then repeated it four times. And then I'd be worried he'd recant. So let's not even go near any so-called one-time offers, okay?"

$A$s they drove back to Manhattan in Devlin's car, Gray was still shaking his head. "Okay, now tell me what this stuff is about your daughter," he said.

Devlin told him.

Gray stared at him, incredulous. "This guy Estaves threatened a police inspector's kid? Who the fuck does this cowboy think he is?"

"He'll know who he is when I get my hands on him," Devlin said. He gave Gray a long look. "You still looking to make a deal with Valdez?" He tried not to laugh as he asked the question.

"Yeah, sure," Gray said. "I just can't wait to put that little shit on the witness stand. I can't wait to hear him tell a jury how he turned a little twenty-something nun into a fucking drug mule and then gutted her to get his product back. Or how he hooked up with some lunatic who hates priests who take it up the ass and how he offed them too. It'll make all the newspapers and all the networks; especially the part about how I gave him immunity. I'll have the biggest win of my career. Then, when it's over, I can start applying to dental schools."

"You should have listened to your mother and become a dentist years ago," Devlin said.

Gray turned to him, sneering at the suggestion. "And what did your mother want you to be, Paul?"

Devlin grinned back. "She wanted me to go to law school," Devlin said.

"So where do we go from here?" Sharon asked.

They were in Devlin's office, together with Ollie, Stan Samuels, and Boom Boom. Red Cunningham was gone for the duration, nursing his leg wound.

"First," Devlin said, "we need to find out everything we can about Charles Meyerson. Everything about his past, his present circumstances, right down to the type of toothpaste he uses." He turned to Samuels, "the mole." "I'm going to lay most of this on you, Stan. Use everything Boom Boom downloaded—everything about Meyerson that Opus Christi has on its computer and everything we found on Meyerson's computer—including that new list of people we don't know anything about yet. In the meantime, Boom Boom will keep searching both computers until they change the passwords." He turned to Boom Boom. "We need everything the bank has in its personnel records, no matter how insignificant it seems. In the meantime, Stan, use your connections at the newspapers and see what they have on Meyerson, then find some people who know him, both personally and from a business standpoint. See what *they* can tell us. We need to get a lot on him fast. We need to know what makes this guy tick, what buttons he has we can push." He smiled at his own language. "You got enough metaphors there to get an idea of what I want?"

"What about us?" Sharon asked, inclining her head toward Pitts.

"Ollie's going to arrest Estaves." He turned to Pitts. "Take some uniforms with you and bring him in."

"What's the charge?" Pitts asked.

"Conspiracy to commit murder, for starters. We'll add on other charges as we need them. Anything we can dream up to keep his lawyers hopping. When you bust him, grab any records you find in his apartment. I've arranged to have some narcs there with a search warrant. They'll also have one for his office, and they'll check that out after we bag him. I'm also asking our Colombian friend at the UN to get the feds involved if we need them. We want to be sure we can hold this guy for the next forty-eight hours before some sharp ambulance chaser cuts him loose. After that it won't matter. What I have in mind is going to have to work within that time frame, or it's not going to work at all." He held Ollie's eyes. He had already told all of them about Estaves's threat against Phillipa. "It wouldn't break my heart if this guy fell down a couple flights of stairs," he said.

Ollie grinned at him. "Hey, you know how these Colombians are," he said. "Clumsy little fuckers."

Devlin nodded and turned back to Sharon. "In the meantime, you're going to an impromptu press conference with me. It's time for you to become an official hero."

"Really?" Sharon said. "A real-life hero, huh? Long overdue, if you ask me. But maybe you should tell me why I'm a hero. Specifically, that is."

"We're going to announce the capture of a prime suspect in Sister Manuela's murder," Devlin said. He paused. "We're also going to tie him in to the murder of Father Halloran, and let the press know, without coming right out and saying it, that we believe he was involved in the murders of the other priests as well."

"I thought we didn't want to do that," Sharon said.

"Now we do. It's time to put a little pressure on Mr. Meyerson." Devlin leaned back in his chair and steepled his fingers in front of his face. He stared through them, as if looking into the future. "We're going to tie it all together: the attempted hit on you, the attempt on Sister Margaret, you and Red capturing Valdez in Westchester, the whole ball of wax. We're also going to tell them we've taken Estaves into custody as a possible co-conspirator."

"What about motive?" Sharon asked. "I mean, that's a little touchy . . . politically . . . right? What are we going to tell them about that?"

"We're not. But we'll imply very strongly that we've been dealing with a religious lunatic. We're going to give the press enough to run wild, while we go after the real lunatic."

Sharon smiled at him. "You're going to panic Meyerson. That's it, isn't it?"

"We're going to do more than that. We're going to make him believe that his big dream is evaporating. His plan to rid the archdiocese of gay priests is headed straight for the toilet, and there's nobody left to help him."

Sharon's smile widened. "You're going to ruin that poor man's day."

"Could be," Devlin said. "But that's just for starters. Charles Meyerson's life is about to become a real nightmare." He turned to Ollie again. "After you lock Estaves up I need you to make some phone calls to set up something else." And he explained what he wanted.

John Barger moved along the corridor with his medications cart, a corrections officer trailing closely behind. He was a large man in his mid-twenties, with a shaved head and a badly trimmed goatee. The medications he dispensed were nothing special, mostly Advil and other over-the-counter painkillers. There were also fresh dressings and a bottle of alcohol on his cart so bandages on wounds could be changed, all treatments that did not require the assistance of a doctor or a registered nurse. Barger was neither. He was a prisoner who, off and on, had spent a total of nine years behind bars.

Barger's criminal history went back to his early teens, when he had specialized in mugging elderly women who had just cashed their Social Security checks. Within a few years he had graduated to petty stickups and then to the street sale of narcotics. Soon he had expanded that business by running a handful of addicted whores. His "women"—mostly teenage girls—worked the low end of the trade, offering themselves on the dark, seedy avenues west of Times Square. Barger had killed two of those young prostitutes when they had failed to meet his financial expectations. He had also killed a rival pimp who had tried to lure one of his women away. He had beaten all three to death with a metal pipe. It was his preferred method of violence; he had often told other inmates about the pleasing sound the pipe made on the fourth or fifth blow—a soft wet splat, like hitting a ruptured melon.

Barger had never been charged with the three murders. NYPD investigations of crimes against prostitutes and pimps were cursory at best. His last arrest had involved an assault against an undercover cop, for which he had received a severe beating and a two-year sentence. Within months of his incarceration, the New York City Department of Corrections had decided to make him a trusty.

Barger moved down the hall, dispensing Advil and Tylenol through small openings in the solid steel cell doors. Most of the patient inmates on the hospital ward were ambulatory, those needing more serious medical attention being housed in the less secure prison ward at Bellevue.

The young thief, pusher, pimp, and murderer had come to the attention of Ricardo Estaves when he had put out feelers among the drug dealers housed in the prison. Using one of those men, he had offered Barger five thousand dollars, along with the guarantee of a job when he completed his current sentence. Barger had no idea who his benefactor was but had been assured by his fellow inmate that the offer was "money in the bank." He was also assured that the corrections officer now following him along the corridor had been paid "to take a walk" when they reached the cell occupied by Emilio Valdez.

*V*aldez lay on an ancient hospital bed that was bolted to the floor. Unlike beds used in regular hospitals, this one was raised and lowered with a hand crank at its foot. Since orderlies only visited the ward to deliver meals and medications, this meant that the position of his bed could be changed only at those times. Inmate patients could, of course, operate the beds themselves if they were physically able. Emilio was not. The hip-to-ankle cast he wore on his left leg, together with the pain in his smashed femur, made it impossible.

Now, as he lay in his eight-by-eight-foot cell, Emilio anxiously awaited the arrival of the orderly. He had been flat on his back since breakfast, when he had cajoled a corrections officer into lowering the bed again to ease the pain in his leg. Now his back was getting stiff from lying in a fixed position, and he wanted the bed raised to ease that pain.

Emilio heard voices outside his door, then a voice explaining that Emilio's cast had to be checked. He heard a key rasp into the lock and another voice saying that something had been left behind but the speaker would be right back.

When the door opened, only the orderly entered the cell. This was unusual, since a guard had always been present when anyone entered his cell in the past. Emilio, intent on the repositioning of his bed and the easing of his pain, paid no attention to that anomaly. He also failed to notice that the orderly had closed the solid cell door behind him.

"Hey, man, I need this bed up," Emilio said. "My fucking back is killing me."

Barger nodded and moved forward, the hint of a smile on his lips. He liked it when people trusted him. He liked the sense of power he felt when he knew he had fooled them into complacency. He liked it even better when they realized their mistake, that sudden awakening that came into their eyes just before the fear set in. He liked the fear, too, of course. That was always the best part, the icing on the cake—that and the cries of pain. The cries of pain were good, too.

"You want an aspirin or anything?" Barger asked as he reached the bed.

Emilio shook his head. "Just the fucking bed, man. My back feels like somebody hit me with a bat."

Barger placed a hand behind Emilio's head, raised it slightly, and removed the pillow. "It'll just take a minute," he said. He smiled. "They told me it should be fast. No unnecessary pain."

Emilio didn't seem to hear the words at first. Then they registered, and his eyes darted to the closed door. "What are you doin'?"

The sudden realization of what was happening came to his eyes now. Barger smiled again. Then the fear hit full force, and Barger's smile widened. He jammed the pillow down on Emilio's face and pressed his considerable weight against it. Emilio's body began to thrash wildly, and Barger placed a knee against his chest to hold him to the bed. Muffled cries came through the pillow; Barger wished he could hear them more distinctly. He couldn't tell if they were curses or a plea for mercy. He liked the latter better. The concept of mercy denied appealed to him.

After three minutes Emilio stopped moving, but Barger held the pillow in place for another thirty seconds, just to be sure. Five thousand bucks was a nice piece of change. So was the promise of a job with a major drug dealer. He didn't intend to screw up and lose either one of them.

Barger removed his knee from Emilio's chest and placed the pillow behind his head again. He used two fingers to close his partly opened eyes and rearranged the bedsheets. It was only then that he noticed he had an erection. Later, back in his own cell, he would think about the killing again and satisfy himself.

Barger left the cell and went back into the corridor to await the corrections officer, who was already headed back in his direction.

"Everything okay in there?" the officer asked, when he reached Barger.

"He's sleepin' like a baby," Barger said. "Didn't even have to give him a fuckin' aspirin."

The officer slid his key into the lock. "Let's finish this medications tour," he snapped. "I go off duty in half an hour, and I'm takin' my old lady out to look at new cars."

# *Chapter Twenty*

*T*he media were gathered in the press briefing room at One Police Plaza, an auditorium off the main lobby that was also used by the NYPD brass to host civilian awards ceremonies, high-profile promotions, and the presentation of service commendations and medals.

Devlin had planned a smaller event, but when he had informed the mayor what he was about to do, Howie Silver had insisted it be more high profile so he could make a personal appearance before the cameras.

Silver had also required the attendance of several chiefs, who would have preferred to be cleaning washrooms rather than take part in any event that acknowledged the achievements of Paul Devlin's squad. They were gathered in a grim line behind the mayor, who was flanked by Devlin and Sharon Levy, the designated hero of the hour.

The mayor began by announcing the arrest of Emilio Valdez, identified only as a Colombian national who was being held at the Brooklyn House of Detention pending arraignment. Valdez, he said, would be charged with the murder of Sister Manuela. He had also been connected to the death of Father William Halloran in the Flushing section of Brooklyn and was considered a prime suspect in the deaths of the three other priests. He also informed the press that a second man, another Colombian named Ricardo Estaves, had also been taken into custody and was being questioned as a possible co-conspirator. Additional arrests were also possible, he said.

When the mayor finished his announcement the press erupted with its usual cacophony of questions, and the mayor turned the briefing over to Devlin.

Laying it out much as he had with his staff, Devlin gave the press the high points of the various crimes, placing heavy emphasis on the attempted murder of Sergeant Levy and her subsequent capture of the suspect when he tried to murder a second nun. He also praised Red Cunningham, whom he credited with saving the life of the second nun by taking a bullet intended for her. Estaves, he said, was being questioned because of his known ties to Valdez, along with certain evidence gathered in the course of the investigation. Additional charges were being considered against both men, he said, adding that the police department, through the district attorney's office, would ask that each be held without bail when those charges were lodged against them.

The press erupted again, asking for more details about the murder of the four Catholic priests, but Devlin deftly sidestepped each query, claiming that the district attorney's office had asked that additional details of the crimes be withheld. He then redirected the press's attention to Sharon Levy, stating that she had agreed to give a full account of both the attempt on her life and the subsequent capture of Emilio Valdez in Westchester County. Previously the press had been told only that a "deranged man, dressed as a custodian" had opened fire at a religious retreat. Devlin apologized for "this ruse," as he termed it, but said it was needed to avoid alerting Estaves and other possible suspects.

"There was a little more to it," Devlin said, with a smile tinged with regret. "We just couldn't tell you about it until we had all the evidence in hand. Now we can. Or, rather, the very courageous Sergeant Levy can."

Sharon shot Devlin a look and stepped up to the bank of microphones. She was perfect for the role of reluctant hero. Tall, willowy, redheaded, and beautiful, only her automatic holstered at the waist gave any hint that she could also be a lethal adversary. The fact that she was a lesbian and one of the toughest cops on the force—with a mouth to match—was known only to her peers. Devlin wondered how the story would be played if the media, especially the tabloids, were to find out.

Standing before the microphones, Sharon played her part as the demure woman detective who had twice faced death at the hands of a deranged religious fanatic. She declined to speculate on the motivation of either suspect, insisting that any comments she might make could jeopardize the district attorney's case.

But the press seemed satisfied. The story had everything they required—murder, madness, and a cop who looked like a photographer's model to provide "art" for their copy. When they left the auditorium, Devlin had what he wanted: news accounts certain to shake up Meyerson, and the media off on a tangent that would give him the time he needed to play out the rest of his script.

That plan took a major hit before he reached his office, when the mayor's voice crackled over his cell phone. "Get the hell over here quick." Silver paused as though fighting hyperventilation, then added, "I just got a call from Corrections. They just found Valdez dead in his cell."

*H*owie Silver paced his office like a caged cat. "So where the hell does this leave us?" he demanded. He glared at the corrections commissioner, who except for Devlin was the only other person in his office. "I just get through taking bows for what my cops did, and now I've got shit all over my shoes for what my Corrections Department *didn't* do— keep a goddamn killer from getting knocked off in one of my prisons. Explain this to me, please."

"It's bad, but maybe we can get around it," Devlin said, before the corrections chief could respond. He didn't want to waste time with recriminations.

Both men turned to him, expectantly.

"How many people know Valdez is dead?" he asked.

"Only a handful. We haven't even moved his body. In fact, we haven't even gotten a forensic team into his hospital cell," the commissioner said. He was a nondescript middle-aged politician, an African-American who had come up through the ranks of the party machine. He had no idea how a prison should be run—let alone a murder investigation—but was smart enough to accept the advice of professionals when decisions had to be made.

"You let us handle that," Devlin said. "We'll get them in quietly, dressed as corrections officers. As far as anyone else is concerned, Valdez isn't dead. He was attacked but he survived, and he's being moved to the Bellevue prison ward for treatment. Fortunately the ME's office is right next door, and we can slip the body in there without anybody knowing the difference." He looked hard at the commissioner. "But you've got to sit on your people. Every one of them who knows the truth has got to keep his mouth shut. I need forty-eight hours, maybe less, but if this gets to the media I'm dead in the water."

Silver glared at his commissioner. "Can you at least do that?" he snapped. Then he turned to Devlin. "What the hell are you planning?" he demanded.

"You don't want to know," Devlin said. "But if it works, we'll be out of this thing clean."

"Politically clean?" There was open wariness in the mayor's eyes.

"As clean as possible," Devlin said.

Silver's eyes narrowed. "I'm not sure I like the way that sounds," he said. "We can't afford any more trouble with the archdiocese. I am *not* going to let those people take me down. Remember our meeting. The clock is ticking. Understood?"

Devlin arched his eyebrows. "I'll do the best I can, Mr. Mayor. Let's put it this way. If it doesn't work, I know we're in a pile of shit. I also know what it means for me."

"Also understand it's not something I'll want to do," Silver said, "but I will. So don't make any more mistakes, Paul. Make sure this time it's clean. Not just as clean as possible. Clean."

"I'll do my best," Devlin said. "Let me get out of here so I can make it work."

"So where do we go now?" Sharon asked, when Devlin returned to his office and told the team about Valdez.

"We move everything up twenty-four hours." He turned to Ollie. "Have you set things up the way I told you to?"

"Everything will be in place by seven tonight," Pitts said. "Oh, by the way, Estaves is in the prison ward at Bellevue. Silly bastard tried to make a run for it when I collared him." He shook his head. "Fell down and broke his fucking leg. Sorry about that. I should have been more careful with him. Never thought he'd make such a dumb move."

Devlin fought off a smile. "Pity," he said, "but it can't be helped." He turned to Stan Samuels. "What did you come up with on Meyerson?"

Samuels was also fighting off a smile. He picked up a long yellow legal pad, several pages of which seemed filled with copious notes, and turned serious. "This is a silver-spoon guy," he said. "What I got came from half a dozen different places, but it all paints pretty much the same picture. Boom Boom really milked the Opus Christi computer and the one at Meyerson's bank, and there were some articles about the guy in the *Wall Street Journal,* the *Times,* and *BusinessWeek*. I also got some background from his old college roommate, who doesn't seem to like our boy very much, some business people who feel pretty much the same, and oddly enough from his aunt, his mother's sister, who likes him even less."

Devlin had been making some rapid notes. Now he looked at Samuels. "That's quite a bit of contact in a short time. You find out what toothpaste he uses?"

Samuels kept his usual stoic expression. "Crest," he said.

Devlin laughed. He was reasonably sure "the mole" wasn't joking. "So give us a thumbnail, and go as heavy as you can on things that tell us where this guy is coming from."

Samuels flipped some more pages. "Our boy comes from what my Jewish mother would call 'a family that is very secure financially.' Big bucks on his mother's side. I mean not just comfortable. These people were so comfortable they were almost asleep." Samuels flipped another page. "Meyerson's father left when he was five. According to the aunt, the sister married beneath her, realized it, and tossed the guy out. Funny thing is, no other guy came knocking on her door after that, despite the big bucks. Auntie moved in, then later another woman named Christine Moore. All of them living there with our boy, all of them, from what I can get, pretty dominant women."

"You get anything that indicated they were gay?" Sharon asked.

Samuels shook his head. "Nothing at all. But they weren't women who were enamored of men."

Ollie Pitts grunted. "What the hell does that mean? Women who weren't *enamored* of men? You saying they were man-haters?"

Again Samuels shook his head. "No, I'm not. I got nothing to indicate they were lesbians, or man-haters, or anything like that. According to the sister, they didn't need them and didn't want them around."

"Maybe they were just smart," Sharon said, grinning.

Devlin held up his hand. "Okay. Okay. Let's get back on track here. What else, Stan?"

Samuels flipped some more pages. "Anyway, Charles got shipped off to boarding school at seven, and pretty much saw his mother and aunt only on holidays. They even sent him to a fancy boys' camp every summer. Then, when he was thirteen, his mother had a religious epiphany."

Again, Ollie interrupted. "A what?"

"She suddenly got religion, big-time," Samuels said. "Trotted down to church every day with her rosary."

"That's better," Ollie groused. "Speak fucking English, will you?"

Samuels glanced at Devlin.

Devlin rolled his eyes. "Go on, Stan."

"Okay. At that point Meyerson was going to Phillips Exeter, a pretty upscale boys' prep school, but his mother decided to pull him out and put him in Saint Anselm, an equally pricey Catholic boarding school. She did send him to Yale after that—it was sort of a family thing to go there—but apparently religion stuck with Meyerson. His roommate at Yale says he was very big in the Cardinal Newman Club and was always bugging people about their morality. This could have been sour grapes on the roommate's part, because Meyerson was also a member of Skull and Bones,

Yale's very exclusive secret society. His maternal grandfather and great-grandfather were in it before him, but even that family connection isn't enough to get you in. It helps, but if you're a real loser the door shuts on you pretty fast, so Meyerson must have had something going for him."

Samuels flipped some more pages in his notebook. "Anyway, Skull and Bones was a key factor in the big banking job he walked into when he graduated. His grades didn't hurt either. This guy is one very smart cookie. Started pretty high up the ladder and has gone even farther on his own ever since. He's a legit expert on foreign banking and currencies, and even his business enemies say that on any given day he's got the economies of half the world's nations floating around in his head, right down to the nickel. So nobody takes him lightly when it comes to international banking. They just don't like him."

"What about Opus Christi, where does that fit in?" Devlin asked.

Samuels searched his notes, stopping when he had found the right page. "Early in his banking career, Meyerson did a stint in Europe—first Madrid, then Rome. He got tied into Opus Christi in one of those places—I really can't pinpoint which—but I know he was pretty well placed in the order when the Banco Ambrosiano scandal hit. One business adversary claims he played a key role in the bailout of the Vatican Bank—the deal that gave the order its personal prelature. Right after that, according to Opus Christi computer records, he was ordained as a priest. There's no record of his ever going through any formal training. It looks like it was a reward, or something, for what he did."

"It's not supposed to work that way, is it?" Sharon asked.

"Not according to anything I've ever heard," Devlin said. "But this is a strange group. They seem to be a religion within a religion."

"Anyway," Samuels continued, "when he got back to the States he played a big part in financing the order's move to this country. His bank holds a lot of paper for these people, and according to the order's records he's donated a good chunk of money to them as well." He glanced at Devlin. "Serious money," he said. "We're talking high six figures."

"So he's got his own dough," Devlin said. "He lives like he does, so you'd think so, but you can never tell how much is really behind the flash."

"He's got it," Samuels said. "His mother died five years ago. Up till then Meyerson lived with her. He'd moved back into the old lady's brownstone on East Fifty-third after he graduated from Yale, and again when he came back from his stint in Europe."

"The other women still there then?" Devlin asked.

"Oh, yeah," Samuels said. "But not anymore."

"What happened?"

"The old lady's will divided her estate into thirds, after leaving a chunk to the Catholic church. One third went to Meyerson, one third to her sister, the aunt, and one third to her friend Christine Moore." Samuels flipped to another page. "Meyerson was pissed about the will, and according to the aunt hired an attorney to break it. But the mother had had a better lawyer. The way it was set up, Meyerson couldn't do a thing. He did get the Fifty-third Street house, though, so he threw the other two old babes out and sold it."

"Vindictive little prick," Sharon said.

Samuels shrugged. "He thought he got screwed." He smiled. "Only ended up with about ten mil, plus the couple he got for the house."

"Poor baby," Sharon said.

"Hey, this is a guy who knows money," Samuels said. "Picking up ten million when he expected thirty didn't exactly bring a smile to his face."

"Did the old lady give any money to Opus Christi?" Devlin asked.

Samuels shook his head. "Not according to their records. And the aunt told me the old lady didn't approve of them. Called them a bunch of Catholic Moonies."

"Even though her boy was a big shot?" Sharon asked.

Again, Samuels shook his head. "To that old broad, big shots only included presidents and popes. Everybody else was an employee."

"But Meyerson was definitely a wheel in the order, right?" Devlin asked.

"Oh, yeah," Samuels said. "Right up at the top they know our boy Charles. Hell, the boys in the Vatican know him." Samuels paused. "There's one other thing. I checked this list of people Boom Boom came up with. I'm not sure how it fits in, but it may explain why the archdiocese is backing these Opus Christi clowns."

"Spill," Devlin said. "I can use anything I can get on the archdiocese right now."

Samuels flipped a few more pages. "I talked to everybody on that list, the one with names and addresses and dollar amounts next to them. All these people were in foster care, or orphanages, or group homes when they were kids, and in each case those places were run by Catholic Charities of New York. Also in each case, these people claim they were subjected to physical or sexual abuse, and each one filed a claim against the archdiocese within the past year. They're all adults now; these are old cases. They happened a long time ago, and most of the priests and nuns involved are long dead or at least retired. But it would still have been a big scandal, and these people who were supposedly abused were threatening one big-assed lawsuit if the archdiocese didn't pay off." Samuels stopped and smiled. "And guess who contacted each of them and negotiated an out-of-court settlement?"

"Meyerson," Devlin said.

"You got it. Paid them off personally with cashier's checks written on his own bank. Funny thing is, no money came out of his personal accounts when those checks were written. I know that for a fact. I had Boom Boom check them all. But somehow he paid all these people off. So suddenly we have no more threats against the archdiocese. No more impending lawsuits." He cocked his head to one side. "Hell, who knows, maybe that's how our boy got that special invite to the installation of the new cardinal," Samuels added.

Sharon eyed Devlin. The others followed her gaze. "You thinking what I'm thinking?" she asked. "That our boy used the drug money he got from Estaves to buy his church out of a little scandal?"

Devlin nodded. "And then decided to make sure it didn't happen again, by knocking off priests he considered a risk."

"What about the heterosexual priests?" Sharon asked.

"He had no way to find them," Devlin said. "Not anybody who might be doing the same thing today, anyway. As far as the old priests and nuns who might still be alive, he couldn't just ask the archdiocese for *their* names. He'd become a prime suspect if somebody started knocking *them* off."

Sharon nodded. "But the gay priests were threatening his church with a different type of scandal, because all of them had AIDS." She shook her head. "I dunno, boss. This guy may be a lunatic, but he's also carrying some heavy weight with the archdiocese, and that makes him a dangerous guy to go after. Especially the way we plan to nail him."

Devlin considered her words. "I don't think so," he said. "I think Mr. Meyerson may have given us a way to get the archdiocese off our backs. Or at least decide to turn their backs on their Opus Christi friends until they see which way this is all going to fall out." He thought about that for a moment. "I think I'll pay Father Arpie a little visit, before we make our move against Meyerson, and see what he thinks." He looked at each of the detectives in turn. "As far as Meyerson goes, I don't think we have any other way to nail him, other than the one we've worked out. Estaves won't rat him out. He knows we don't have enough on him, personally, to do more than push for deportation. Valdez was the only one who could finger Meyerson, and I wasn't willing to cut a deal with that murderous little prick." He gave them a wan smile. "I don't think the DA really wanted him after he found out what he was going to say. But it's a moot point, anyway. Valdez doesn't figure in anymore, except as a way to push Meyerson the way we want him to go. As long as he thinks he's still alive, we can use him."

"Maybe we should have cut a deal," Samuels said. "If you're wrong about how the archdiocese is going to react, your ass is really on the line this way."

Devlin pondered Samuels's words. He knew they weren't intended as criticism, only concern for the potential political quagmire that lay ahead. "Maybe," he said. "All of our asses are on the line on this one. Maybe I was thinking too much about my kid. Maybe I should have pushed to have Valdez handed over to the witness protection program and put him where Estaves couldn't reach him. But it's too late now."

"Don't second-guess yourself, boss," Ollie snapped. "The scumbag shot two cops. You don't make deals with assholes who shoot cops. And as far as protecting your kid goes, nobody's gonna question that."

Devlin smiled at the words. It was typical cop. In the poker game of life, two wounded cops beat four murdered priests and a murdered nun anytime. And a threat against a cop's family trumped everything. "Too late for second guesses anyway," he said.

They were all quiet for several moments.

Sharon finally broke the silence. "So now we go after Meyerson."

Devlin nodded. "First I'll pay a little visit to Father Arpie. Then we go after our boy. I want you with me for both," he told Sharon. "I want a witness for my conversation with Arpie. As far as Charles Meyerson goes, you're the one who took Valdez down. I want Charlie-boy to see the woman who ruined his little game. I think you being there might push him the way we want him to go. Especially if we script it the way I have in mind."

Devlin turned to Ollie. "You go and set everything up." Then, to Samuels: "I want you and Boom Boom on Meyerson. Stay on his tail. I want to know everything he does, every place he goes. Make sure your cell phones are charged so you can tip me about it step by step. And stay close. If we need you, we're gonna need you fast." Devlin hesitated, thinking over everything he had told them. "I guess that's it," he said. "Let's do it."

## Chapter Twenty-one

*F*ather James Arpie stared at Devlin and Sharon with horrified eyes. His mouth moved for several seconds before any words finally emerged.

"Narcotics? You're sure?"

Devlin folded one leg over the other and answered slowly, keeping his voice soft and confident. "We know Meyerson was paid off for helping ship drugs into the United States. The shipments came into the country in religious artifacts that supposedly belonged to Opus Christi. We also know those payments came directly from the drug dealers. In addition, we know the money was never deposited in any of Meyerson's accounts. And we also know that Meyerson personally paid off every person who had made a claim against the archdiocese. He made those payments with cashier's checks written on his own bank. I don't think it will be very hard to show where that money originated."

Arpie began to stutter. "We . . . didn't . . . know . . . any of this."

"Did you ever question where the money was coming from?" Devlin asked.

Arpie stared at Devlin. "No. There didn't seem to be any need. The problem with those people . . . the fact that we could end it . . ." His eyes took on a pleading quality. "We knew Charles, knew he was a good Catholic." His final words seemed to come back at him like a slap to the face. "Certainly you don't think we would have accepted

the money if we knew it came from something so . . .
so . . . ?"

"Of course not," Devlin said. He paused. "But that doesn't
change the facts. And it certainly offers no guarantee what
other people—people not friendly to the Roman Catholic
Church—will think."

Arpie straightened in his chair and fought to put some
force in his voice. "I insist that you protect us from this. We
were innocent of any knowledge. We were—"

Devlin's voice became sharper. "You're not in a position
to insist on anything, Father," he snapped. He let the statement sit for a moment, then softened his voice. "But I'll do
everything I can . . . providing you help me."

Arpie stared at him. He began to stutter again. "This . . .
is . . . this . . . is—"

"A request for help," Devlin said, cutting him off. "That's
all, Father. Just a request for help." He turned to Sharon.
"Isn't that how you understand it, Sergeant?"

"Oh, yeah," Sharon said. She looked at Arpie and smiled.
"That's all it is, Father. A request for help. So help me, God."

Arpie's face reddened; then he seemed to get control of
himself. He turned to Devlin. "What do you need?"

"First I need you to call the mayor and back off on all
your earlier threats." He waited until Arpie had nodded
agreement. "Then I want you to call a couple of your
parishes. And this is what I want you to tell them."

*R*asheed O'Neil stood in the lobby of Meyerson's building
like a block of black granite. When he saw Devlin and
Sharon approaching the front door, he stepped out onto the
sidewalk to meet them.

O'Neil was a first-grade detective out of Midtown South
who was closing in on his thirty years. Devlin had worked
with him as a rookie detective, and when he needed additional manpower to keep Meyerson under surveillance,
Rasheed was the first to come to mind.

"You see our boy?" Devlin asked. There had been no
handshakes, no outward sign that they knew each other, just
in case anyone was watching.

"He's up in his apartment," O'Neil said. "Came in about two hours ago. Kept lookin' over his shoulder like he expected somebody might be right behind him." He gave Devlin a big-toothed grin. "Spotted me and wanted to know who I was; where was the regular doorman. I just give him my 'Yes, massa' smile, an' tol' him I was fillin' in because the regular dude was sick."

"He seem to buy it?" Sharon asked.

O'Neil turned his toothy grin on Sharon. "Hey. Who's gonna doubt an honest-lookin' guy like me?"

"I saw you coming down the street I'd head the other way," Devlin quipped.

O'Neil's grin widened. "I get that sometimes. Usually from chickenshit white boys. No offense intended, Inspector."

"No offense taken, Rasheed." Devlin looked down the street. It was seven in the evening, and the traffic along Central Park West was heavy. Rasheed, as directed by Devlin, had blocked off a parking space twenty feet from the front entrance with orange traffic cones, so Samuels and Boom Boom would have a place to set up for their tail. Rasheed also had a radio so he could alert them when Meyerson left the building.

"When he leaves, after you alert our unit," Devlin said, "I want you to use your passkey and check his apartment. Then call me and let me know if anything looks out of place. Okay?"

"No problem," Rasheed said. "You want me to stay after he bugs out?"

Devlin nodded. "Just in case things don't work the way we hope they will, and he heads back here."

"You got it," Rasheed said. He grinned at Devlin. "You come a long way since you was that little-squirt detective used to tag along behind my big black ass."

"That's little-squirt detective, *sir*," Devlin said.

"Oh, yeah. I forgot," Rasheed said. He gave Devlin a serious fatherly look. "Watch your ass with this dude, Paul. He got that look in his eye. Like a real crazy scared motherfucker."

"I'll watch him," Devlin said.

Rasheed turned to Sharon. "You too. Don't trust him for a minute."

"I never do," Sharon said.

*I* don't like to be disturbed at home," Meyerson said, when he opened the door to his apartment. He was dressed in a white collarless shirt that seemed almost clerical, black slacks, and shoes. He was surprised to find Devlin and Sharon facing him across his threshold. From what the doorman had said, he had expected two uniformed officers, not detectives, and certainly not the police inspector who had interviewed him at his office. He attempted to hide his surprise with feigned annoyance. Inside, his stomach was churning.

The nervousness was not lost on Devlin.

When Rasheed had buzzed Meyerson's apartment to tell him that two police officers wanted to speak with him, Meyerson had initially claimed he was too busy. Rasheed, experienced in such games of avoidance, had told him the police insisted it was urgent and were coming up anyway, and there was nothing he could do to stop them.

They were pushing him, keeping him off balance, making him feel everything was moving quickly out of his control. It would get worse.

"It will only take a few minutes," Devlin said. "You can refuse to let us into your apartment—it's your right—but we still have to talk to you. We'll just have to do it at the nearest precinct."

Meyerson glared at him, but Devlin knew it was all bluff. "Do I need my attorney?" The question came out with a sneer: more bravado.

"It's not that kind of talk," Devlin said. "If it were I would have read you your rights as soon as you opened the door. But, again, it's up to you."

Meyerson glanced past Devlin. "Who's this?" he demanded, raising his chin toward Sharon.

"This is Detective Sergeant Sharon Levy," Devlin said. "She's the lead detective in the Sister Manuela murder investigation."

Meyerson stared at Sharon without expression. It was the

woman he had sent Valdez to kill, the homosexual filth who . . . who . . . who had destroyed everything he had planned. He fought down his anger and revulsion. "I read about you in tonight's newspaper," he said. "You seem to be the hero of the hour."

Sharon remained silent, just stared him down.

The lack of response seemed to unnerve Meyerson, and he turned abruptly and started back into his apartment. "You may as well come in," he said, almost as an afterthought.

Sharon preceded Devlin into the spacious living room, turning in a slow circle, taking everything in as though looking for some treasure she might want to buy. The act seemed to annoy Meyerson, and he pointed to a large sectional sofa and suggested they sit.

"I hope we can do this quickly," he snapped, as he took a seat across from them.

"As quickly as we can," Devlin said, unperturbed. He crossed his legs, holding one knee with both hands. "As I told you earlier, we've arrested Sister Manuela's killer," he began. "A Colombian named Emilio Valdez."

Devlin watched Meyerson's face as he spoke. The blue eyes remained cold and unmoved, but a slight tic hit one corner of his mouth at the mention of Valdez.

"I'm pleased you solved the case," Meyerson said.

"Oh, it's not wrapped up yet," Sharon interjected. "That's why we're here." She paused, letting Meyerson sweat the words, wondering if the other shoe, when dropped, would be for him.

Devlin picked up the next line they had loosely scripted. "We know Valdez did the murder. The evidence is all there," he said. "We also know he was involved in the Colombian drug trade. He was heavy muscle for a drug lord named Chavarría. Here in the States he took his orders from one of Chavarría's top people, guy who runs a phony import business in the city, goes by the name of Ricardo Estaves. We've got him locked up too."

"We've got him solid on a couple of things," Sharon said. "We expect we'll have a lock on conspiracy to commit murder in the Sister Manuela case in just a few more days." She gave Meyerson a small, knowing smile. "Seems he made a serious mistake, really blew it. Tried to have Valdez killed in the Brooklyn House of Detention but didn't quite get the job done. Now Valdez knows he's a dead man as far as his drug bosses are concerned, and his lawyer has told us he's ready to sing as soon as the DA cobbles a deal."

Devlin leaned forward. "That's why we're here, Mr. Meyerson. We need to ask you some questions that might clear up a loose end we can't seem to crack."

The tic was jumping at the corner of Meyerson's mouth, and he raised a hand, rubbing the spot lightly to conceal it. "I'll do what I can, of course. But I really don't know much about this matter."

"It's Sister Manuela we need help on," Sharon said. "Valdez has been hinting things. Things about the drug shipments he was bird-dogging." She paused, then looked to Devlin as if concerned she might be saying too much. Devlin nodded his okay for her to continue.

"Valdez has been jabbering about religious artifacts being brought into New York. This makes sense, of course, with a nun being involved." Sharon held up her hands. "Maybe two nuns. He did try to kill the other nun who was traveling with Sister Manuela, so we've got to think maybe he was trying to shut her up." Sharon shook her head. "What we can't figure is how these two nuns got involved. Sister Margaret insists she knows nothing about the drugs—and to be honest, I believe her. But that leaves us with Manuela, a twenty-two-year-old woman who worked for a bank and then joined a religious order. So we're asking ourselves: What's her motive? Obviously she didn't care about money. If she had, why not stay at a bank? Helluva lot more chances to be dishonest there than a convent. And if she were mixed up with drug dealers back when she worked for you, a bank would be a great place to be. Drug lords are always looking for connections in banks to launder their money."

Meyerson stiffened visibly. "I assure you, Sister Manuela was doing nothing of the sort when she worked for us."

Devlin raised a hand. "And I assure you, we have nothing to say she was." He shook his head. "But something was going on with this woman. Somehow this Valdez had enough of a hold on her to get her to swallow condoms filled with heroin. You only do that sort of thing for two reasons, greed or fear. I mean, it's hard to imagine some nun being convinced she's gotta do something like that for some greater good, right?"

The tic at the corner of Meyerson's mouth was flying again. Devlin decided to turn the pressure cooker up one more notch.

"Then we've got the fact that Valdez was behind the murder of four priests. Were they involved in this drug business?" Devlin dismissed the rhetorical question with another shake of his head. "The only connection between the four of them that we can find—" He stopped, leaned forward to make his words more intimate, and then continued. "This has got to be kept in this room. Okay?" He waited again as Meyerson nodded. "The only connection we can find is that all these priests were gay, and all of them had been diagnosed with AIDS. So how does this fit? Did Sister Manuela facilitate this drug shipment as a price for getting these priests knocked off? And, if so, why would Valdez still murder them after he had already killed her?"

"There's got to be someone else involved," Sharon interjected. "Somebody who was using Manuela. Somebody who had the power to do that."

"And that's why we're here," Devlin said, picking up the thread of their script. "Do you know anyone who had that kind of influence on her, anyone who could have exerted the kind of pressure needed to get this nun to play mule for a group of scumbag drug dealers?"

Meyerson was momentarily unable to speak. Everything he had done, everything he had planned was coming back at him from the mouths of these . . . people . . . these police officers. He felt shattered, defeated. All he wanted was to rush to his cell, his sanctuary, and pray to God for deliverance. He looked up at Devlin and shook his head. "I didn't know anything about this woman's private life," he said. He wanted out of here, *now*. "She was just . . . just an employee."

"Damn," Sharon said. She shook her head, imitating

Meyerson. "We were hoping you might have something we could use to get a handle on this last piece of the puzzle. Well, at least one good thing is coming out of it."

Meyerson stared at her, confused. "I don't understand."

"The priests," Sharon said. "There were more than just four on Valdez's list. At least the others are safe now." She paused for effect. "And the way it's working out, it may end up being a good thing for the archdiocese—for the church, even."

Meyerson's confusion deepened. "I don't understand what you're saying. Are you saying these deaths were a good thing for the church?" A hint of suspicion came to his eyes as they darted back and forth between Sharon and Devlin.

"No, of course not," Sharon said. "The fact that it's over—that these other priests are safe—that's good. But it's also done something else. It's given these other priests, the ones who are safe now, the courage to do something that might help their church."

"And what is that?" Meyerson snapped. He was having trouble controlling his emotions now, and he struggled to keep himself in check.

She glanced at Devlin, then shrugged. "Well, it won't be a secret much longer, so I guess I can tell you. These priests—the surviving ones, I mean—have decided to out themselves. They're going to make their homosexuality public. They're even going to acknowledge that they contracted AIDS when they . . . when they"—Sharon waved her hand in a small circle—"sinned, I guess you'd say."

Sharon watched Meyerson struggle against his anger. She could almost see the outrage boiling up inside him, see him fight to keep the words down, words that might give away his hatred of those men.

Devlin saw it too and pushed ahead, twisting the knife even deeper. "They're actually going to do more than just acknowledge their own homosexuality and their . . . medical problems."

Meyerson snorted, unable to hold it in any longer. "I would think that would be quite enough," he snapped.

"Hey, easy there, Mr. Meyerson," Sharon said. "I'm homosexual myself. It's not all that bad."

She watched Meyerson's eyes widen, his lips tighten in a thin line as he fought back some unspoken rebuke. Her open acknowledgment also made him shrink back, to push himself farther into his chair. It was as if the word *homosexual* itself produced a need for greater distance between himself and any person who used it.

"I didn't mean to imply anything adverse," he finally said.

Sharon thought the words almost choked him.

"We know you didn't," Devlin said. "What I was getting at was that these priests plan to form a group, an organization of some kind."

"Of gay priests," Sharon said. She tried to put some sense of pride in the words to goad Meyerson even further. "I guess there are quite a few more than just them."

Devlin picked it up again. "I spoke to them—when we told them they were out of danger, that the killer had been caught—and several of them told me they intend to lobby the archdiocese and the church itself. They're going to press for an acknowledgment of gay men in the priesthood. They want the church and the laity to accept the fact that homosexuality exists within the clergy."

"Kind of give up the *don't-ask-don't-tell* approach," Sharon interjected.

Devlin again: "They said they're also going to press for an end to celibacy. Get the church to recognize that priests and nuns should have the right to marry."

"Gay priests?" Meyerson's entire body had stiffened. He seemed to realize that his outburst was untoward, and he forced himself to relax. Everything about him seemed to slacken; everything except the inner rage that remained in his eyes.

"I don't think they meant that," Devlin said. "I think they meant heterosexual priests and nuns." He hesitated, scratched his head, and looked at Sharon. "You don't think they meant gay priests should marry, do you?"

Sharon shrugged. "I don't think so. At least not as part of any first step to overturn celibacy. I think they know that won't fly. At least right off."

Devlin stared at her, incredulous. "You think somewhere down the road, they'll want that? Gay priests, I mean, getting the right to marry?" He shook his head. "No, you're off base there, Sergeant."

Sharon shrugged. "Hey, gays are getting married in Vermont. People are starting to accept the fact that this isn't some kind of perversion."

Devlin continued to shake his head. Meyerson was watching them both now, almost as if it were some kind of tennis match. There was no question in either Sharon's or Devlin's mind about which player he was rooting for.

"Okay. Okay. I agree these murders are going to raise people's consciousness about homosexual members of the clergy. It might even force the church to formally accept them. But marriage? No way. Not in our lifetime."

Again, Sharon shrugged. "Hey, wait and see, Inspector. Once you acknowledge gay men in the priesthood; once you acknowledge the right of heterosexual priests to marry . . . All I'm saying is, what's fair is fair. And people are going to see that."

Devlin waved away her argument. "We're getting off base here." He turned back to Meyerson and shook his head. "Anyway, these priests aren't in danger anymore. And we're still stuck with the same problem—Sister Manuela and how she fits in all this. We were hoping you might be able to help us—some hint, something she said, some person she mentioned as being very influential in her life."

Meyerson shook his head. He looked numb, Devlin thought. The little boy at his own birthday party who had just seen his party balloons all burst at once. "I can't help you," he said. "I can't think of anyone. I wasn't that close to the woman."

*R*asheed was waiting for them when they got off the elevator. "You get what you wanted?" he asked.

"Oh, yeah," Sharon said. "He's almost fucking catatonic."

"You think he's scared enough to run?" Rasheed asked.

They moved out onto the sidewalk. Devlin glanced down

the street and saw that Samuels and Boom Boom were in place. He nodded an acknowledgment. He would not go to the car and speak to them, wouldn't risk drawing attention to their presence.

He turned to Rasheed. "I can't read the guy at all. He's scared. But how can you tell what a scared nutcase will do? He might sit up there in a corner, suck his thumb, and rock himself to sleep."

"I think he'll move, and move fast," Sharon said.

"I hope you're right," Devlin said. He turned to Rasheed. "He comes down with a suitcase in his hand, you blow the alarm fast."

"Like Gabriel with his fuckin' horn," Rasheed said.

---

# Chapter Twenty-two

Charles Meyerson sank to his knees in the small cell-like room that had once served as a maid's quarters. The bare hardwood floor pressed into his knees, the discomfort, normally pleasant to him when he prayed, unnoticed now.

The room was dimly lighted by a votive candle placed before the statue of the Virgin on his bedside table, the light flickering so the photograph of his mother beside it seemed strangely animated. Charles did not see any of it. His eyes were closed tightly, his mouth moving with prayers that flowed by rote. He had placed a repentance belt around his thigh and tightened it so the small spikes on the inside of the strap cut into his flesh, causing a small trickle of blood to seep into his black trousers. There was a knotted rope in one hand, a scourge, and he methodically whipped his buttocks as he prayed until it, too, caused blood to stain his slacks.

Sister Manuela filled his mind as he prayed for guidance. He had offered up similar prayers months ago before he had approached her about the first step in his plan. She had been reluctant at first, but he had pressed her, told her The Holy Order had become victims of Chavarría and his drug cartel and his minions would seek vengeance against her family in Colombia if she refused to help.

He told her it was his fault that he had fallen into Chavarría's clutches, because he had trusted him. The man had the same name as the founder of their holy order, Father José Chavarría de Mata. He had taken it as a sign from God, he had said, the lie burning in his throat. Now he too was being threatened. She had only to help bring the religious artifacts into the country, to protect her family, to protect him and The Holy Order itself. Maria Escavera had looked at him with pleading eyes, begging him to allow her to escape this task. Finally, she had agreed. She had grown up in Colombia and she understood the ruthlessness of the cartels, the brutality of the men who ran them—men who brought government officials to their knees out of fear. She believed what he told her, and she reluctantly said she would do as he asked. Yet her eyes had held something else even then: the promise of disaster, some inner understanding that all would not go as he planned. But the pressure he had exerted had worked, and it had led to her death. He had not known that Valdez would use the same pressure, the same threats, to force her to do more.

"Forgive me," he whispered. Charles squeezed his eyes tighter as he continued to whip himself. He was not asking the young nun for forgiveness. That would have been pointless. He was asking forgiveness of his God. Forgiveness for his failure. The young nun, all the others, he believed, lived to serve, to do the work of Christ. How God chose to reward or punish that work was beyond the ken of man.

"I have failed you," Charles whispered. "I have failed to serve your church, to save it from the stain of disgrace others would place upon it. Tell me what I must do. Tell me how to serve you."

Charles slumped forward, his cheek coming to rest on his small narrow bed. The scourge fell away from his hand, and his eyes opened. The votive candle flickered on the nightstand, making his mother's photograph dance erratically. Her face seemed to twist and turn, her cheeks quiver, almost as though she were laughing at him.

"Bitch," he hissed. His hand swung out, sending the photo crashing to the floor.

He looked at his mother's image, shards of glass now scattered around it, surprised by what he had done. *Honor thy father and thy mother*. The words of the commandment came at him like a curse. He looked at the photograph again, and his lips curled into a sneer of unadulterated hatred.

Then calm descended, smoothing every line in his face. He raised his head and clasped his hands before him, elbows on the bed, the clasped hands pressed against his forehead. Again, Charles prayed for guidance.

When he emerged from his monklike cell, Charles was calm. He was dressed in his clerical garb now, a long black cassock hanging to his ankles. He walked to the windows that looked out over Central Park. Below, far to his left, the lights that festooned the trees surrounding the Tavern on the Green restaurant seemed like fireflies on a calm summer night. But the night was not calm. Rain had begun to fall; as Charles watched, heavy winds began to whip the trees below, set their boughs swaying violently, almost as if they were engaged in some great lamentation.

A black leather satchel sat at Charles's feet. Normally it held the accoutrements of his priesthood, used when he was called upon to offer up God's sacraments. Now it held the things he would need this night.

He glanced down at it, unwilling for now to pick it up and begin the journey God had set before him. He needed strength to build within him. He needed purification of his mind and body before he set out. Briefly, he thought of telephoning Ginger, asking her to come to his home, asking her to help lead him to the purification he sought, to purge his mind and body of the temptations that had plagued him throughout his life.

There was no time. Midnight mass would begin in one hour, and that had been ordained as the starting point of this new, perhaps final journey he would take. Charles closed his eyes in prayer as the wind suddenly changed and sent a torrent of rain crashing against his window.

God would sustain him in all; he knew that, accepted its truth in every sinew of his being. His mature years had been dedicated to the work of Christ—Opus Christi—and now God had chosen a new direction for him to follow. He had learned not to question those decisions. God had granted him knowledge of his will, and he had followed that will in complete obedience. He would do so now.

Charles bent and retrieved his satchel, its heft comforting

him. The satchel held the only clothing he would take with him and the implements of the work ahead. Now there would just be his priesthood. The world of banking would be but a memory. It was another of the mysteries of God's will. Just as Peter had abandoned his fishing nets to follow Christ, so Charles too would leave his past behind him.

Charles turned away from the window, pausing to take in the room, the comforts God had given him. He would miss them. But God would provide other comforts. He possessed an almost Presbyterian view of life, one of predestined glory for those chosen by God. There would be trials, of course, tribulations God would set before him to test his worthiness. The task ahead of him was one such trial. He was certain he would prove worthy and seize the glory that lay ahead—the reflection of God's own glory in the humblest of ways it could be known by man.

Charles closed his eyes, shutting out his life as he had known it. He started for the door, eyes open now, staring straight ahead. Only the work of Christ mattered now. The words *Opus Christi* played across his mind like a mantra driving him forward. A small smile came to his lips and his eyes were filled with a serenity he had seldom felt.

*R*asheed watched Charles step off the elevator, noting the black leather satchel he carried. He was wearing a trench-coat, and beneath the hem he could see what looked like a black dress. No, it was that thing priests wore—a cassock. Yes, that was what it was called.

He gave Charles his "Yes, massa" smile, but the man didn't even seem to know he was there.

"Do you want a taxi, sir?" he asked.

Charles nodded once but said nothing.

"Can I take your bag, sir?"

Again Charles ignored him, holding tightly to the bag. Rasheed picked up an umbrella that stood by the door and stepped outside under the long awning that stretched to the curb. On the sidewalk he glanced toward the unmarked car that held Devlin's men. He nodded once toward them. He would raise them by radio once the man had left, but wanted to alert them now so they would be ready. A plume of exhaust suddenly rose from the rear of their car, and he knew they had seen his signal. He opened the umbrella and stepped from the curb to wave at passing taxis. One pulled up immediately—a miracle, he thought, a cab on a rainy New York night.

Rasheed watched as Charles entered the rear of the cab, still silent as a stone, eyes fixed straight ahead.

"Can I tell the driver where you want to go?" he asked.

Charles remained silent, then reached out and closed the door. Rasheed continued to lean forward, trying to hear the instructions to the driver, even to read Charles's lips through the closed window. A passing truck and the fast-fogging window made it impossible.

As the cab pulled away, Rasheed looked to the unmarked car that held Stan Samuels and Boom Boom Rivera and gave an exaggerated nod. Then he pulled a mobile radio from the back of his doorman's coat. "Your boy is off and running. I don't know where," he snapped. He watched the unmarked car pull out and fall in behind the cab. He keyed the radio again. "Good hunting," he said. "I'll let the inspector know you're on him."

Rasheed watched the two cars move away, satisfying his professional need to know that the tail car was properly positioned. Then he turned and headed back into the building. He would have a quick look at the man's apartment. Then he would call Devlin.

"*Y*ou think he's running?" Boom Boom asked, as he steered the unmarked car west to Columbus Avenue.

"He's got that black bag," Samuels said. "We gotta figure it's a possibility."

"You think we should check with the boss, see if he wants us to pull him over?"

"Not yet," Samuels said. "Let's see if he's headed for the airport or one of the tunnels to Jersey. If he does we'll call it in. The boss said to let him run, see where he goes."

They swung around Columbus Circle and headed east on Fifty-ninth Street. Hansom cabs lined the north side of the street, tops up, the drivers hunched inside, waiting for the rain to subside so they could resume their quest for tourists.

Boom Boom inclined his head toward the waiting horse-drawn buggies. "Can you imagine shelling out forty bucks for a ride behind some stinking horse?" he asked.

"It's romantic," Samuels said. "Women love it."

"You been on one of those rides?" Boom Boom asked.

"Sure," Samuels said.

"No shit."

"I got laid once in the back of one of those rigs," Samuels said.

Boom Boom looked at him longer than he should, incredulous. It wasn't that someone had gotten laid in the back of a hansom cab. It was that Samuels claimed to have done so. "Stan the man," he said. "I didn't think you did that stuff."

"Shut up and drive," Samuels said.

At Fifth Avenue the cab sped through a yellow light. Boom Boom was two cars back, and he floored it, determined to make the light himself. A city bus pulled into the intersection, then came to a halt, blocking all eastbound traffic. Boom Boom pounded on the steering wheel, then leaned on his horn. The driver of the bus ignored him.

"Motherfucker! What's wrong with this asshole!" Boom Boom shouted.

Samuels reached down and picked up the red bubble light on the floor, placed it on the dashboard, and turned it on. Boom Boom hit the siren in short bursts, and the bus driver finally looked down. He gave them a sneer and slowly pulled his bus ahead, giving them just enough room to pull around him.

Ahead, farther down Fifty-seventh Street, the road was clear all the way to Madison Avenue. Beyond that intersection they could see three cabs approaching Park.

"It's gotta be one of them," Samuels said. "Floor it."

Samuels turned off the bubble light, and Boom Boom killed the siren. Ahead, two of the cabs continued across Park Avenue. The third, the middle one, turned south on Park.

Boom Boom pounded the wheel again. "Which one?" he shouted. "Which fucking one?"

*D*evlin answered his cell phone and heard Rasheed's rumbling baritone.

"The dude is off, bag in hand," he said.

"Does it look like he's running?" Devlin asked.

"Hard to tell," Rasheed came back. "It's a small bag. But with a guy like that, big bucks and all, it's hard to tell. He could buy himself new duds wherever he lands. Banker like him probably has money stashed outside the country."

"You check the apartment?" Devlin asked.

"Yeah. Only activity seemed to be in this small room. Strange fucking place. Very bare. One small bed, a table, a crucifix on the wall, a statue of a saint, the Virgin, I think. Like one of them monk's cells you see in the movies sometimes. Oh, and there was a picture on the floor, photograph of an old lady. All smashed to shit like our boy threw it or somethin'."

"You do a search?"

"Best I could. Didn't find nothin' we could nail him on. No drugs. No weapons. No kiddie porn. Zilch. He got a computer here and plenty of empty disks. You want me to copy his hard drive, I can. Just make sure the tail lets me know, he heads back this way."

"No," Devlin said. "Forget the computer. We don't have a warrant, and Boom Boom's already had a look from an outside location."

"*He* have a warrant?" Rasheed asked.

"I can't hear you," Devlin said. "My cell phone's breaking up."

Rasheed laughed. "I'll wait for him, then. Downstairs in the lobby. I'll call you if he drags his lily-white ass back here."

Devlin disconnected the cell phone and looked at Sharon and Ollie. "Charles is moving. He's got a small bag with him."

"Running, you think?" Sharon asked.

Devlin shrugged. His cell phone interrupted any other answer.

He listened, then snapped out an order. "Keep looking, then get your asses down here if you draw a blank." He disconnected the phone again. "Shit," he said.

"Don't tell me they lost him," Sharon said. "Who was driving?"

"Boom Boom," Devlin said.

"Stupid little bastard was probably playing with his dick," Ollie said.

"It was Stan on the phone. He said it wasn't Boom Boom's fault."

"So what do we do now?" Sharon asked.

Devlin looked down at his shoes, the black leather spotted from the rain. "We keep our fingers crossed and we wait," he said.

## Chapter Twenty-three

*T*he mass was beautiful and soothing, and Charles awaited the miracle that always brought tears to his eyes: the transubstantiation, the changing of the bread and wine into the actual body and blood of Christ. Only one thing would spoil its beauty.

Charles watched Father James Janis move about the altar, preparing to defile the host with his vile filthy hands. Charles's stomach churned with the thought, and his limbs trembled with a barely withheld rage. He moved his leg, feeling the satchel with his foot. The knife inside was a religious artifact, a jewel-encrusted dagger once owned by Saint Thomas More and taken from him before his martyrdom at the hands of Henry VIII. Charles had purchased it at auction, never knowing how God would one day seek its use. Yet he had sharpened the blade to a razor's edge, undoubtedly lessening its value. He had not known why at the time, but perhaps he did now. Perhaps that, too, had been the will of God, preparing the blade for its holy use.

Charles continued to follow the mass, continued to watch Father Janis as he prepared the host for consecration. When the host was at last elevated, he lowered his eyes, but not out of reverence this time. He lowered his eyes to keep the sight from view, to keep himself from seeing the sacrilege that was taking place before him. He feared that if he watched he would rise up and strike the man dead before the mass was ended.

Charles kept his eyes lowered throughout communion. Normally he would take every opportunity to accept the body of the Lord into his own. But not from the hands of this man—this so-called priest—who made a mockery of the church and of everything for which it had stood for two thousand years.

When the final blessing was given, Charles sat back and watched the priest leave the altar. He waited until the parishioners had made their way to the exits. Then he stood and slipped off his trenchcoat, revealing his cassock. Now he would be just another priest, moving through the church, and if anyone should return they would pay no mind when he entered the sacristy.

Charles reached down and picked up his leather satchel, opened it, and withdrew the bejeweled dagger. He offered a silent prayer to Saint Thomas More, asking that this weapon he himself had never used would now perform a task for the greater glory of God.

He slipped the dagger into the sleeve of his cassock, stepped from the pew, and froze in mid-stride. The priest had just returned to the altar, still in the vestments he had worn at mass. His head was lowered, hands raised before his face, pressed together in an attitude of prayer, the tips of his fingers touching his forehead. Charles watched as he knelt, facing the altar, his back to the rows of pews. Then he started forward.

Charles Meyerson had never killed another human being with his own hands. He had been raised in a capsule of wealth, in an atmosphere protected from violence. Even the meaner streets of the city had remained foreign to him, places he had never felt the need to visit. He had never served in the military, had never received any training, formal or otherwise, in the so-called *killing arts*. He had destroyed lives as a banker, and on at least one occasion his victim had committed suicide. But it was something that had occurred at a great distance, and Charles had neither grieved nor taken pleasure in that death. If he thought of it at all, he considered it inconsequential.

Now, as he moved slowly down the center aisle of the church, he studied the kneeling priest, suddenly uncertain of exactly where and how he should stab him. He understood human anatomy, knew where the vital organs of the body were located, but the best method of reaching them with a single killing blow suddenly seemed beyond him.

Charles closed his eyes momentarily and whispered a quick silent prayer, seeking God's intervention. Guide my hand, he thought. Guide my hand to do thy will.

Charles slipped the dagger from the sleeve of his cassock and felt his hand tremble as he seized its jeweled handle. He uttered another silent prayer to Saint Thomas More, then clasped the handle in both hands and raised it high above his head.

He was only two long strides from the priest when a sharp, clear voice called to him—a woman's voice.

"Don't do it, Charles. One more step, and I'll send you straight to hell."

Charles's eyes snapped to the sound and found Sharon Levy standing to his left, pistol held in both hands, eyes staring along the barrel.

"And if she misses, Charlie boy, I won't."

Charles turned to the second voice. Ollie Pitts stood to his right in a wide combat-shooter's stance, a pistol steady in his hands. It was leveled at Charles's chest.

The kneeling priest stood and turned, drawing Charles's attention. Paul Devlin stood before him, dressed in the same vestments Father Janis had worn during mass. He held a pistol down along his right leg. His left hand was extended toward Charles.

"It's over, Charles," Devlin said. "Give me the knife. No one else has to die."

Confusion spread across Charles's face, as he tried to understand how Father Janis could suddenly turn into a police officer. Then he understood what had happened, and his features twisted with rage.

"*Nooooo!*" he screamed. He leaned forward as if preparing to launch himself at Devlin.

Devlin's hand came up and joined the other, the barrel of the weapon only five feet from the center of Charles's chest. "Please don't make me kill you," Devlin said.

Charles faltered; his eyes blinked. "They have to die," he

said, his voice suddenly soft, melodious, distant. "It's the will of our Lord."

Devlin shook his head. "Can't happen, Charles. Not today. All the priests on your list have been taken out of the city. The archdiocese moved every one of them at my request. They're in a place where no one can reach them, surrounded by police. No matter which priest you went after tonight, you wouldn't have found anything but cops—all waiting for you. It's over." Devlin kept his pistol leveled on Charles but released the two-handed grip and extended his left hand again. "Give me the knife," he said again.

Charles ignored him. His eyes darted to Sharon, then to Ollie, as both moved in on either side, their weapons still held out before them. He turned back to Devlin.

"They must die," Charles said. "It is the only way the church can be saved."

"Why must they die, Charles? Why will it save the church if they do?" Devlin momentarily wondered if this conversation would be considered an interrogation by the courts, if he should Mirandize the man now. It was the kind of hesitation the court's recent decisions had produced; the kind that got cops killed. He pushed the idea away. He was simply "talking him down," trying to get him to surrender his weapon so they wouldn't be forced to kill him. That was how he would testify, and so would Sharon and Ollie.

Charles was blinking again, apparently confused by the question.

Devlin made his voice even softer and asked again, "Why do they have to die, Charles?"

Charles continued to blink, then suddenly focused on Devlin's face. "They're homosexuals," he said. "They defile their priesthood with their sins, with their very being." As he spoke, his mouth twisted with hatred.

Sharon was only five feet away from him now. "Do I defile *my* job, Charles?" she asked. "Does my very *being* offend you?"

Charles's eyes snapped to the sound of her voice. "Yes, it does," he hissed.

Sharon gave him a cold smile. "Is that why you sent Emilio Valdez to kill me?" she asked.

It had gone too far now. Devlin turned to Ollie. "Read him his rights," he snapped.

Ollie did so. Charles remained fixed on Sharon.

"Do you understand your rights?" Devlin asked.

Charles looked at him briefly, then turned his gaze back on Sharon. The dagger, still held above his head in both hands, had dropped slightly but was still poised to strike. "I understand," he said. "I understand everything." He smiled at Sharon. "Yes," he said. "That's why I sent him."

His voice held an arrogance that made Sharon blink. "What about you, Charles?" she asked. "What about your sexuality? What part did that play?"

Charles glared at her. "I am a priest of God," he hissed.

"So is Father Janis. So were the four men you had killed."

Again, Charles's face twisted with hatred. "No . . . they . . . were . . . not." His voice was sharp, each word spat out, each standing alone like an individual truth.

"We spoke to Ginger, Charles," Sharon said. "She told us what you like."

The hands holding the dagger began to tremble. "Shut up!" Charles shouted. "Shut up, shut up, shut up!"

Devlin saw Ollie inching closer and realized what Sharon was doing. She was drawing Charles's attention, forcing him to concentrate on her, so Ollie could slip from his peripheral vision and move up behind him. If Ollie could get his big hands on Meyerson's wrists it would be over.

Devlin moved to his right, until he was beside Sharon. "It confuses me, Charles," Devlin said. "Hiring a prostitute to do those things to you."

Charles's eyes blazed with rage. "She kept me pure," he snapped. "She kept me from temptation." The trembling in his hands increased, causing the dagger above his head to wave back and forth.

Sharon stepped in closer, forcing his eyes to her. "Is that why you had her use a strap-on dildo, Charles? So she could do the same thing to you that someone did to Father Donovan . . . Father Falco . . . Father Hall . . . Father Halloran?"

She snapped out the names of the murdered priests, watching as each one caused Charles's head to jerk back as though he'd been slapped. Sharon's eyes hardened. "Did you think if a woman fucked you in the ass you wouldn't be a homosexual yourself?"

"Is that what you thought, Charles?" Devlin asked. "Is that how Ginger kept you pure, how she saved you from temptation?"

Charles staggered back, one step, then another. The movement brought Ollie into view, closer now than he had expected. Charles spun to face him, then quickly lowered the dagger, bringing the blade against his own throat.

Devlin watched him press the blade against the skin, just above the carotid artery. A trickle of blood ran along his neck. "Don't do it, Charles. Suicide is a mortal sin."

His hand shook, causing the dagger to cut deeper. "God will forgive me," Charles said.

Devlin knew he should step back; knew he should move Sharon and Ollie back as well. If Charles cut through the artery it would send out a spray of blood that would hit all of them. Hit their faces, their eyes. If he, too, had AIDS, they could all be infected. But he couldn't move, couldn't step away. Sharon and Ollie also remained in place.

"No, he won't. God won't be able to forgive you." Devlin kept his voice soft, calm. "Think back to your catechism, Charles. Suicide is the product of despair, a loss of all hope. It denies the sinner a chance to seek forgiveness. If you do this, God will be helpless, Charles. You'll be condemned to hell."

"No one has to know, Charles," Sharon said. "You won't go to prison. You'll go to a hospital. You can be a priest there, Charles. There are people there who need priests."

"It'll hurt, Charlie," Ollie said. "It'll hurt real bad. Then you'll lie there and drown in your own blood, and everybody will know why you did it. We'll have to tell them why, if you kill yourself."

Charles blinked repeatedly. He looked at Ollie. "You won't tell them?" His voice sounded like a small child.

"No," Devlin said. "No one will tell. No one will ever know."

Charles dropped his hands to his side. Ollie's arm flashed out and his oversized fist wrapped around Charles's wrist in a viselike grip. Devlin stepped forward and eased the dagger from his hand.

Charles looked down at the bejeweled dagger, then his eyes rose to Devlin's face. "Did you know that dagger once belonged to Saint Thomas More?" he asked.

# *Epilogue*

**D**evlin put down the Sunday *Times* and took a sip of strong Cuban coffee. It was the last of the beans they had smuggled into the States a year ago, when they had returned from Cuba, the last evidence of the federal crime he and Adrianna had committed by "trading with the enemy."

Adrianna came up beside him and looked down over his shoulder at the front-page story that told of Charles Meyerson's arrest.

"You think the mayor will be happy?" she asked.

"Should be," Devlin said. "So far nothing has come out to make the archdiocese squeal."

"You think it will stay that way?" she asked.

Devlin shrugged, looked up at her, and smiled. "You're hoping it won't, right? You're hoping something will happen to get Howie in an uproar, and he'll fire my sorry butt."

"I didn't say that."

Devlin laughed. "You never say it. You only think it."

"I just don't like you putting yourself in danger all the time," she said. "Kneeling there, all dressed up like a priest, while that madman came down the aisle with a knife in his hand."

"It was a dagger," Devlin said. "And it once belonged to Saint Thomas More."

Adrianna exhaled heavily and rolled her eyes. "So what really happened will never come out?"

Devlin shook his head. "Not if the mayor and the DA have anything to say about it. And the archdiocese and Opus Christi sure aren't talking."

Adrianna smiled like a teacher who had caught a clever student cheating. "So Charles Meyerson was just a madman."

"That part's true enough," Devlin said. "So's the part about a powerful banker who got involved with a Colombian drug cartel—and used them to carry out his fantasies about killing Catholic priests."

"And there won't be anything about the priests being gay or having AIDS?"

"Not unless the archdiocese decides to acknowledge it." He laughed. But there was no joy in it, Adrianna realized.

"I guess that's one big snowball in hell," she said. "What about the nun, Sister Manuela?"

"The wiser heads in the mayor's and DA's offices have decided she was coerced by Charles and the drug lords, that they needed her to front for them with the religious artifacts they used to get heroin into the country. That Charles picked her because she had worked for him, and he knew she was vulnerable; they could threaten her family in Bogotá." He shrugged again. "That's true enough too. According to what Charles told us, at least."

"And the case will never go to trial?"

"Not a chance. Charles's attorney has agreed to have him committed. And Estaves is being deported. We don't have enough to try him."

"What if Charles is found competent someday?" Adrianna asked.

"I hope he is," Devlin said. "But by that time I'll be on some beach, using my walker to chase young women in thongs."

Adrianna slapped his shoulder, then eased herself onto his lap. "You think I'd look good in a thong?" she asked.

Devlin let out a low grunt. "I'd sure like to find out," he said.

Phillipa bounced up to the table, ending their game. It was the way she walked now. She bounced. It was as though she had springs in her toes, Devlin thought.

"Daddo," she said. It was an ominous start—a name she used only when she wanted something.

Devlin eyed her suspiciously. "Yeees?" he said, drawing out the word.

Phillipa grinned at him. "Joslyn solved the Madison Square Garden problem," she said.

"What problem was that?" he asked. "And who's Joslyn?"

Phillipa rolled her eyes. "Daaad. Joslyn's my friend. The one who had two tickets to the concert at Madison Square Garden. The one you said I couldn't go to unless an adult came with us."

"I seem to remember some other parts of that story," Devlin said. "Something about taking tickets from a stranger. That's just a minor detail, of course."

Phillipa shifted from foot to foot. "Yeah, I guess I remember that part," she said. Her face broke into a beatific grin. "But that's history, right?"

Devlin narrowed his eyes. "Okay, it's history. So?"

Phillipa's face exploded into a grin. "So Joslyn's mother got *three* tickets. She bought and paid for them herself."

Devlin groaned inwardly. He was trapped. He could feel Adrianna's body quiver with silent laughter as she sat on his lap. He thought about pinching her but decided against it.

"So Joslyn's mother is going to take you," he said. It wasn't a question, but a statement spoken as a deeply regretted fact.

"Uh-uh," Phillipa said.

Devlin felt a moment of reprieve. "I'm sorry, honey, but three kids going together is the same as two, as far as I'm concerned." He looked up at Adrianna for support. "Don't you agree?" he asked.

"Oh, yes," she said. There was a clearly false tone in her voice. She knew something he did not. It was a plot, the two of them were suckering him. They had done it before, too many times.

"If Joslyn's mother isn't going with you, what's the deal?"

Phillipa gave him a look intended to melt the strongest father's heart. He immediately steeled himself against it.

"Tell me," he snapped.

Phillipa maintained the look, her eyes large and round

and very innocent. "Joslyn's mom said she'll give the ticket to you. She said she'd feel really good if you'd go with us. She said what could be safer than having a police inspector right there with her twelve-year-old daughter?"

Devlin closed his eyes and groaned.

"You will, won't you?" Phillipa asked. The tone of her voice now was something on the brink of devastating disappointment. Devlin wondered where she had learned how to do that.

Adrianna kissed his forehead. "It will probably be fun," she said.

Devlin gave his daughter a cold, malicious smile. "Who's the group?" he asked.

Phillipa glanced at Adrianna, then back at her father. "The Rat's Nest Girls," she whispered. "They're new, and they're really, really cool. I think you'll really, really like them."

"The Rat's Nest Girls," Devlin repeated. He looked into his daughter's beautiful face. "Hip-hop?" he asked.

Phillipa nodded. "But really, really cool," she said, her eyes still wide and pleading.

Adrianna's body was shaking uncontrollably now. This time Devlin did pinch her.

## Author's Note

Opus Christi, the religious order depicted in this novel, is purely fictitious. There is, however, within the Catholic church today, a religious group called Opus Dei, whose history, practices, and beliefs closely resemble those fictionalized within these pages. It is a controversial religious order that many within the church have questioned and condemned in a manner not unlike what is written here.

To the author's knowledge, neither Opus Dei, nor any of its members, has ever been accused of a criminal act, either as a group or individually. This is purely the author's imagination at work.

This is a novel about religious fanaticism, its dangers to the people caught up in it, and what *could* occur when it is allowed to exist unquestioned and unchallenged. It is intended as nothing more.